UNTIL
I
MET
HER

UNTIL I MET HER

NATALIE
BARELLI

Previously self-published as *Until I Met Her* in the United States in 2016.

Published by Thomas & Mercer, Seattle

www.apub.com

Amazon, the Amazon logo, and Thomas & Mercer are trademarks of Amazon.com, Inc., or its affiliates.

ISBN-13: 9781611099829
ISBN-10: 161109982X

Cover design by Mark Swan

Printed in the United States of America

But to be furious, murderously furious, is to be alive.

— Claire Messud, *The Woman Upstairs*

1

I didn't think I would survive this day.

But thankfully, it's almost over now, for her friends, her husband, the many people here I have never met. There are a great many of us who've come to say goodbye, standing together by Beatrice's gaping grave, below a sky so bright it makes my eyes hurt.

Her coffin's lying beside it, waiting to be lowered into its final resting place. That's the part I dread. We're about to put her into this black hole and cover her up with dirt and mud, then turn around and walk away. Later, when it's cold and dark, will she be frightened? Will she hate us for turning our backs and leaving her there?

The minister tells us that God has plans that none of us are privy to, although not in those exact words. God, it seems, knows how hard it is for us to understand that someone we love can be snatched away suddenly, with no warning, in the most mundane of accidents, but that we must trust Him in His wisdom. I'm not sure what the point of that is. I would think that a warning to be more careful with stairs lest you fall and stupidly break your neck—a reminder to us all of the dangers we face at home—would be a more appropriate community message.

Jim has his arm around me and gives my shoulders a squeeze; it makes me aware I'm weeping. I turn to look at him and catch sight of George a little farther away. He's standing close to the coffin, looking down. There's an older woman by his side whom I recognize as his mother; even though I only met her once, Margaret Greene isn't someone you forget easily. She's holding his arm, as if to support him. I think she's crying, but it's hard to tell from here. Still, I have to fight the urge to pull her away, to tell her that she doesn't belong here, that she never liked Beatrice, and Beatrice knew it. But I do nothing of the sort, obviously. She's there for George. I understand that.

He looks up at me, as if he's realized I was watching him. His eyes are puffy and red; he's crying at least as much as I am. Poor George, he's going to miss her so much. How will he ever cope without her? How will he bear to live in that big apartment without her?

The minister must have concluded his eulogy because the coffin's descending into the hole now. I quickly bend down and grab a fistful of earth and throw it on top. I'm unsure what I'm trying to tell her—that I love her, that I miss her, I always will. Oh, Beatrice, why did you come home?

Jim has taken hold of my elbow, and is gently guiding me away. I look up and see that everyone is moving, slowly, in unison. I had a nightmare last night: All these people here had grabbed a shovel and were filling the grave with soil, except it was me in there, at the bottom of the hole. I was shouting at them to stop but they couldn't hear me. I woke up because I couldn't breathe. But it seems I won't get to see that part, the final sealing of the tomb, which is just as well because I don't think I could take it.

George comes over and engulfs me in his arms, and we collapse into each other, each sobbing on the other's shoulder.

"I'm so sorry," I repeat, over and over. After a long time, he releases me, just nods at me; that's all he has the strength to do. I watch him being led into his car, his shoulders hunched under the weight of his grief.

There are people all around me as we reach our own car. "I'm so sorry. You two were so close," they mumble. "It must be so hard for you." Craig gives me a hug. Dear Craig, the first friend of Beatrice's I ever met.

"How are you holding up?" he asks, his eyes searching mine. "Sorry, dumb question." He takes my face in his hands. "It's written all over your face," he says, and my features crumple with misery. "I'll call you later, all right?" Now it's me who's nodding, who doesn't have the strength to do anything else.

Jim's waiting by the car, holding the door open for me, and I'm about to get in when I feel a hand on my shoulder. It's Hannah. She whispers in my ear, "I'm sorry," then she adds, "I really need to talk to you. When you're ready." She puts her hand on my arm and squeezes it, studies my face, her head tilted at an angle, then walks away.

She made it sound like she had something serious to tell me, something bad. What could be worse than this? Maybe I'm imagining things.

"Who was that?" Jim asks.

"Hannah, Beatrice's agent. Remember her?"

"Vaguely."

Everyone is gentle with me, their eyes full of sadness for themselves and especially for me, knowing that I have lost my best friend, my mentor—this wonderful, generous, talented woman who took me under her wing and changed my life.

I'm inconsolable, wretched, heartbroken that my very dear friend Beatrice is dead.

Which is kind of odd, considering I'm the one who killed her.

2

I spend the next few days in bed. I feel like I will never get out of it, will never want to. I expected to feel crushed by sadness, sure, but a little bit of relief as well. It's nothing like that. Every single night I dream of killing her; not the deed itself, but the knowledge of it, and I'm shattered because I know without a doubt that my life is going to be over soon. I will be found out any minute now. I'm waiting for the knock on the door, consumed by overwhelming regret. Oh, how I wish I could turn back the clock! How I wish I hadn't done it!

And every morning I wake up, groaning with a relief so profound it makes my eyes water. Thank God. It was just a dream.

And then I remember, and it's devastating.

Surely it's just a matter of time before I get caught, before the knock on the door. Murderers get caught, right? So I go back to sleep, because anything's better than waiting.

Jim's very kind and attentive. He thinks I'm so sad because she's dead. He's even taken time off work to look after me—that's how intense my reaction has been. "You've taken this really hard, Em. Just rest, sweetheart. It will get better." He brings me food, and endless cups of tea. He doesn't say much, just sits on the side of the bed, patiently looking after me, eyebrows drawn together with worry. But he must be relieved that Beatrice is dead. It's back to being just him and me now, even if he would never say that.

"You're awake, Em." He has brought me some coffee. I sit up slightly. "How are you feeling?"

"Better, I think." The coffee is lukewarm. I wonder how long he's been standing there.

"Frankie called. He said he can cancel the interview tomorrow if you don't feel up to it."

"The interview?" I try to gather my thoughts, struggle to put them in some kind of order.

"*Books and Letters*, sweetheart. Do you still want to go? You don't have to, you know."

"But that's not until Thursday, Jim. I'll be fine by then, I'm sure of it." I put the cup on the small table beside me and slide back down. I just want to go back to sleep for a while.

"Tomorrow *is* Thursday, Em."

"Are you serious?"

"I think we should cancel it. What do you think?"

I sit up properly now, jolted. "No! Of course we're not canceling! I'll go."

"Are you sure?"

"I have to go. I want to go. Call him back, please, darling? Tell him I'll be there?"

He looks at me, then gives a hesitant nod. "Okay, I'll call him."

"I'll take a shower," I say, getting out of bed.

"You're really sure you're up to it?" he asks.

"Yes, I'm sure. I have to do this, Jim."

I'm shortlisted for the Poulton Prize, you see, one of the most prestigious—if not *the* most prestigious—literary prize of all. I daresay I'm even a hot favorite, and *Books and Letters* is the most pretentious, intellectual, literary TV program on earth. Right now, it's the only thing I'll get out of bed for.

◆ ◆ ◆

"My guest today is Emma Fern, author of *Long Grass Running*, a novel that is as surprising as it is engrossing—a novel that is bold, timeless, and yet speaks to the heart of every generation. Hello, Emma. Welcome to *Books and Letters*."

"Hello, Richard, thank you. It's wonderful to be here." My voice is weak.

"Well, first, congratulations. This wonderful book, your first novel, has been shortlisted for the Poulton Prize—a great achievement."

"Thank you, yes. I'm very happy, very humbled too, of course. It's every writer's dream."

"Indeed. And it's also a bestseller, which, as we know, does not necessarily go hand in hand with being a prizewinning novel."

"Yes, again, I feel so fortunate, on every level. It's a dream come true."

"Now, this novel, *Long Grass Running*, is highly unusual in its structure. It's not a traditional narrative—the time frame jumps around. We begin in the Second World War, where we meet three sisters who are left behind, shall we say, when their brothers . . ."

I can't concentrate. The lights in the studio are hot and disorienting. I feel sweat beading on my skin; I hope it doesn't show. I'm dizzy, tired, confused. I answer the questions almost by rote—after all, I've been doing these interviews for months now. Still, I'm zoning in and out. I just hope I come across okay.

". . . that's terrific, Emma, and I wish you the very best with the Poulton. I bet you can't wait for the outcome."

"And you'd win that bet, Richard." We both chuckle. "But, look, of course it would be wonderful to win, but to be shortlisted is already far, far beyond my wildest dreams, so you know, if I don't win, I'm still incredibly proud and happy to be where I am."

"It's an impressive achievement, and especially for a first novel, so—"

"Richard, let me correct you there, it's not exactly my *first* novel—it's my first *published* novel." His eyes widen and I can't help raising an eyebrow. That must have looked a touch smug. I hope the camera didn't pick it up.

"So there's another one?"

"Languishing at the bottom of a drawer, yes."

"Well, folks, you heard it here first," Richard says to the camera. "Can you tell us a little about that other book, Emma? I know we would all love to hear about it."

"No, look—it's not ready anyway. Give me a little more time to dust off the cobwebs and we'll see. And anyway, I'm not quite over this one yet." I laugh, sadly of course, and he laughs with me, but then I take a more serious tone. "But also, I want to say that I had a lot of encouragement from my dear friend Beatrice Johnson Greene in writing this novel. And I really want to acknowledge that. I'm here because of her support and incredible friendship."

He nods, thoughtful now. *Right, yes, let's take a moment.* "Thank you for bringing up Beatrice Johnson Greene. I can speak for all of us here when I say we have been especially touched by her passing away. She was a well-loved writer."

"Yes," I say, taking a breath. "Very well loved."

"It's so very sad. A terrible accident that robbed us of a wonderful author, way before her time, at the peak of her career even. And you knew her well. Is there anything you'd like to share with us? A special memory?"

It takes all my power not to burst into tears. "Beatrice and I were very close. And I want to say it again: I'm here today because of her. She became my literary mentor, if you will. She guided me and advised me, and without her, I'm not sure I would even have finished the novel. It probably would be lying on top of the other one in the same drawer right now."

My chin trembles and the corners of my mouth droop down, and I can't stop it happening. Maybe this was a mistake, coming here so soon.

7

Richard takes a moment; looks serious, reverential even. "I'm very sorry for your loss, Emma. And for all of us, because who among us hasn't been kept up all night by a novel by Beatrice Johnson Greene?" He smiles.

"She's caused a few sleepless nights for me, I assure you," I say, managing to smile back.

And she's still keeping me awake at night. What am I doing here? I shouldn't have come. I should have listened to Jim and Frankie, I should have—

". . . we never had the pleasure of her company on this program, unfortunately . . ."

I've zoned out again. I force myself to concentrate. I can't be falling to pieces here, on national television, for Christ's sake. *Pull yourself together, Emma, this is your big moment—don't waste it.*

". . . you say she mentored you, but your novel, *Long Grass Running*, it's not crime fiction as such, not in the genre that Johnson Greene excelled at." He says this as a statement, not a question. "Could you tell us a bit about that mentoring process?"

I nod. "Yes, you're right, Richard, we did write in completely different styles. It takes special skills to write crime fiction, as Beatrice did so well. I never put any thought into what style or genre I wanted to write in, I just, you know, wrote what was inside me, but to go back to your question, Richard, Beatrice took me under her wing almost as soon as we met. I had started my novel years earlier, but I didn't have the confidence, I guess, to finish it, to see myself as a writer. That's what she helped me with, mostly, and instilled some discipline into me as well." I laugh.

"She certainly was prolific."

"Wasn't she? So no, it wasn't so much tutoring in that way, but we used to talk every day about our writing, about how it was going, and she gave me enormous amounts of encouragement. I'll always be grateful to Beatrice for that."

He nods thoughtfully. "How did you meet her? Such a life-changing event for you. Do you ever think about that?"

I don't know why the question takes me by surprise, but I'm momentarily speechless as the memories tumble over each other and Richard goes out of focus for a second.

"She came into my store," I finally manage to say. I tell him a little about that day, how I used to own a home decor store and I'd never dreamed I would become a published author. I tell him about meeting Beatrice, and how quickly we bonded over our shared love of writing, about her kindness to me, and how fortunate I was that she believed in me. She semi-adopted me as the daughter she never had, I tell him. Until I met her, I had never shown my work to anyone, but she made me open up and trust myself, I tell him. It became important to her that I fulfill my potential, and she worked very hard at it. I will always be grateful to her for that.

I tell him.

It's all a crock of shit, of course. Except for the first bit.

She came into my store.

3

It was a Saturday. I remember because Jim came with me that morning. Fall was well underway, but the sun was out and it was still warm for the time of the year. We came out of the subway and joined the leisurely crowd of young families, parents pushing strollers and carrying small children, and people bursting out of coffee shops onto the sidewalk. When I first bought the store there almost a decade ago, that part of Brooklyn was quiet, a neighborhood of ordinary folks going about their ordinary business, but you could get a taste of things to come—literally, as it turned out, since it was food—the haute-cuisine kind—that first replaced the old closed stores. Restaurants serving artfully presented dishes, the type of place you could imagine reading about in a fancy magazine and taking a taxi to. After that, the trendy wine bars followed, then fashion retail, organic food stores, and finally, art galleries. Which is when you know for sure a neighborhood is well and truly gentrified.

On that sunny morning, Jim wanted to go to the bookstore a couple of doors down from the store, which is why we were walking together, arm in arm, and we were only a hundred feet away from it when we heard a loud crash just ahead. The traffic was heavy, but slow, and a car filled with far too many people had driven straight into the one in front of it. They weren't going fast—no one was—and they were probably distracted by all the activity along the street and hadn't been looking ahead. But still, it was loud. The back door opened and a little girl, no more than seven or eight years old, jumped out, screaming at the top of her lungs, and ran.

We were a little crowd who had stopped on the sidewalk to watch this minor road accident, and to my amazement, people parted to make way for this child, this frightened little dark-haired girl, running away from her fear. I shouted something and pushed the people in front of me out of my way, jutting my arm out just as she came level with me, and stopped her in her tracks, my hand on her chest.

"Hey," I said gently, crouching down. Her face was inches from mine, and she was still screaming, her eyes, big and desperate, boring straight into mine.

"It's okay, you're okay, honey. It's over now," I said to her again and again, bringing her into my arms, quickly doing a visual check up and down her body to make sure that she was indeed fine, until from somewhere above us a pair of hands descended and picked her up. I looked up and watched as her mother took her away. From me.

Afterward, Jim told me he was so impressed, but I was baffled, upset that none of the adults watching had tried to stop her; she could have run into traffic or gotten lost. "She was in shock, poor little thing," I said to him. "What's wrong with everybody?"

He squeezed my shoulders with one arm as we resumed walking. "Brave, fearless Emma," he said, to no one in particular, "throwing herself into the throng of people."

"Stop it!" I punched him in the shoulder.

"Willing to risk everything to save one poor child—"

"Cut it out!" I laughed.

"—from danger that only she, Super-Emma, could prevent."

"Okay, that's enough. You've made your point."

He turned his handsome, smiling face to me and kissed the side of my head. "Maybe you're starting to feel a little motherly yourself?"

Motherly? What did that even mean? That I was thinking of having children? Of course I was—*we* were. We talked about it occasionally. And maybe that's what it was, because I kept thinking about this child, the way she was looking at me with despair in her eyes, like she was screaming for me to help her, and I did, I was there. And truth be told, I was sorry when her mother took her away from me. I could have held on a little longer. It stayed with me all day, that memory.

But then Beatrice came into the store.

She was beautiful, radiant, elegant, and I knew exactly who she was. I was so shocked to see her that for a split second I was unsure where I was, or if I were dreaming. She smiled at me briefly, then scanned the items closest to her. A vase, I think, a large wooden chess set definitely, a set of stone coasters maybe. She ran a fingertip along a walnut cutting board, and I couldn't take my eyes off her.

"Could I take a closer look at this lamp?" She was pointing to a high shelf and I followed her gaze. It was part of the Celia Sherman collection, with a blue ceramic base and large blue shade, decorated with exotic birds. I was pleased, because it was one of my favorites. It made me feel validated that she had noticed it.

"Of course." I smiled, outwardly professional, but giddy beyond belief that she had spoken to me. I pulled my little stool from behind the counter so I could reach the lamp, and took it down from its perch and handed it to her.

"It's lovely," she said, turning it in her hands with great care. God, she was even more beautiful in real life, her black hair in a loose chignon at the back, wispy strands at the front; her makeup impeccable, although more of it than I'd expected; and her outfit elegant and relaxed at the same time. She didn't look her age, not even close. It wasn't that she looked younger, so much as she looked timeless. She was mesmerizing.

I had seen her many times on television of course, and even a couple of times in the flesh in the distance at some book signing—but this, this was incredibly special, and the little girl who had been in my mind all day long vanished quietly.

"If you don't mind my saying . . ." I started.

"Yes?" Her eyebrows rose, the beginning of a smile on her lips.

"I'm a great admirer of your work. I just love your writing. All of it," I blurted. I felt myself blushing, wishing it to stop, which made me blush even more.

"Thank you so much." She beamed, looking genuinely delighted by my comments. She put a warm hand on my arm. "You're so sweet to say so. It means a lot to me."

It made my skin tingle slightly, the feel of her skin on mine, the touch of her hand, and I really fell in love with her. She looked kindly at me, and I found myself thinking that she liked me.

She handed me the Sherman lamp. "I'll take it."

"Of course."

"Could you gift-wrap it, please? It's a gift." She caught herself and laughed. "Obviously."

"Certainly." I set out to perform the most accomplished wrapping I'd ever done, but slowly, deliberately, to keep her there as long as I could, as I frantically searched my mind for things to say, things that would spur on a conversation. But she spoke first, looking around.

"I walk past this store sometimes. I've often wanted to stop and browse, but I'm always in a rush."

"Thank you. Do—do you live around here?" I stammered, even though I knew exactly where she lived. In fact, I'd read about it just the other day, in a magazine interview, and it wasn't even close to this neighborhood.

"Oh no, but my editor does. Right around the corner."

She'll go away. I had to say something smart—anything—quickly. "Well, I'm very glad you had the time to stop in today."

13

She was lightly fingering a candleholder on the counter. "So am I," she replied. "You have such interesting things here."

And I did. I loved my store. When I first started out, I was selling a mixture of French provincial and contemporary furniture, but then I moved on to mostly handcrafted, reclaimed materials: lots of wood, iron, glass, vintage leather; mostly small furniture pieces and objects, all beautifully made. It was my passion back then, beautiful things for the home. That, and books.

"Are you working on a new novel?" I wanted to tell her what her work meant to me, to explain that I thought her writing was wonderful. I wanted to tell her how her phrases often surprised me when they took a turn for the unexpected; that she had a gift for expressing sentiment; that I reread her when I needed cheering up, because the recognition I found in her words made me feel that I wasn't alone and that I wasn't crazy. I was rehearsing all this inwardly when I caught her looking at her watch, and she made a small, frustrated sound between pursed lips. I felt silly for wasting her time, and my hands moved faster on the wrapping.

"Almost done," I said as I cut and folded paper and made curls from ribbons. I was missing her already, knowing that she'd be gone soon.

She pulled her wallet from a surprisingly large handbag and gave me a credit card. "Do you deliver?"

"Of course." I was about to tell her I'd happily waive the usual charge.

"Now? Could you do it this afternoon?"

"Now?" It was almost four o'clock. "Not now, I'm afraid: I won't be able to get a delivery guy on such short notice. I'm sorry. But tomorrow morning, certainly."

"Oh no, it can't wait until tomorrow morning. It's a gift for my mother-in-law, you see, for her birthday today. I mean her birthday is today. I'd take it to her myself but I have to be somewhere else."

She looked at me with pleading eyes and put that warm hand of hers on mine.

"Would you do it for me? Could you deliver the lamp? It's not very far from here." Then she rushed to say, "I'm very sorry to be asking such a thing. But I'm in a bit of a bind, you see. You'd be doing me a huge favor."

I also had to be somewhere. Jim was expecting me to be at a charity function, the fundraiser for his research consortium, and it was a big deal for him. Anyway, I couldn't just arbitrarily close the store early—it was just me that day. Jackie, my assistant—well, she was my friend too—wasn't there. Normally there were two of us. But she was off that day.

"I'm sorry. I can't just close up. I have customers." I pointed my chin in the direction of a young couple who had just walked in and were browsing. "But definitely first thing tomorrow. Definitely. Absolutely."

"After closing then? I'd be so very grateful." She said it as if I hadn't spoken that last part. Her pleading eyes again.

Who was I kidding? I'd go to the moon and back if she asked me.

"Of course," I said finally. "I'd be glad to help."

She looked so relieved, and I felt a tinge of pride that I had brought that on.

"Thank you so much. You really are so kind." She lifted the hand that was still resting on top of mine and held it out to me. I noticed an almost-imperceptible tremor that made me feel disappointed. That's how much I wanted her to be perfect.

"I'm Beatrice, by the way," she said.

I know you are.

I shook her hand. "I'm Emma." The inconvenience suddenly didn't matter one bit. I was on a first-name basis with Beatrice Johnson Greene.

4

As it turned out, Margaret Greene did not live close by, and I found myself in a taxi negotiating city traffic smack in the middle of rush hour, wondering yet again why anyone would call it that.

I was peering out of the window to read the numbers on the front gates of the elegant houses, although by then it was too dark for me to appreciate the architecture or the landscaping. I should have been at the fundraiser by now.

The package was quite large and awkward to carry from the car to the porch, and having instructed the driver to wait, I was fumbling around reaching for the bell when the door opened before I could ring.

"Hello? Can I help you?" a very thin, very attractive, rather haughty older woman said coldly, in the tone you'd use with someone who might have been picking your lock.

I introduced myself and explained the purpose of my visit. If she was at all pleased to receive a birthday present, she wasn't letting on.

The hallway was magnificently furnished and made me gasp. It was much grander than I had expected, and even though I couldn't see any farther inside, I could tell the lamp wasn't going to fit in with the decor, which was far too classic. Exquisite, expensive, and very, very classic.

"Is there a card somewhere?" she asked. I had put the package on a narrow hall table, and Margaret Greene was peering inside the layers of tissue paper.

"A card? No, I don't think so," I replied, which was a stupid thing to say since I'd wrapped this gift myself. "Beatrice didn't give me a card." Was I supposed to write a card? I tried to remember.

She turned to look at me for the first time, from head to toe, literally sizing me up. I found myself admiring the chandelier above her head.

"Are you a friend of Beatrice's?"

"Oh no. I'm just delivering the package."

"I see."

She turned around and started walking away from me, her heels clicking on the parquet floor. "One moment. I'll fetch my purse," she said over her shoulder.

I was confused. Did she mean to pay for the lamp? Then it dawned on me that she was going to give me a tip.

"Oh no!" I raised my hand to stop her, feeling crimson patches rising up my throat, hoping to recover before the telltale signs of embarrassment reached my face. "There's no need for that. I delivered it as a favor to Beat—your daughter-in-law. She purchased it from my store, you see. She wanted you to receive it today."

"Really?" She turned back and faced me. "And she couldn't come herself?"

What, because you'd have liked to see her, you old hag? I don't think so. There was no warmth in her tone, just pure reprimand. "She said she had to be somewhere." *Anywhere but here*, I thought.

Margaret Greene did a quick shake of her head, closing her eyes. A disparaging gesture, one used on a regular basis, probably.

"Well, I need to get going," I said. I was annoyed now that I'd let myself be dragged into this errand. I walked toward the door, which had remained open the entire time. "Goodbye, Mrs. Greene."

She moved in front of me, placed one hand on the door handle, her body half facing the other way, waiting for me to leave so she could put this interruption behind her. She said goodbye dismissively, and shut the door as soon as I crossed the threshold.

I glanced over my shoulder, and through the frosted, decorated glass pane I watched Margaret Greene walk back into the house without so much as a glance toward her gift, which was still sitting on the table.

It was my turn to shake my head disparagingly before walking back to the waiting taxi.

◆　◆　◆

"You missed all the speeches."

I was standing on my tiptoes to kiss him, my Jim, but he drew slightly away from me.

"Which is to say you haven't missed much," Carol said, jumping in to give me a quick kiss on the cheek.

God bless Carol; she was always nice to me. Jim was lucky to have her as a colleague, and I was lucky too.

"Did you get my texts?" I asked.

"Yes, I did."

I leaned closer to him. "The most incredible thing happened this afternoon," I whispered conspiratorially. "You will never believe who I met!"

I'd been looking forward to telling Jim about meeting Beatrice ever since it happened, but it was coming out all wrong. The excitement I was feeling sounded forced, and anyway, this was not the time.

"I've been waiting for you for an hour, Em," he whispered back. "Can we talk about something other than you now? You think you can manage that?"

"What's wrong?" We must have looked ridiculous, leaning in, whispering to each other.

"What do you think, Em? Hello? Fundraiser? Very important occasion for me. Months in the planning—ring any bells?"

He was about to say something else when a distinguished-looking man tapped him on the shoulder, sparing me a lecture.

"Well done, Jim, this is brilliant. Fascinating." They shook hands, and engaged in conversation. *Oh Lord*, I chided myself, *you really screwed up, Emma.* Jim had put so much work into this; he and his research team, Carol and Terry especially. He had talked of nothing else for weeks. I was so proud of him, and I wanted to be by his side, to be part of the team as we all worked together to make this night a success, except I'd screwed up, because I got star-struck, and I wanted Beatrice Johnson Greene to like me. What an idiot! Of course he was angry with me; he had every right to be.

I took the glass of champagne that was offered, and chatted to Carol for a while. She must have picked up on our tiff, but she didn't show it. Her eyes were darting left and right.

"Go," I said. "Don't stand here talking to me, you have things to do." I had a hand on her arm in a gesture that reminded me of Beatrice.

"You're sure?"

"Of course. You won't get a big fat check from me! Your talents are wasted here."

She laughed. "Thanks, Emma. I should, really."

"That's right, you should, so go already!"

I stood there awhile, sipping my champagne, checking out the room. I picked up one of the canapés off a tray that glided past me. This event was great; the room was packed. I recognized a few of the guests, but not many, which wasn't surprising: they were mostly politicians or the people who worked for them.

I saw Jim make his way toward me. He touched my elbow as he reached me.

"What do you think?" he asked, looking around the room.

Thank God. I was so relieved he had forgiven me already. How lucky was I to be with this wonderful man? I wanted to grab his face and kiss him full on the mouth.

"Great turnout, Jim, really. Hey, why don't you introduce me to some people?" I said, determined to help. I was going to do everything I could to make this night a success. "That's what we're here for, right? I'm ready for duty." He smiled at me briefly, just as Carol walked past and he quickly reached out and grabbed her arm.

"Carol, come talk to Alan Bunting with me. It's going to take two of us to tackle his questions," he chuckled.

He turned back to me quickly and shot me a small smile, and I nodded. *You two go*, I wanted to say; *go forth and prosper*. But they'd already gone.

I watched him laughing at something this Alan Bunting guy said, my heart filled with love, and no small amount of pride. I knew most people would not consider Jim an especially good-looking man on first meeting him, and he was carrying more weight than he should have, which blurred his features somewhat, but his physical appeal was something that crept up on you. One moment you thought he was just ordinary-looking, and then boom! You couldn't take your eyes off him. It had to do with the power he projected, his self-assurance, his intelligence. Everyone admired him, everyone wanted to be liked by him, and that made him very sexy.

"Don't look so bored." Terry materialized at my side. "You'll put off the donors."

"Bored? Certainly not! Just, you know, choosing my prey," I replied.

I adored Terry. Jim and Terry knew each other from working together at NYU, so when Jim was invited to lead the Millennium Forum, he'd asked Terry to join him.

"All right. This man here, we need him on our side, and he's hardly spoken to anyone yet." He pointed his chin toward a man in a grey suit, but tried to look nonchalant at the same time, which made me ask, looking from person to person, "Who? You mean him? Oh, him? No?" until he picked up on my teasing and shook his head, eyes heavenward.

And then, said man in the grey suit appeared in front of us and extended a hand to Terry.

"Hello, I'm—"

"Professor McCann," Terry said before he got to finish his sentence.

"Michael, please."

Terry introduced me. "It's good of you to come, Michael."

"Not at all. To be honest I thought I might poach some of your donors before you get every last cent out of them," he replied, which made Terry guffaw. Michael turned to me. "I'm in politics. Senate. I'm not one of them, but I advise them."

"In what area?"

"Economics."

"Of course." Right. That's why everyone was here tonight, to raise money for the Forum, as it was known—the most cutting-edge, progressive economic think tank in the universe, as Jim called it.

"Jim's white paper was astounding," he said.

"I don't think Emma's read it, Michael." Jim's voice, behind me.

No, I hadn't read it, but did he really need to say that?

"It's true that I haven't read it, and that's clearly my loss, so, Michael, why don't you explain it to me?"

"Surely you'd want to hear it from the horse's mouth?"

"No, good idea," Jim said. "I'd like to hear it from you myself. How would you describe it? I'd be really interested to hear your take on it."

Michael took a deep breath. I felt a bit sorry for him, having put him on the spot.

"In one sentence," I said, holding up an index finger helpfully.

"One sentence—okay, let's see. The old adage of 'wealth trickles down,' as we call it, is a complete fallacy, but it's made its way into accepted theories that are now being tied to policy. Or rather have been tied to policies for decades."

"Not a bad take," Jim said.

"I don't actually agree with it, by the way." Michael shook his head. "Also, I think you're taking the moral high ground."

"How so?"

"That there's a right way to make money, something like that?"

"No. I don't care how people make money as long as it's legal. My work is about the principles of economics that underpin society; economics derived from work, trade, productivity. That's why it works, Michael—the modeling. The part of economics that deals with making money out of money? Interest, loans, stock exchanges? That's up to the individual, or groups of individuals. Our work is about wealth as an index of societal well-being."

Jim was glowing. This was what he lived for, someone asking him what his work was about. Michael started to interrupt, but Jim put a hand up.

"All I did is take that idea—making money out of money—out of government economics, and bingo! The picture changed completely and the variables were clear. A tiny tweak here or there, on the order of point-zero-zero-one percent, whether applied to taxes, or to subsidies, or to welfare, can affect the balance."

A few people had stopped speaking, and a little circle had gathered around us, all of them listening closely, Alan Bunting among them. Alan spoke then, shaking his head. "I have no idea what all that means, sorry."

"Think of it as a magic formula," I said quickly, "that will not just balance your budget, but pull it out of deficit and still achieve everything you want." Jim stared at me, but I was better at explaining his work than he was. I didn't need to read his paper; I already knew what it was about. How could I not? He'd spoken of hardly anything else in all the years that we had been together—seven years now—besides his dream to come up with the perfect government economics model.

"We keep hearing so much about your magic formula, so where is it?" Michael asked.

"I'd prefer to call it an EMT—efficient modeling template—and you can see it when enough generous people such as those here tonight contribute to the project," Jim replied. "We're so close, Michael. We're at the finish line, but we need support to get over it."

"It's ironic, isn't it? Your model will be more likely to benefit the poorer members of society, and yet it cost a cool two thousand to even get in the door of this event tonight."

"It's not designed to *benefit* anyone," Jim corrected him. "We're data miners, and we have so much of it available to us, for the first time in history. So, what if you, being an economics adviser, had a template, a recipe, where you could just tweak this parameter or that value, very slightly, on the order of less than one percent, but very precisely, and come up with policies where everyone in this country gets an education; everyone gets a job"—Jim was counting on his fingers to make his point—"no one is poor; the rich are still rich; the roads are built, and so are the bridges; everything works; housing is affordable to everyone; everyone is healthy because healthcare is available and affordable, including preventive healthcare; water is available and clean; pollution is negligible. And that's just to start with. Would you use that template?"

There was a beat before Michael roared with laughter. "You're serious? It sounds a lot like some socialist propaganda to me, buddy!"

"Well, it's not. It's pure, sustainable, demonstrable, political economics."

"You show me that template, as you call it, and I'll tell you whether I'll use it," Michael said.

Jim smiled. "Okay, in good time, you'll see it."

"I think you may have to show Jim a check to get that template," I said, because, hey, I was sold. "Get in on the ground floor."

"Ha! You're right." And to my delight, Michael literally pulled out a checkbook from his inside pocket. "You do have my curiosity piqued,

Jim, I'll give you that." Terry offered his back as a surface to write on. I heard people laugh and turned to see quite a few more people had joined us.

"There you go," Michael said with a flourish. "Ten thousand dollars. I hope that will go some way toward that template, or whatever you call it, and it better be a good one."

Everyone clapped, and then hands shot up. If Michael McCann was prepared to pay that much, then they would too. The scene was amusing, with Jim, Terry, Carol, and I all offering our backs for people to write checks upon.

I was very pleased with myself.

5

"Wow. How good was that? Amazing! Congratulations, my darling! Are you pleased?" I clapped my hands, did a fist pump. I was exhausted but exhilarated too. It was almost midnight and we were in a taxi, going home, finally. I beamed at Jim, expecting him to look like I did, on the top of the world, but he was staring straight ahead, silent. The taxi moved off the curb.

I waited until we had joined the traffic and put my hand on his knee. "Everything okay?"

Silence, then a sigh.

"You've known about this for ages, Emma. Tonight was crucial to me. Not just for the Forum, for the money, but for me. It's my work; I need to impress the people who believe in me." His mouth was tight, angry. "And you waltz in late because you had something more important to do."

He paused, and I waited; I knew it wasn't over. We were both looking in opposite directions.

"I don't understand you. How hard can it be to get there on time?"

"Darling, I'm sorry. Really. I didn't think I'd be so late, and yes, it all happened at the last minute, but—"

"I know, you told me. Never mind, Em."

We drove in silence for a while. It started to rain.

"I did text you, you know. Twice," I said.

"Yes, I know."

"You could have replied."

"What for? It's not like you were asking me anything, you were just telling me that you couldn't be there."

"I'm sorry," I said again. I was saying that a lot to Jim lately and wasn't sure why. I worked hard to keep him happy—not that I minded. I loved him so much. My Jim. My husband. My life.

He had seemed a bit on edge of late, but I thought it was the pressure of the new job. It was a dream job. A Research Director in economic policy—tailor-made for him. They'd sought him out, head-hunted him. He was so smart, and so experienced, so passionate. So when he'd found out he was the successful candidate, we danced in the living room, we drank champagne—we were so happy, both of us. I was as happy for him as he was for himself.

"This is a great opportunity for me. For us. And I want you to be by my side, you understand? Make a good impression. Be a part of the team, Em. We talked about this."

"I know. I'm sorry, Jim. I really am." I didn't know what else to say. Neither of us spoke again until we reached our little house, some forty minutes later.

Jim had started to hint recently that we should move to an apartment in Manhattan, so we could be closer to work. We could afford it now, he said. But I loved my little house in Woodhaven, and I loved our neighborhood. I was in no rush to leave.

Jim paid the driver. He didn't look at me, and I had that too-familiar feeling in the pit of my stomach that he was disappointed in me. I was exhausted by how much I wanted him, because I knew, deep down, that I was the one who loved more in this relationship, and my entire existence was a balancing act between being desirable enough that he would love me, but not so needy or dependent that I'd drive him away. Everything I did, everything I was, was underpinned by the fear that I might get the balance wrong and slip off the tightrope. One false move and it would all be all over, or at least that's how it felt. Like he was waiting for that excuse to extricate himself from me.

It was stupid. *I* was stupid. I didn't know why I did that to myself.

"I'm sorry too, Em," Jim said finally as we both got out of the taxi, and my heart sang, the tension that had gripped my stomach instantly releasing its hold. He turned to look at me, gave me a little smile, and said, "Come on, let's go in."

We walked up to the front door, hand in hand. *I'll feed us*, I thought. *That's it, that's what we need.* I was about to go straight to the kitchen but he stopped me, put his hands on my shoulders, and said, "I overreacted, I know, I'm just—God, overwhelmed by this job, I think. I wonder if I'm in over my head sometimes."

It was such a candid thing for him to say that tears pricked at the back of my eyes. I led him to the kitchen and poured us each a glass of wine. We stood on either side of the kitchen island, and I looked into his adorable face.

"Jim, look, it's completely normal to feel that way. It's a huge step in your career, darling. And you will find your feet, you'll see. Not long now."

"I know. I'm just overtired. I don't actually feel that way. I don't know why I said that." He took a swig of his wine.

"I love you," I said.

"I love you too."

"Hungry?"

"Famished."

I laughed and pulled ingredients from the refrigerator to make us a snack. We didn't speak, but we were in a sweet place, just gentle with each other.

While we ate our sandwiches, I told him about Beatrice's coming into the store, but I didn't tell him exactly how excited I was, how impressed, how pleased that she seemed to like me so much. He didn't really know who she was anyway. I'd given him two of her novels, but I don't think he'd ever read them.

Then I told him about my delivery experience, and I made it sound funny, playing it up completely. We laughed a lot. I did a not-too-bad imitation of Margaret Greene's snobbery, her wanting to give me a tip. He said I should have accepted it, and he pretended to be me receiving the tip, making faces of shock and outrage at the meagerness of it. He called her Lady Gan-Greene.

It was nice, really nice.

6

I was still thinking about her two days later, at the store, trying to concentrate on some paperwork at the same time, when the phone rang.

"I wanted to thank you, Emma. For bailing me out the other day," she said.

My heart took a leap. Lord, what a beautiful voice she had, a little deeper than most women, which gave her even more . . . What was it—confidence, class? It was a warm, honeyed voice and I was thrilled to hear it. I told her I was delighted to help, instantly forgetting the trouble it had caused me.

"Emma, the reason I called is I want to thank you properly," she said. "I'm not joking when I say you helped me out of a tight spot. You met the dragon, I presume?"

I laughed. "I did, yes." I wasn't going to elaborate, but there was no point in pretending I didn't know who she was talking about.

"Well, then you see why I stayed away. Emma, I know it's very short notice, but are you free for lunch? I was hoping I could take you out somewhere."

"Oh, you don't need to do that." It was my stock response to anyone wanting to do something nice for me.

"Please, I'd like to. You really did me a huge favor—let me take you out for lunch. I enjoyed meeting you so much yesterday, so this is a selfish act on my part, really. I'd like your company. No, I would *very much* like your company, if you're free."

I found it so strange, the way she said exactly what she felt, without stopping to think about how it would sound, how it would look. I admired her for that—me, who was always second-guessing myself. I wanted to learn from her.

"Thank you, Beatrice. I'd like that very much."

"Oh, I'm so pleased. I'll book us a table at L'Ambroisie. Is that all right?"

"Oh Lord! Are you sure?"

"Of course. Shall we meet at one? Or is that too soon?"

I checked my watch. That gave me barely forty minutes to get there, but I could do it. "That's great. Thank you, Beatrice. I'll see you there."

◆ ◆ ◆

As soon as I entered the restaurant, I wished I'd worn something more special for the occasion, but then I decided not to dwell on it. It was such a generous gesture on her part, and I was sure she didn't care what I wore.

She hadn't arrived yet, but the maître d' was expecting me and escorted me to our table. I was surprised she'd gotten a reservation on such short notice; the restaurant was completely full. But, of course, she could get a table there whenever she liked. This was Beatrice Johnson Greene: they'd have fallen over backward to accommodate her. I couldn't help feeling a touch smug, sitting there at one of the best tables in the room, scanning the menu while I waited, relieved that the prices were not listed.

I looked around at the decor, as I usually do. I can't help it. When I first walked in, I thought it a little too dark for my taste, with its wood-paneled walls and draped windows, especially for a lunch date, but now that I'd adjusted, I realized it was perfect.

I checked my watch discreetly. Maybe I'd misunderstood the time. I tried to remember: Did she say one? But then there was a shift in the air and there she was.

"I'm so sorry I'm late," she said, sitting down. "Oh, who am I kidding, I'm always late, I don't know why. It's in my bones. Well, never mind, we're here." She smiled. "It's lovely to see you, Emma."

"It's nice to see you too, Beatrice." I had to pinch myself. Here I was, with this incredible woman I'd admired from afar for a long time. I expected everyone to be staring at her, but they hardly noticed her, or if they did, I suspected it was because of her looks. She was a stunning-looking woman. Could it be that not everyone knew who Beatrice Johnson Greene was? Was it possible they didn't realize she was there, in their midst, lunching with me?

"This is a wonderful place," I said, stating the obvious.

"You haven't been here before?"

"No, never."

"Well, you're in for a treat," she replied as the maître d' arranged the napkin on her lap. He nodded his appreciation of her compliment. I rushed to set my own napkin, feeling embarrassed at the thought of him doing it, telegraphing how out of place I was there, how out of my league.

"Will you have some wine?" she asked.

"Oh, I don't know, I don't usually drink at lunchtime, to be honest."

"Go on, it's just us girls, let's let our hair down and live dangerously." She quickly scanned the wine list.

I laughed. "Okay, let's, then." And it felt great to say it. God, I was happy.

"I'll get the sommelier, madam," the maître d' said. He made a quick gesture to attract his attention, but she stopped him.

"No need, Alain, I know what we'll have. A bottle of the Barth. Thank you." She handed him the wine list and turned to me. "I'm glad you could make it, Emma, and let me apologize again—wait, did I apologize at all?"

"What for?"

"For dragging you into my life's complications." She shook her head.

"It wasn't that complicated, Beatrice." *Beatrice.* I loved saying her name. My friend Beatrice. I tried it on for size: *Have you met my friend Beatrice? Oh, do you know her? Beatrice Johnson Greene! The writer! Yes! That's my friend Beatrice!*

"Well, it was generous of you to help me. So, thank you," she said.

I snapped back to the present. I was here, for goodness' sake.

I was about to contradict her again, but the sommelier arrived with a bottle of something that looked like pink champagne.

"Monsieur Raymond, as always, your timing is exquisite." She winked at him as he served us. I didn't think I could get through half a bottle, but never mind. We were letting our hair down.

"No, leave it here." She put out a hand to stop him from taking the silver ice bucket to the sideboard a few feet away. She leaned toward me conspiratorially. "Do you think they do that to stop us from drinking too much?" she whispered. "Making us ask for a refill every time? You'd think that would be bad for business."

We ordered food, and as we were sipping our drinks, we asked about each other's lives. *Where do you live? Are you married? Do you have children?* It turned out we were both married with no children, although I still wished for one or two very much, and at the age of thirty-two I still had a very good chance, I thought. I hoped.

"Not me," she said. "Well, obviously not me—even modern medicine isn't that good yet. Or maybe it is? Anyway, I've never wanted children, and children have never wanted me."

"What about George?" I asked, then quickly regretted it. "I'm sorry, that's none of my business."

"George doesn't care one way or another," she replied, ignoring my discomfort. "He knew when he married me I didn't want a family, not like that. He's never asked me if I've changed my mind in the thirty-four years we've been married."

"Really!" I blurted out.

"Is that so surprising? My books are my children. My friends are my family. We live a charmed life, George and I. Why ruin it with children?"

I burst out laughing. I was surprised they'd never really had a conversation about children, but I let it go. She helped herself to another glass of pink champagne. The sommelier materialized by our side, horrified.

"Oh, Monsieur Raymond," she scolded him gently, "we've known each other long enough, and it's just us women here—we can look after ourselves." She shooed him off as he muttered his *very well*s and *as you wish*es. I smiled at him apologetically. I wouldn't want to disappoint the sommelier.

"Come on, catch up," she chided. I had barely touched my glass, and she was onto her second. I did as I was told and finished my drink obligingly so she could replenish it.

"Can we talk about your books?" I asked. She smiled a little and I took that as encouragement. "I just wanted to tell you, you really are my favorite author. I just love everything you write."

And I was off. I couldn't stop babbling about my admiration for her. That's what one glass of pink champagne will do to me. "They're so unusual and gripping! Where do you get your ideas? Your characters? They're so—I don't know—I want to say *real* but it's more than that."

She looked genuinely pleased. "Oh, you know, it's hard to say exactly. A lot of my characters are based on myself, especially the weak and nasty ones!" She laughed, and I did too, but I was struck by the fact that I'd heard her say those exact words recently on the radio. Maybe that's what happens when you're asked the same thing over and over.

And why wouldn't she give the same answer every time? It only showed it to be the truth, after all.

The food was divine, in the *nouvelle* tradition, and every bit as delicious as I was expecting, but Beatrice barely touched her plate. Just as I was thinking I'd had enough to drink, she motioned to the sommelier for another bottle.

"But tell me about you, Emma."

"Oh, there's not much to tell."

"Of course there is. Tell me everything. Tell me about the store, to begin with, and we'll go from there. How did it come about?"

So I told her about the life insurance payout when my mother died in my early twenties, and how shocked I was to receive the money: I'd had no idea she even had insurance. I told Beatrice how much I missed my mother, and that she'd loved beautiful things, but I didn't tell her that we hadn't been able to afford any of them. Or that we used to spend hours together, poring over glossy home-decorating magazines I'd stolen from the doctor's waiting room, constructing our ideal home, room by room, piece by piece, knowing full well that we would never get out of that hellhole of an apartment in a crummy area of Queens.

No, I didn't tell her any of that, and anyway, it was a tale of another time and another place. But I did tell her that, almost on a whim, I had taken the money and bought the store, so that I could stock all the things my mother would have loved, and in my own way I could live among them, just as she'd wanted me to.

We talked about my favorite designers, about how I sourced new stock. Then I told her more about Jim, what a wonderful man he was, and how lucky I felt that he had chosen me. She shook her head at that.

"Please, Emma, you're a beautiful, accomplished businesswoman. Jim must have been beating men off with a stick."

I laughed, not just at the rush of pleasure that her words brought me, but at the imagery. That afternoon I pretty much told her everything

I was willing to share about myself, short of my social security number. I was tempted to tell her that as well.

I didn't pay attention to how many times she refilled our glasses, but I was definitely light-headed. The entire time I told her my stories, she looked at me intently with her large brown eyes, frowning in concentration, like she didn't want to miss a single morsel; asking questions, prompting me to go on about certain topics. I felt, literally, fascinating.

And then I blurted out the one thing I'd been dying to tell her but hadn't had the nerve to.

"I wrote a novel once."

She jerked her head up, eyebrows raised high. "Did you? Really? Tell me more, tell me everything!"

"Oh, it was a silly thing. I just did it for myself. It was years ago."

"A novel is never a silly thing, my dear. Was it published? Can I get a copy?"

"God, no." I laughed, embarrassed now. "I tried. I sent the manuscript to a few people but nothing happened."

Why did I lie? My "novel" had been no more than twenty pages at best.

"What was it about, tell me. Was it a crime novel? A romance, maybe? I love a good romance."

So I told her, reluctantly, making it up as I went along, and wished I hadn't said anything at all, but she wouldn't let me change the subject.

"You know, Emma, my novel *The Man in Winter*? I wrote that ten years—wait, more, thirteen years I think—before it was published."

"My Lord, that's one of my favorites! Or maybe it is my favorite. So, what happened?"

"Well, my agent didn't think it was ready. She wanted me to make changes that I wasn't comfortable with. To cut a long story short, I refused to change anything, put it in a drawer, and moved on to other books. Then one day, I pulled it out again and reread it for the first time in more than a decade, and I realized right away that she was right!" She laughed. "And I knew in a flash that if I made those changes, it would be perfect! So I did, and here we are. What I'm trying to say, Emma, is why don't you dust off your manuscript and take another look at it, with fresh eyes?"

"Oh no, I don't even have it anymore anyway. I threw it out years ago."

"Threw it out? No, Emma! No! Never throw out a manuscript! Never!"

"Oh, that's history now. But you know"—I paused, and took the plunge—"I have an idea for another one," I said. "I think this one might be worth the effort." I shook my head. "Lord, I'm drunk."

"Emma! How coy you are!"

"It's hard to find the time, really, or maybe the motivation. I don't know. But I'd like to give this one a good try. Meeting you, and talking about this, it's inspiring me." I smiled at her and raised my glass.

"I have an idea: why don't you show it to me? I'll tell you what I think."

"Oh Lord, no! I'd never! I—"

She stopped me with one hand raised. "No, hear me out."

I sat back and listened.

"I'll tell you what I think, and I'll be honest, but I can also show you some tricks of the trade. I can even help you finish it, if you like. I'll be your mentor! It would be so much fun. We'd have a project to do together. What do you say?"

I didn't know what to say. I was dumbstruck, but I knew I'd be a fool to pass this up, and I was drunk enough to do something about it.

"Thank you, I'd be honored. I really would. I accept your offer."

With her other hand, she lifted her glass and we toasted for the umpteenth time that afternoon, this time to literary successes all around.

7

I rode home in a taxi, having gotten Beatrice into one first. She was far drunker than me, and that was saying something. I was supposed to do inventory that afternoon, but it was out of the question now. And anyway, I wanted to work on my outline. That was my first piece of homework from Beatrice. She wanted me to bring her an outline of the novel, along with any snippets of writing I had. I had none at that point, but I was excited at the prospect.

"Outlining your story is a great starting point. Make it as long or as short as you like, I don't care. In some parts it'll be vague probably, but it will help you see the arc of the story. And me too."

I was happy to find Jim home when I got there. I couldn't wait to tell him my news. He worked from home often: one of the perks of an academic research position. I could hear him on the phone in his office. I opened the door and knocked lightly at the same time to let him know I was there. He looked up at me and smiled.

I was in no state to do anything productive, so I went upstairs to the bedroom to have a nap.

I was lying on top of the covers with my eyes closed, replaying the hours Beatrice and I had spent together, step by step, word by word, savoring every morsel like a lovestruck teenager after a first date, when I heard Jim opening the door quietly, checking in on me. I kept my eyes closed; I was enjoying my reverie too much. Eventually, of course, these thoughts led to a delicious fantasy where my novel was a resounding success. I was going to be profiled in a glossy magazine, my journey to published author written up for all to read, telling the world what it's like to have a friend and mentor like Beatrice. I imagined different lunches where we discussed our latest manuscripts, used each other as a sounding board, asked for each other's feedback on particularly tricky plots.

I couldn't stand it anymore—I was too excited. I got up and went to the kitchen to make a pot of strong coffee.

"Are you okay?" I turned. Jim was leaning against the doorjamb with a mildly concerned look on his face, his arms crossed against his chest.

"I am! Lord, Beatrice and I had a rather boozy lunch at L'Ambroisie, if you can believe it! I needed a bit of recovery time." I smiled. I felt like I was sparkling. Scintillating at the thought of my new reality. Boozy lunches with Beatrice Johnson Greene at L'Ambroisie, discussing my latest novel. Words failed me.

"Beatrice?"

"You know, I told you about her the other day. She bought something from the shop and I—"

"Ah yes, I remember. I didn't know you were seeing her today."

"Neither did I, but she wanted to thank me, you know, for the—"

"Yes. Lady Gan-Greene's delivery girl. I remember."

Except he wasn't making it sound as funny as last time.

"You're okay?" I asked.

"Yes, I'm fine. Working on my paper for the conference. Some of us can't take time out whenever we like to go and get sauced in the middle of the day."

"Hey, come on! I—"

"Only joking! I'm just jealous, that's all. I'm drowning in work over here."

I had completely forgotten about the conference. "How's it coming along?"

"Hard work. You know how it is—no wait, you don't."

"What's wrong, Jim?"

"Nothing. I'm joking."

Okay, here we were again. I recognized the signs. This was Jim at his most stressed. No wonder, really: he *was* working very hard, and good for him, because he was making a name for himself. That was one of the things I loved about him—his ambition.

I sat down at the kitchen table and tapped the chair next to me, inviting him to sit. "Please stay and have coffee with me. I want to tell you my news."

"Tell me quickly, because I still need to pack," he said, sitting down.

"Oh, honey! I can barely say the words! It feels so unreal. I don't want to break it by saying it out loud!"

"What is it?" He poured a cup for himself.

I blurted it out. "Beatrice is going to mentor me, help me finish my novel! I'm *so* excited! I'm beside myself! I can't stop thinking about it!"

"Sorry, what? What novel?"

"You know, the one I started in college. The story about—"

"That's the first I ever heard of it. I have no idea what you're talking about."

"Well, anyway, I started writing a novel back then, and it wasn't bad, actually—"

He shook his head. "In college? Really? Oh, Em, sweetheart, that was a lifetime ago! And it wasn't exactly *college*, was it? It was secretarial school or something, right?"

"I did take creative writing for a semester. Who knows what I could do with Beatrice's help?"

"Oh, come on! I know how much you love reading, and that's great, but that doesn't make you a *writer!*" He was actually laughing at me.

"Well, obviously I know that, thanks very much. She offered to look at my chapters and an outline of the story. She's going to help me. She says there are techniques I should know about. What's so funny about that?"

"Oh, sweetheart, honestly, she probably wants something delivered." He laughed heartily at his own sense of humor.

"Okay. Go away. Go back to your work, and leave me be. You're annoying me now."

"Don't be mad, Em. But honestly, listen to yourself. You're great at so many things, Em. You have a great eye." He made a sweeping gesture to show that this room, our beautiful kitchen, was a testament to my good taste. Which it was. "You're a visual person, Em. And you're very good at it. But you're not a writer. You can't be great at everything. Writing is an intellectual pursuit, a cerebral exercise more than anything else. You're visual."

"I'm sure there's a compliment in there somewhere." I crossed my arms defensively. "I'm not sure what you're trying to tell me, Jim, but it sounds an awful lot like you think I'm stupid."

"Of course not, sweetheart! I don't think that at all! There are many different forms of intelligence and as I keep telling you, yours is visual, which is wonderful! You're lucky! I wish I could be like you!"

"Right. Because you're the cerebral one, obviously."

Of course he was. It was silly of me to even try to argue. Jim had gotten his PhD a few years back, and his research was so impressive, his conclusions so groundbreaking, they had been published in some journal or other that apparently was almost impossible to get published in. That was why he'd gotten his new job. Out of Lord knew how many international applicants, they had begged him to accept it.

"Uh, yes?" he said.

"Well, go and do something cerebral somewhere else then. Go away. Leave me and my stupidity alone, we have a book to write."

"Don't be like that," he said, but he got up anyway, taking his coffee with him. "I don't know what this Beatrice woman is trying to do, but I don't want you to get hurt. That's all." He kissed me on the top of my head and gave me a smile before walking back to his office, shaking his head with a chuckle.

I wasn't feeling fantastic anymore. He had thrown me completely. There I was, raring to go, imagining the words flying from my fingers onto the page, convinced I'd complete my outline in no time at all and have it ready to show Beatrice. And then Jim had ruined it.

I kept telling myself to ignore him, that he was being insensitive because he was stressed. But a part of me knew he was right. I wouldn't have put it quite as sharply as he did, but I wasn't particularly scholarly, shall we say. To be honest, I didn't even know what that meant. I had gone to college, but not for long, and I'd always thought people discovered literature and philosophy and science and music or whatever through their own interests. Being given a reading list and ticking off all the items to receive some degree seemed like cheating to me.

I stood up and put aside all thoughts of starting anything, and instead decided to prepare dinner. As I went about my tasks, I tried not to cry.

Beatrice emailed me. She wanted to talk about the project. She'd been thinking a lot about it, she said, and was eager for us to get started. When should we meet? But now I had a problem. I didn't want to do this project anymore.

"What do you mean, Emma? Of course we're doing this!" she said when I told her.

I felt guilty. She'd been so kind to suggest it and there I was, wasting her time, not up to the task. It would have been easier to be vague—*Let me think about it some more; I'm not sure I'll have the time but I'll see;*

maybe we could start after the holidays, depending; we'll see—but no, I needed to be clear about this.

"Beatrice, I really mean it, it was a silly idea over far too many glasses of pink sparkling."

"Don't ever let Monsieur Raymond hear you call a bottle of NV Barth rosé pink sparkling. He'll have you thrown out of L'Ambroisie and neither of us will ever be able to go there again."

I laughed with a rush of pleasure that she'd described that scene as a shared predicament. It was like we were friends. Real friends.

"But seriously, Emma. Don't give up before you've even started. The whole point of the exercise is for me to show you how it's done, and it's normal to feel doubt, by the way. There, let that be your first lesson, my dear. Don't give in to doubt. You need to push through it to see what's around the corner, otherwise how will you know?"

She had a point, of course, and I found myself telling her about Jim's reaction, and how thrown I was by it. I said probably more than I should have, but the resentment that had been bubbling up in me had found a way out. I told her how, since he'd gotten his new position, he'd made me feel somewhat—I don't know—dismissed. It wasn't the right word of course, but the feeling belonged in that family.

I don't know why I said all these things, since that wasn't really the state of our relationship. We were great together, I felt loved and I loved in return, but something had been niggling at me. Maybe I wanted to try it out, talk to someone, see how it felt, how it fit.

"I'm sorry, Emma, but he's jealous of you," she said, and I burst out laughing.

"Hardly. He's got nothing to be jealous about, trust me."

"You'd be surprised. Men like Jim are very competitive. Take my word for it: I know."

Men like Jim. I knew she meant well but her words sent a rush of guilt through me.

"Hey, Beatrice, look, I shouldn't have said all that. I'm giving you a really bad picture of Jim here. He's not like that at all."

"Trust me, darling. You're a beautiful, accomplished, intelligent businesswoman making her own way in life. You are remarkable. You're someone to look up to. He's the one trying to keep up with you."

I should have been delighted to hear those words, to have someone like her stand up for someone like me, but she didn't know Jim from a bar of soap, so instead I found it presumptuous of her to say those things about the man I'd spent so many years with, as if she could read him better than I could. I had done him a disservice and I knew it. He'd be livid if he found out. Anyway, I wasn't beautiful—not then—and I didn't care. I wasn't particularly accomplished either, and it was a stretch to call me a businesswoman. I didn't need to hear this.

"I was sharing a moment, Beatrice, not the whole picture. I'm sorry I said all those things. I shouldn't have, it was unfair of me. I can't take it back, but I wish I hadn't said it."

"Well, never mind. It's just us girls. And I do understand, really I do. But I will say this—he's lucky to have you."

"Okay, let's leave it at that then."

"Of course. But don't think you're off the hook. We made a deal, you and me, and I'm not asking to see *War and Peace* here, just two pages. After that, who knows?"

I felt myself relax, enjoying the conversation again. "Okay, you're on. Two pages, then."

"Tightly spaced, eleven-point type. No cheating."

"Got it."

"That man of yours, when is he back? Because I want to steal you for myself this evening. Would you mind?"

"He's back tomorrow, but—"

"Wonderful! Come with me to Craig Barnes's little soiree. He's a friend of mine. You'll love him, and you'll meet all sorts of fascinating people who write fascinating things. Please say yes?"

I hesitated for a moment, but only for a moment.

Do something different, Emma: meet different people, nurture this new friendship with this amazing woman.

"I'd love to."

"Wonderful! I'm so glad! Will you meet me here? At my apartment? We'll go from here?"

I spent the rest of the day giddy with excitement.

"Emma, darling, look at you! You look beautiful!" I was wearing a knee-length dress with short sleeves. It was red with large poppies. I loved that dress. It had been a gift from one of my suppliers, who designed the most wonderful printed fabrics. Beatrice looked stunning in a black and white dress—maybe a bit too much jewelry for my taste, lots of gold bracelets, that sort of thing, but on her, it worked.

I thought we both looked pretty good, but she looked way better.

I'd never been in an apartment as beautiful and opulent as this. It was even better than my mother's and my ideal home. "Come in, darling—this way." She took my arm and guided me down a long, bright hallway.

"Oh my gosh, this is something else. I suppose you have a den? A morning room? A hall of mirrors?"

"A morning room? Hardly. What would I do with it? I'm never up in the morning. The hall of mirrors is through there, however."

We both burst out laughing. She put an arm around my shoulders and we walked into a very large, modern living room. It was beautiful, with a polished stone floor and colorful rugs positioned here and there that helped define inner spaces. But it was the windows at the far end that drew the eye—wide and tall, curved at the top. Dominating the room was a large curving staircase with a blue carpet running down the center of it.

"My God! It's a duplex!"

"Yes, darling. The bedrooms are upstairs, and my office—my writing room. George's office is downstairs, along with, you know"—she flapped her hand vaguely—"everything else down here."

At the far end of the room was a large sitting area, and to the left, an alcove, and as we reached it I gasped in surprise and wonder. Water cascaded down a large copper wall into a stone riverbed. The sound was quiet and delicious.

"Ah yes, the water feature."

It was mesmerizing. I put my hand through the water and touched the copper wall behind it. "Amazing, really."

"Isn't it? And you know, it helps cool the room in summer."

I gazed at the fountain a while longer, until Beatrice took me by the hand. "Come on, let's get you a drink."

We walked over to the bar. I couldn't stop admiring everything— the tall ceilings, the lovely rugs, the colors. *What would she think of my much humbler home?* I thought. I'd always loved my home. I'd decorated it exactly as I wanted, to make it comfortable, light, warm, and welcoming. Now I wondered for the first time if I hadn't made it ordinary instead.

She handed me a glass. "Try this. I made it especially for you."

I took a sip, spat it back out. "It's revolting!" I said, wiping my mouth with the back of my hand.

"Really?" She took it back from me with an exaggerated sigh. "I really thought I'd nailed it this time. I'm trying to invent cocktails: it's my new hobby. I was experimenting with vermouth. Does anyone drink vermouth anymore? Never mind. Here, have a Pinot Gris instead." She retrieved a bottle from the wine cooler and poured me a glass.

"George isn't here?" I'd have liked to meet her husband.

"Yes, he is, somewhere. Probably in his office looking at numbers on a screen, the phone stuck to his ear." She made a vague gesture toward the other rooms.

She told me George was some kind of financier, that he ran his own investment fund, and that he was very successful at it. "He must be very clever," I said. "I can't imagine working with things so—intangible, values that may or may not materialize."

"Yes, I know exactly what you mean. I like to think he trades in hope."

"More of a dream catcher hopefully," said a voice behind me.

"Ah, there you are! Darling! Come and be met!" She stretched an arm toward him to welcome him into our little fold.

I knew there was an age difference between them—that he was about ten years younger than Beatrice—but seeing them together you'd never have known. He was very handsome, and very . . . *dignified*, I thought. The two of them were a perfect match, and in their beautiful surroundings, they looked like royalty.

"I'm not staying. I have masses of work to get through, but I heard the door."

I put my hand forward to shake his, but instead he took mine and bowed slightly to kiss it. A gesture that would have been pompous coming from most people, but not from him. He was charming.

"It's nice to meet you, Emma. My wife talks about you often, and I'm delighted to meet a new friend of hers."

I blushed instantly. "It's nice to meet you too, George." He turned to Beatrice and kissed her gently on the cheek.

"I really do have piles of work. Please don't think me rude," he said. "Have fun, both of you." And he walked out of the room.

"We will!" Beatrice replied cheerily, then turned to me. "Let's go, I'll get my coat."

8

"Are these the right size?" Jackie was unpacking a set of brass bookends, frowning. "They look smaller, don't you think?"

I took a closer look at the items, which were shaped like small, sitting elephants. A bit of a novelty item for us, but they sold well.

"They look fine to me. Do they even come in another size?"

She shrugged and we continued in silence for a few minutes.

"Do you feel like getting a drink later?" Jackie asked, polishing the trunk of one of the elephants with great concentration.

I sighed inwardly.

"Can't—we're going to Beatrice's for dinner, Jim and I."

She looked up. "Is that why you're so quiet today?"

"Am I?"

Was I? Probably. I'd been thinking about this dinner all day. Jim had still never met Beatrice, incredible as that sounded, considering how much time I'd been spending with her over the last month or so. I was so pleased that we'd been invited to dinner. I really thought that if he got to know her, he'd love her as much I did. I wanted us all to get along. In my fantasy world, which I had probably been inhabiting far too much lately, I'd started to imagine the four of us as close friends—dreaming up occasions where we dined together, visited an exhibition, went on a trip—so this invitation was certainly a step in that direction.

"Sorry, Jac." I felt a tinge of guilt.

"It's just that . . ."

"What?"

"Oh, no big deal, it's been weeks since we've had a drink together, that's all. I miss it." She had polished that elephant to within an inch of its life.

Weeks. Had it been weeks? Of course it had. I'd been ignoring Jackie, but it had been a blur of luncheons and parties, Beatrice and I dashing off together every other day, seeing more or less the same people, the same faces. These were the people who made up Beatrice's circle and they were all wealthy; almost all famous, or so it seemed to me; and very, very fun. I was a bit of a mystery to them, and they were very complimentary to me, as if they had never met someone who did ordinary work for a living and inhabited an ordinary house—as if it were a lifestyle choice, like joining a nunnery.

But they were friendly, welcoming even, and when we talked about this film or that exhibition, fashion week or the latest art prize, I gradually stopped feeling intimidated by their sophistication, their ease at being in the world. I had even started to think of them as my friends. They called me "Bea's protégée."

I always drove us to our "dos," as she liked to call these outings. "Come along with me to this do," she'd say. "It'll be fun." She always said that, and it was invariably true. I'd always drive her home. That was our ritual now, and I didn't mind in the least. For one thing, I knew she'd get home safe, and that was important to me. Alcohol has never been my thing, and she did like to party, as they say.

"I hate catching taxis," she told me early on. "Who wants to stand on the sidewalk doing semaphore anyway? What if someone took a photo of me—can you imagine? The embarrassment?"

I wanted to do that for her, and she was grateful. I loved doing things to help Beatrice, and why wouldn't I, when she was so good to me? But even Jim had been making remarks about this friendship.

"You should get out more, Em. You're shutting yourself up in here," he'd say sarcastically. It was funny, but there was a tinge of something slithering through these jokes. Something like resentment, maybe.

And now Jackie.

I gave her a hug. "I'm sorry," I said into her hair, "I really am. I miss you too."

She snorted. "It's not you I miss, it's the alcohol."

I chuckled.

"Seriously, Em," she said as I released my embrace, "I'm happy for you that you have a new friend, but you know, you don't need to completely ignore your old ones."

"I know, you're right." Then I said, as if I'd only just thought of it, "You should come with us sometime. You'd love Beatrice. I know you would. And she'd love you! She *will* love you!"

She raised her eyes at me without lifting her head.

"Maybe," she said finally, looking back down to her task.

We both knew I wasn't exactly being genuine. I did want Jackie to join us, but not just yet. This friendship with Beatrice was new and exciting, and I was learning to be myself, my better self, around her. I needed to be comfortable with that before I brought in my "old" friends, as Jackie called them.

We were both relieved when the phone rang.

"I've got it," I said.

"Brian called," I said to Jim. We were in the car, on the way to dinner, my stomach in a knot. I'd waited for him—I couldn't wait to tell him—but he'd been late and we'd had to leave right away if we were going to get there on time.

"Brian?" He was focused on the road.

"Yes, Brian Moreno, from First National—our banker, remember him?" I hadn't meant to sound so flippant.

"Yep, Brian. Okay, what about him?"

"What about him? He called to get my approval on the loan you applied for."

"The loan?"

"You put our house up as collateral, so of course he called me. He needed my signature. Want to share why you need a hundred thousand all of a sudden?"

"I'm sorry, Em, but I have no idea what you're talking about."

Was he lying to me? He seemed relaxed enough, but Jim was very particular about his finances. The news that someone had tried to borrow money against our house should have sent him into a spin.

"You didn't try to take the money out today?"

"Nope."

"Well, someone logged in with your details and applied for the loan. Does that not worry you at all?"

He snapped his head my way. "Did Brian approve it?"

"Of course not. I just told you, he called me and I told him I wanted to talk to you first."

"Thank God, Em! Sorry, I was really distracted there, it didn't sink in, what you were saying. I'll have to change my login details. I'll do it as soon as we get home."

"I got Brian to put a stop on your login."

"What?"

"What was I supposed to do? You can talk to him tomorrow. He'll issue a new password or something."

"Oh good, good, great. Thanks, Em."

"So it wasn't you then?"

"No! Of course not! What would I do that for?" he said, echoing my thoughts.

"Okay."

"I'll talk to Brian tomorrow. It'll be okay, Em. Don't worry."

I started to let go of the tension I'd been holding in my stomach. I felt more relieved than I should have. Was that normal? After hearing that someone had tried to hack into our bank account?

◆　◆　◆

"No problem with parking?" George asked as he reached for our coats.

"No, none at all! Thank you, George, your instructions were perfect," I replied brightly.

"Some guy in your garage thought we were burglars, I think," Jim said, by way of greeting.

"Not really." I shot a look at him, then turned back to George. "One of your neighbors was parking at the same time as us. He wanted to know who we were, and who we were visiting. You can't be too careful, I'm sure."

"I'm surprised he didn't call you to check," Jim said, sneering.

"Maybe *he* was the robber," I suggested lightly. God, I was already trying too hard. I needed to relax. *It will be fine. Everyone will have a good time and live happily ever after.*

"What did he look like?" George asked, welcoming us into the main hall.

"Thin-rimmed glasses, leather jacket, trendy haircut."

"Sounds like Marcus. He's harmless enough, just not used to his new surroundings. He thinks there aren't enough CCTV cameras in the parking garage; that sort of thing. That's what being young, running a start-up, and landing a billion-dollar IPO will do to you."

Jim let out an admiring whistle as we walked into the living room. I couldn't help feeling a little proud. Actually, the word is *smug*. There was a fire going, and the apartment was warm and welcoming.

"Not bad, hey?" I whispered, accompanied by a gentle elbow-bump on his arm.

"It's like Louis Quatorze and Dolly Parton had a child who became an interior designer," he muttered, not so loud as to be overtly rude, but close enough to make my spine snap straight.

"It's nothing like that, Jim, really," I said, whispering.

He looked at me with a half-smile. "I know—teasing."

Beatrice joined us and went straight to greet Jim, arms spread wide, and enveloped him in a warm embrace. I knew this was awkward for him—he wasn't a touchy-feely guy—but he'd come ready for a party, and gave back as good as he got.

"I'm so happy to finally meet you." She hooked her arm into his. He was trying to contain his smile, I could tell.

"I have heard *lots* about you." She winked at me. I wished she hadn't done that. It made us look like we'd been gossiping.

"Well, it's all lies. I'm actually a really nice person," he said. Beatrice shot me a quizzical look, but it was just one of Jim's little jokes. He always said that when someone said "I've heard a lot about you."

We moved toward the windows, where George was preparing us drinks, and I showed Jim the lighting between the exposed rafters on the ceiling, with maybe more enthusiasm than was warranted.

"You must come here often," I heard a voice say behind me.

The first thing I noticed about the woman who was facing me was her gray hair. It looked great. She was attractive, elegant. I shook the hand extended to me.

"I'm Hannah, Beatrice's agent," she said.

"Beatrice's friend, surely!" Beatrice exclaimed. She had seated herself on the couch and was patting the place next to her. "Jim, please sit with me, so I can talk to you without having to shout across the room."

He did as he was told, slowly. I wanted him to hurry up. *Don't keep Beatrice waiting*, I almost said. Hannah and I stood together as George handed out the drinks.

"I've been here a few times, yes," I said, a bit unsure of myself. Was I supposed to reply literally, as I had? I had this awful feeling that the evening was about to descend to that place where everyone got the joke except me, and the more paranoid I became, the more likely it was to happen. *Pull yourself together*, I told myself. *What's the matter with you?*

"Home decor is a bit of a passion of mine, so I tend to go overboard when I see something I like." I gazed around the room.

"You play the piano?" Jim was asking Beatrice. I turned to look at them and saw him pointing his chin toward the white baby grand.

"No—you?" she replied.

"No," Jim said slowly, turning to me with one raised eyebrow. "Which is why I don't have one," he added with a smirk.

I quickly turned back to Hannah, smiling, pretending I hadn't heard that little exchange, but struggling to stop the vein that was throbbing in my neck.

"So, Emma, you seem to have succeeded where many others have failed," Hannah said.

"How so?"

"You have seduced Beatrice! Many have tried, I assure you!"

"Oh, I think it's the other way around," I giggled.

"I understand you're a bit of a writer yourself?"

"Me? Oh no! Not really. I mean, I did think, once, a long time ago, but that was, no . . ." I was rambling now, feeling myself flush deep red. To my great relief, the maid came in announcing that dinner was served.

Beatrice stood up. "Please, everyone, this way," she said, indicating the archway that led into the formal dining room.

She put a hand on Hannah's shoulder.

"Sorry, dearest, Craig canceled on me tonight, and it was too late for me to make up the numbers."

"Oh, don't be silly, Beatrice. I don't need to be matched, especially not with your trendy gay friends, unless you're allergic to odd numbers."

"Jim, walk with me, will you?" Beatrice took his arm, and Hannah and I walked together. It was all very old-fashioned, I thought.

"I love your shoes." Hannah was looking down at my feet.

"Oh, thanks. They're Kate Spade. I do love what they do to my feet, I must say." I too was looking down.

"Are they comfortable?"

We'd reached the table then, and I rested a hand on the back of a chair and pulled off one of my shoes with the other to show Hannah. "Very—you'd be surprised."

"Do you mind?" She took it from me and pulled her own shoe off.

"Not at all. I think we're probably the same size."

It made me feel better, this. Checking out each other's shoes, talking about fashion—not that I was a big follower, but I had started to pay more attention since I'd begun hanging out with Beatrice.

"Sit down, you two, stop dawdling. It'll get cold," Beatrice scolded. Hannah was seated between George and Jim, and after a little while the three of them were deep in conversation.

The food was wonderful.

"I wonder how she can bear it, talking to those two. Doesn't she know that finance and economics are the two dullest subjects on earth?" Beatrice said.

We laughed.

"Did you bring it?" Beatrice asked.

I knew she meant the outline of course. She'd been asking me about it all week, but it had turned out to be harder than I thought, writing up a summary of my story. I told her it was all her fault: if she was going to take me out to parties every night, how could I possibly find the time to write up my outline? *I'm not a superwoman*, I'd told her. *Yes, you are*, she had replied. *That's why I love you so.*

That's what had spurred me on, to get on with it and get it done.

"Yes, I did, it's on the table in the hall."

"Good," she said.

"But it's very rough," I blurted. "Just a couple of pages, like you said, Beatrice—an outline of some kind."

"I know," she said, putting a hand on my arm. "Don't worry, darling, I'm sure it's perfect."

"You won't show it to anyone, will you?"

"Of course not . . . I was thinking we need some new things in here," Beatrice said, changing the subject. "What do you think? One of those big country dressers—you know the ones, where people put their plates to show them off."

"Seriously?"

"Why do you say that?"

"It wouldn't fit in here, Beatrice. The style would be all wrong for the space. But I know a piece that would work in this room. It's low and wide"—I had my arms outstretched, emphasizing the width aspect—"with tapered legs, which would go really well with this table. In fact, it would be perfect."

She smiled at me. "You're so clever, Emma. I'm so glad I asked you." I felt a tinge of pleasure as she kissed me on the cheek.

After dinner, we had a nightcap in the living room. Jim and George were still engrossed in their conversation. They had barely acknowledged the rest of us all night, but I didn't mind. I was pleased that Jim was having a good time.

When Hannah made noises about calling it a night, we took the opportunity to say our goodbyes as well, and a few minutes later our little group was standing by the front door, putting coats on and kissing each other good night.

"Wait! Where is it?" Beatrice was spinning around the hall in search of something.

I groaned inwardly. I hadn't mentioned it to Jim since that day, and I didn't really want us to have that conversation again. I didn't want him to make me feel bad about it.

"There." I pointed to the envelope that was sitting on top of the narrow table.

To my horror, she picked it up, and for a moment I thought she was going to open it right there and then, with Hannah peering over her shoulder.

"Good girl," Beatrice said.

"What's this?" Jim asked.

"A fat wad of cash, of course!" Beatrice said. "No, not exactly. Although by the time I'm done with your wife, it'll be worth much more than that."

Jim raised an eyebrow at me. There was no escaping now.

"You know what it is, darling. I told you, Beatrice is helping me with my writing."

"Are you?" George said. "That's kind of you, Bea."

"I thought you weren't going ahead with that," Jim said. "Obviously you've changed your mind."

"Obviously she has," Beatrice said, a little sharply.

I rubbed his shoulder gently. "I thought I'd give it a go, that's all, and Beatrice is so kind to offer."

"Doesn't bother me," Jim said. "I'm just surprised, that's all." George, Hannah, Jim, and Beatrice were all looking at me, waiting for me to say something, to explain. I felt exposed.

"It's just a little thing, no big deal." I made a vague gesture in the air with my fingers. I just wanted to leave. I thanked Beatrice one last time, and she took both my hands in hers.

"Sorry," she whispered. "I didn't mean to put you on the spot."

I nodded, a little embarrassed, a little disappointed.

9

"What do you think of this?" I was sitting on Beatrice's bed and she was standing in front of me, looking down at some kind of pantsuit she was holding up against herself. "I bought it from that vintage shop I told you about. Isn't it divine?"

"Stop! No! It's too strange, I can't let you wear that!"

"Why? It's my throwback to the seventies, which as you know is back in fashion—luckily for me, too. I have miles and miles of this stuff."

"It's lime green, Beatrice! Please!"

She looked down at it. "Ah yes, so it is," she said. We burst out in hoots of laughter. We'd been doing a lot of that lately—laughing, lounging around in her bedroom. Once I'd called it her boudoir and she'd said, "You know *bouder* means 'to sulk' in French? So by extension, the *boudoir* must be the sulking room." After that we always called her bedroom the sulking room. The fun we had—how I loved her.

She took a sip from the charming little silver flask she kept on her dresser. It had an inlay of mother-of-pearl on the front. Highly unusual and very feminine. Of another time. She took a swig every now and then as we chatted, and it looked dainty. I was strangely moved by this old-fashioned quirk of hers. It was as if she'd stepped out of a 1920s novel.

"Oh, all right. After all, you're the queen of good taste, so I suppose I should listen."

"Just this once, yes, you should." She passed the flask to me and I took a sip.

She changed, finally, into a surprisingly demure outfit. Black pants and a white shirt. And she looked as gorgeous as ever. I stared at her and sighed.

"You're so lucky, Beatrice. I don't understand how you do it. I don't know why you take so long to choose an outfit since it never matters what you wear—you're always stunning."

"Oh, you're a dear to say that, my love. Truth be told, it takes a bit of money to get there. Ask my hairdresser, manicurist, and the rest of that army. But look at you! What are you talking about? You look absolutely scrumptious! Oh, don't look so sad. You look far too sad, far too often. It's that husband of yours. It's all his fault."

Did I look sad? Maybe. Things had been a little strange at home. I'd never gotten a full explanation about the attempted withdrawal of money. Brian thought someone must have come across Jim's login details. "It's not like it's unusual, Emma," he'd said. "It must happen hundreds of times every day. Welcome to the Internet."

There was no reason for me to believe anything else. What would Jim want with all that money? It made no sense. But there was something— some shift that I couldn't quite understand, couldn't quite put my finger on. He'd been a bit distant lately, more than usual. When I asked him if he was okay, he blamed it on his work.

"There's a lot going on, Em. We're building up to a huge milestone. I need to give it a hundred percent."

"For how long?" I asked.

"I don't know, Em. A few more weeks, okay?"

But he'd agreed that I could go with him on his next trip, another conference coming up, in Montreal. I was looking forward to it so much, I'd splurged on some mightily expensive—and, I hoped, sexy—underwear: a little surprise for my husband.

"Did you hear what I said?" Beatrice asked.

"Sorry." I shook my head to brush off the thoughts, get focused again.

"Lipstick?" She pointed to her lips, pulling them away from her teeth.

"Beautiful." I stood up and followed her out and down the stairs.

"Watch out for that top step!" she said in a singsong voice, for the hundredth time. "The carpet's gaping and you'll catch your toe. Oh, I've been having a hell of time trying to get that man to come back and fix it. He's very much in demand, or so he says. I don't know why. How hard can it be to lay down a carpet? I wish George was more the man about the house!"

That night, when I dropped her off outside her building and kissed her good night, she put a hand on my cheek. "Emma, lunch with me tomorrow, will you? I want to discuss something with you, I've been putting it off far too long."

My heart took a little leap. "About my novel?"

"Sort of, I guess. Will you come?"

"Of course I will. Is it that bad?"

"Don't be silly," she laughed, and blew a kiss in my direction.

I'd been asking her almost every day what she thought of my outline, whether she'd read it yet, whether I should redo it, but each time she somehow put me off. I was starting to think it must be really awful if she couldn't bring herself to discuss it with me.

"I'm putting my thoughts together. There's so much to say. Give me a little more time," she said whenever I brought it up.

I got home that night and fell into bed next to my husband, who had long ceased waiting up for me, and dreamed—dreamed of what might be.

◆　◆　◆

We'd arranged to meet at my local café, Altitude. They made great food and the place had a good vibe, and since I needed to be at the store all day, it was nice not to have to travel into Manhattan.

I got my usual espresso and chatted with the owner awhile. Beatrice was always late, but I was used to that by now, and as ever it was a pleasure to see her walk through the door with a warm, wide smile and her arms stretched out above her head.

"Emma, darling! What a day! I've been running around like a madwoman! It's so good to see you!" She grabbed my face and kissed me on both cheeks.

"You just saw me yesterday!" I managed to say through my distorted mouth, holding her wrists to stop her from crushing my cheeks.

"Let's eat," she said as she let go and sat down, grabbing the menu. "I'm starving. What do you recommend?"

We ordered, we chatted. I was feeling tense. I hoped she wouldn't hate it, my outline. It meant more to me than I'd expected, that she would like it at least a little.

"I must say, Emma, I'm feeling a bit nervous about what I'm about to ask you."

"*Ask me?* Really? That's a first!"

"One should never discuss life-and-death topics over lunch, I've just realized that. We should have met for cocktails somewhere."

"Life and death?"

"Well, maybe not quite. But it's important. Very, very important."

"Then I'm glad we're not drinking. You're starting to worry me, Beatrice, you need to tell me now. Please. Should I be scared?"

She didn't answer right away.

"I was joking," I said, bending my head down a little to catch her eyes.

She looked up. "I know." She smiled, then sat up straighter. "You know I've been working on a new book."

"Sort of. You haven't said much about it, just that it's very special. You made it sound quite mysterious in fact."

"Well, I'm about to tell you all about it."

"Okay, so tell me." *How long is it going to take?* I wondered. *It must be dreadful, what I wrote, if she has to prepare me like this. She's going to tell me how shockingly bad her first draft was and that she had to start over, something like that.*

We waited until the waiter finished serving our meals, and then she said, "But you must promise not to repeat any of this. Not to Jim, not to anyone in the world. Nobody. Can you do that?"

I was about to laugh. Surely this was a joke. But her eyes were locked with mine, telegraphing the seriousness of her words. "I can't promise that, Beatrice. I have no idea what you're about to tell me."

"It's nothing illegal or criminal or anything like that. It's just something very private, very personal to me, and I don't want anyone to know about it. Yet. Later maybe, but not now."

I let her words sink in. "Okay, I accept that. I promise." I waited, but she didn't say anything else. "Everything okay?"

"I want you to be the author of my book." Her words tumbled out so fast I didn't think I'd heard her right.

"What?"

She put down her fork and sighed, sitting back in her chair.

"I want you to be the author of my next book." This time she had spoken clearly, deliberately. The shock on my face must have registered, because she put her hand up and said, "Hear me out."

"Don't worry. I'm speechless."

And so began the strangest conversation of my life.

10

"I don't understand why you don't want to publish this under your own name. It makes no sense to me."

"I just want freedom again. You don't know what it's like for someone in my position. The critics will pore over this and they'll go to town. I write crime novels, Emma—thrillers. I may be good at it, but I'm typecast and always have been. I need this one to be fresh."

"But I'm sure everyone will love it! Why wouldn't they? You're a wonderful writer!"

"Thank you, Emma. You're always so kind to me." She opened her mouth as if to say something else, but nothing came out.

"So?"

"I tried this once before."

"You did?"

"Yes, a war story. No crime, no perpetrator, just a story about two people."

"Well, war stories, you know . . ." I shook my head. "Let's face it, does the world really need another war story?"

She looked away. "It was special to me."

"Sorry." I realized I'd hurt her feelings. I put my hand on top of hers. "Tell me, when was that?" I was sure I'd read everything Beatrice had ever published, and this did not ring any bells.

"Years ago." She pulled her hand away and waved it in dismissal. "I published it under a pseudonym, paid for it all—a vanity-press project. I told myself it didn't matter if it sold or not, or what the critics said. I was doing this for me."

"What happened?"

"Nothing, is what happened. I had to rent a storage unit, the walls of which are still lined with unopened boxes of beautifully printed first-and-only editions of *Life After Us* by B. E. Everett."

I didn't know what to say. I waited while she played with her food.

"I realized that it did matter after all, what people thought. At the very least, I wanted people to read it—some, not that many, but I wanted the knowledge that some people had read that book. I wouldn't have spent tens of thousands of dollars printing five thousand copies if I didn't care."

"But, Beatrice, no one knows me! Why would this be any different than, what was it? B. E. Everett?"

"I did get one very good review, in a small newspaper. That reviewer loved the book. He really wanted to interview me and get some interest going in the novel, but of course that was out of the question. I could hardly pretend to not be me."

"So why didn't you come out as you?"

"For the same reason I explained before: I'd have been shot to pieces by the literati police. No one wants a woman crime novelist to discover literary ambitions, trust me. I'm not the first to attempt this, you know. There are very well-known writers out there doubling as crime or fantasy novelists, or 'serious'"—she made air quotes—"writers who do all that under a pseudonym or two."

"Like that author of the Harry Potter books."

She raised her head and looked at me, finally. "Yes. J. K. Rowling, for example, but that's just because you happened to have heard about that. There are many, many more, Emma. Imagine if she'd had an alter ego to do the interviews, do the radio, do just a little publicity. No one would have been any the wiser. She could have happily published whatever she liked."

"You want me to do that? The interviews? The radio? Be the face of B. E. Everett?"

"No, of course I don't expect you to wander around pretending to be B. E. Everett."

Then it was her turn to reach across the table to take my hand, her eyes focused on mine.

"You will be Emma Fern, of course—Emma Fern, the author of my next book."

I was completely confused. I still couldn't see how it would help to put my name on the cover. It wasn't like I had any credibility in that department.

"Emma Fern has written the book I've just written," she said slowly.

"Emma Fern has written the book you've just written," I repeated.

"Exactly!" She clapped once.

Then I got it.

"Forget it. I can't do it, you must know that. How on earth would I pull it off? Me? Are you kidding?"

She squeezed my hand, her eyes still not leaving mine. "How is this any different than you publishing your own novel? You'd do that, wouldn't you? Publish your own novel?"

"It's all the difference in the world, Beatrice! I'd be able to talk about it. I'd know my novel inside out: it would be mine—surely that's the difference!"

"That's beside the point. Obviously, you'd be prepared. I'd talk you through every sentence, every idea, every nuance of the book."

"And I'd be going on radio? Television?"

"Well, I hope so! I hope it generates enough interest for that, but I can't promise. Maybe one or two newspaper interviews. But that's the point, you see? If it's you in the chair, then you'll be able to talk about the work. You come with no baggage whatsoever."

"That's crazy, Beatrice." I sat back in my chair, pushed my plate away. "So, for the sake of argument, let's assume I agree to go ahead with this insane and very unlikely project. Which I'm not, by the way, and I don't think I will change my mind. But let's assume. Then what happens?"

"Well, you do your one or two interviews, and you and I go fifty-fifty on all the proceeds. Don't get too excited, there won't be much. It takes one hell of a machine to make a book successful, and that's not what we're doing here. Think of it this way: It will give you a head start in the business. By the time you're ready to publish your own novel, you'll already have a publisher and an agent, and you'll know how to deal with the publicity machine."

"It's not going to happen, Beatrice."

"Come on, Emma! You're the person I trust the most in the world, apart from George! Speaking of which, George knows nothing of this, all right? I haven't shown the manuscript to anyone. I haven't discussed this book with anyone. You're the only person in the world who knows about this."

I had to admit I was more flattered than I could say. "Your secret is definitely safe with me. I'm good at keeping secrets, actually. So you don't need to worry about anything, I promise you."

"So you'll do it?"

"Certainly not! I will absolutely not do it! I think it's crazy, Beatrice, and I think you completely underestimate the reception you'll get. I think *you* should do it."

"You do not understand how the publishing world works, my dear," she said drily.

"What I don't understand is why you're so paranoid about this."

She sighed. "I know you don't, but please just think about it. Just let it sit with you for a while, maybe a week. Think it through, ask me any questions."

"Will I get to read the book?" I asked.

"Only if you agree. If you agree, then of course you'll read the book!"

"What if I don't like it?"

She looked at me with one eyebrow raised.

"Right. Got it. I'll like it. A lot, probably."

"That's more like it," she said. "So? Does that mean you'll think about it?"

"No. Absolutely not, Beatrice. I'm sorry, but it's a really terrible idea and I'm not doing it. That's final."

She looked away. *I've made her sad*, I thought. I leaned forward.

"I'm sorry, I really, really am. I'd do anything for you, you know that. But this? I couldn't pull it off."

She nodded.

One week later, the longest stretch of time since I'd first met Beatrice that we hadn't spoken, she called.

"So? Have you thought about my proposition?" she asked.

"Well, hello to you too! Where have you been? Did you get my messages?"

"Sorry, darling, yes I did, of course, but I've been insanely busy, and to be honest, I thought I'd leave you alone for the week, so you could have a proper think about it, without me breathing down your neck."

I felt awful. The truth was I hadn't considered her offer at all since that day. I'd told the truth. It was a stupid idea and I didn't need a week to know I wouldn't change my mind about that.

"I'm not doing it, Beatrice, like I said. I really think you should—"

She interrupted me. "All right, I understand. But I'm counting on you, Emma, not to betray my confidence, all right?"

"Of course! God, Beatrice, you can totally trust me! I promise!"

"Good."

"I'm sorry if you thought I'd go along with it, really I am."

"It's fine, Emma, really. I understand."

"Great!" That was a relief. "So, what time should I pick you up tomorrow?"

"Tomorrow?"

"You know, Craig's lunch? I could come earlier if you like."

"Oh no, don't bother. I won't be going. I just got a set of proofs from my publisher. I need to get them back to her before the end of next week."

"Oh."

"Why don't you take Jim with you? It might be nice to go out with your husband."

"Maybe," I said, trying to sound enthusiastic, and failing.

"Sorry, darling, I must run, but thank you for letting me know your decision."

"Of course. I'll talk to you soon, okay?"

"Yes, you will."

I was so disappointed that I wasn't going to see her the next day. I was hardly going to go to this lunch with Jim. She must have known that. I wasn't used to Beatrice being busy, which was silly of me. She had to work sometime.

She'd told me once that she worked in bursts. "I only work half the year," she'd said. "The other half, I let thoughts bubble through, so by the time I'm ready to go to work, I have a fully formed story in my head."

I was being unfair. I needed to leave her alone. I just hoped it wouldn't be six months; I didn't think I could bear it. But there was a positive side to this: Jim and I could spend a lot more quality time together. We could start with our little trip away to Montreal. We were leaving the following night.

Except that I had expected to hear what Beatrice thought about my story, and she hadn't said a word. I called her back.

"My outline, did you get a chance? To read it? What did you think?" I blurted.

"Yes, of course. Sorry, darling—I did make some notes for you. Come and pick them up."

"Oh good! Now? I could come now." I checked my watch. It would mean closing early, but I didn't care.

"No, no, right now isn't good. Come tomorrow, all right?"

Yes! Yes yes yes! Tomorrow! I could get Jackie to cover for me. I was going to see her and we were going to talk about my story, and—how wonderful!—we could both be working on our stories at the same time. I could see it! Both of us sharing her office!

I'd forgotten to ask what time, so I figured it didn't matter to her. I wasn't going to call her again and disturb her. If she had a time in mind, she'd have told me. So I decided to leave it until after lunch so we could even have a cocktail or two while we were at it. Beatrice never needed to wait until five o'clock for cocktails.

Since she didn't know when to expect me, it was understandable that when I arrived the next day, the maid, whose name I had forgotten, was the one to greet me.

"Mrs. Johnson Greene has left a package for you, madam. I'll fetch it."

"Oh, that's fine, she's expecting me," I said, walking into the hall.

"She's working upstairs, madam. She can't be disturbed."

"Does she know I'm here?" Even to my ears I sounded haughty. I didn't mean to. I was more puzzled than offended.

"Mrs. Johnson Greene has instructed me to give you a package. One moment, please, I'll bring it out."

"Please!" I stopped her; she turned.

"Yes?"

"We have an appointment, she wants to see me, really, will you please tell her I'm here? It's Emma. Emma Fern."

"Yes, I know who you are, Mrs. Fern. Mrs. Johnson Greene doesn't want to be disturbed. She instructed me to give you a package," she insisted.

I stood there, confused, rooted to the floor, dealing with the anticlimax of this moment. Surely we were supposed to discuss my outline? Our heads together, going over every part, dissecting the characters, the narrative arc? Had I misunderstood?

The maid returned with the same envelope I'd given Beatrice and handed it to me. I took it, automatically.

"Is Mr. Greene here?" That would be nice. George and I could spend a little time together while I waited for Beatrice to finish whatever she was doing. She'd like that, I was sure. She'd be pleased I'd waited, and I'd love to spend some time alone with George so I could get to know him a little better. We could have coffee together or something. And Beatrice would be so pleased to see me when she came downstairs.

"Mr. Greene is at work."

Of course, George had his main office downtown. That's where he went to work.

"Should I wait for Mrs. Johnson Greene then?" I was clutching at straws, still hoping she might have asked for me to do so.

"Mrs. Johnson Greene is working right now, madam. She said not to wait."

I really expected her to come down the stairs at this point, before I got a chance to leave, saying, "Emma, darling! There you are! Come up immediately!" But she was nowhere to be seen, so I thanked the maid and left with my thin little envelope.

By the time I got to the subway I'd talked myself better. I hadn't seen Beatrice in work mode, and that's what it was like. Good for her—she had real discipline. I should remember that.

I found a seat and settled in, then tore the flap open, my heart beating faster. I couldn't wait. I pulled the sheets out quickly, but was startled at the sight of them. There were red lines throughout—she'd used a marker—and a few perfunctory comments like *unclear*, and *too cliché*, and that was it, almost. There was a brief note at the end: *Shorter than I expected. Needs work.*

Was that what she meant by *mentoring*? The corners of my mouth drooping, I felt like a schoolgirl—chastised. I'd disappointed her. It wasn't meant to go this way; she was supposed to talk me through it. Did she even like any of it? Any of it at all? Was it really so hopeless? Was I? Tears were pricking the back of my eyes. I shoved the pages back in the envelope.

Stupid, stupid, I was being stupid. I could talk to her later about it. If I was going to be this sensitive, then I wasn't going to get anywhere.

11

I turned the corner into our street and saw a man and a woman standing outside our house in the distance. Did I know these people? Then it dawned on me that the man was Jim. Something made me stop and watch. The woman had her back to me. I couldn't see her face but there was nothing about her that made her familiar. I saw Jim take her face in his hands and get real close, like he was going to kiss her. I retreated back around the corner, then peered forward. Was it really Jim? What was he doing?

I walked toward them, watching them all the while. Then she turned. She was no one I knew. She looked very young. She looked my way, then Jim turned and looked also. Then she grabbed a bicycle that was leaning on the side of our steps and took off.

"What's going on?"

Jim looked pale. His lips were tightly pressed together, the thing he did when he was angry. Was he angry with me?

"Jim?"

"It's nothing, Em."

"Who was that?"

"No one." He walked up the steps to our front door, with me following behind.

"Jim! What's going on?"

"Really, Em, it's nothing, I promise."

"Don't brush me off like that. Please! I just saw you. Who is she?"

"It's none of your business." He closed the front door behind us and turned his head my way, then he deflated somewhat. He took my coat from me, and hung it on the rack, and pulled me to him in a hug.

"Sorry, Em, I shouldn't have snapped at you like that," he said.

"So tell me! Who is she? What were you doing out there?"

Because the detail I hadn't been saying out loud was that he'd looked like he was about to kiss her, this attractive young woman.

We walked into the kitchen. He took my hand in his.

"She's an old student of mine. She's been harassing me for a job. She's a royal pain in the ass."

"A job?"

"Yes, at the Forum. You know what it's like. We're getting successful, so young, ambitious people like Allison are knocking on the door."

"She can't call you at the office?"

"She did—she has, a lot. I told you, she's a real pain, that one."

Jim, my Jim, my love, my life, say it isn't true. Don't be that man—the professor who takes up with his ex-student. Make me believe you, I thought. *Try harder, please.*

"I'm going upstairs to pack," he said.

I sighed. "I've already packed, but I'll come and help you." I followed him upstairs. We could talk later, on the plane even.

He sat down on the bed, looking up at me. His suitcase was next to him, already open. He took my hand, and drew me close.

"I'm sorry, Em."

That was a start. Not nearly enough, but a start.

"I can't bring you to Montreal."

"What?"

"I know it was going to be our little trip, but we can't go together now, because something's come up. I'm going to have to work a lot more than I expected. There are some key people up there who want to meet with us—it's a great opportunity."

He looked into my face.

"You understand, don't you?"

I must have looked like a blowfish stranded on the beach, because he pulled me even closer.

"I'm sorry, sweetheart," he continued. "It's the Canadian government. I couldn't pass this up. I got Carol to set up some meetings and this trip has turned into a monster work affair now."

I couldn't stop the tears. They just rolled down, and I let them.

"I'm so disappointed, Em. I was really looking forward to this little trip with you, but now I'm going to be stuck in meetings the whole time."

I couldn't believe what I was hearing. "I'm not going with you?"

"Not this time, darling. Trust me, you'd be bored to tears, but next time, I promise."

"I can still join you! I can do the tourist sights during the day and we can be together in the evenings. You'll hardly know I'm there. You'll see." I sounded whiny, even to my ears. Jim hated whining.

"I already canceled your ticket and got one for Carol, darling. I really need her there with me. You understand, don't you?"

That's how it worked between us lately, it seemed: with me being understanding. That was one thing I was very good at. I understood Jim's needs better than anyone—I understood it was my role to support him so that he could be free to do the very important work he did—so the shock on his face was not unexpected when I said abruptly, "Are you going with Allison?"

He pulled back from me. His face rearranged itself from its usual benevolent, kindly, patient expression into one of serious anger and outrage. He stood, and gripped my shoulders with his hands. I could feel his body tense, but I was angry too, and my own face was rigid with it.

All those conversations with Beatrice must have rubbed off on me, because suddenly I heard myself shout, "No! I do *not* understand!"

I was tired of tiptoeing around, walking on eggshells, hoping each day would be a *good* day, and being sweet and understanding when it was a *bad* day.

He looked at his hands on my shoulders and slowly removed them, straightened his back.

"I'm going to pretend you didn't say that."

"Which part?"

"I'm not going with Allison. Please, Emma, that's the most ridiculous thing—"

"Is it?" I was shaking, standing a little away from him. "Because here's another thing I don't understand: what you were doing outside just now. And don't tell me this bullshit about a job, please. I'm not that stupid."

He stood up, started to pack his case, slowly, deliberately. People get killed for that kind of dismissive behavior, surely. My blood was boiling. I was so angry, I was vibrating.

"Talk to me!" I shouted.

"I don't have the time for this, Emma. Whatever it is you want to say to me, it's going to have to wait until I get back."

"You still haven't answered me."

"Oh, for God's sake! Of course I'm not bringing Allison! Jesus! Get a grip, Emma!"

Jim was many things, but he wasn't a very good liar, and I knew he was hiding something behind all the posturing, but I wasn't completely sure what it was. It would have been a stupid lie, to pretend he was taking Carol with him and then take this Allison woman. Easily found out.

"You don't understand, Em, but what I'm doing, what I do, it's actually very important work."

"Oh, fuck off, Jim!"

I grabbed my coat and bag and ran out the door, sobbing. I hailed a taxi; I wanted to run to the store, to Jackie—*She'll get it*, I thought—but then I changed my mind. When I called Beatrice and George picked up, he could barely understand me.

"Emma! What happened, my dear?"

"Can I speak to Beatrice, please, George? Tell her it has nothing to do with her package, it's about Jim. Would you tell her that?"

"Of course, my dear. I'll get her for you."

"Emma?"

Just hearing her voice brought on another rush of sobs in me, and I managed to pour out my sorry tale, in spits and spurts.

"Come over now, right now, and we'll figure it out, I promise."

She was waiting for me outside her door when I came out of the elevator, and wrapped me tightly in her arms.

"I'm getting snot all over your shirt," I mumbled into her neck.

"That's all right. I never liked this shirt."

"It'll come off, I think."

"Then get some more snot on it. Give me no excuse to keep it."

I just cried my heart out.

She took me upstairs to her bedroom, and lay on the bed with me, cradling my head against her shoulder, stroking my hair, while I spewed out words of anger, regret, frustration, bewilderment. Finally, I could speak no more, and she soothed me like a child while I took in great big gulps of air.

George came in, Lord love him, with two hefty glasses of something. She nodded to him to put them on the bedside table and he left us, with a kind look toward me.

She leaned over, took a glass, and passed it to me. It was strong and warm, and it was helping.

"I got your package, obviously," I hiccupped.

"Yes, I know."

"It hasn't been my lucky day, has it?"

"You better get used to it, darling. It's a cutthroat business out there."

"But still, you could have gone easy on me."

"You think *I* was tough? You should see some of the line edits I get back."

"I don't believe you."

"Then remind me to show you sometime."

"Seriously though, why so dismissive? Was it that bad?"

"It was pretty bad."

"Shit."

I rested my head back on her shoulder.

"So you won't help me then? It's irretrievable—is that what you're saying?"

She moved away slightly so she could look at me straight in the face. Put a finger under my chin and lifted my head up. "Of course not. You just don't know what you're doing, that's all."

I nestled my head against her again. "You could have been kinder."

"You wouldn't help me," she said.

I looked up. "What are you talking about?"

She looked at me sideways, like I should know.

"Really? You're angry with me because I wouldn't go along with your crazy idea?"

"Please stop saying that."

"You're right. It's *not* a crazy idea. It's a *great* idea," I said, because it occurred to me at that moment that pretending to be someone else would be fantastic. Just imagine what Jim would think if I were to publish a novel—and a great one, at that. Because I didn't need to read it to know it would be great.

"Don't be sarcastic."

"I'm not. It's a great idea. I've just realized that."

"What are you saying?"

"If I say yes, will you help me with mine? So that I have something, shall we say, presentable to publish? Once everyone discovers I'm a fraud?"

She laughed. "No one will believe you're a fraud, and yes, of course, that's the deal. I'll help you write your novel, and trust me, it will be a lot more than presentable."

I nodded. "Let's do it."

"You're serious?"

"Absolutely. Let's do it."

She took me in her arms and hugged me, really tight.

George kindly spent the night in the spare bedroom so that I could stay with Beatrice. God knows what he thought about my state of mind, but he was so sweet. Jim could have learned a thing or two from this man.

Beatrice and I stayed up until the wee hours getting drunk on her whiskey, moving on from the glasses to the pretty flask, and then to the bottle, and since Beatrice kept a small refrigerator in her office next door, we even had ice.

She told me vaguely about the story she'd written, and I must have asked her a hundred times why she wouldn't publish it under her own name. I did understand the fear of being judged, only too well, but not why Beatrice—or someone like her, someone so talented, beautiful, admired—could feel that way too.

Eventually we fell asleep, both our heads on the same pillow. I watched her dream, and reached out a hand and caressed her cheek, her breathing slowing down a little.

12

She was up before me, and when I woke up, alone in her bed, it took me a minute to recognize where I was. Then it all came flooding back just as she entered the room in a floor-length white bathrobe, carrying a tray, which she placed beside me on the bed. She sat herself upright against the pillow next to me and brought her knees up.

"Good morning! How does the world look today—better?"

"So far, so good," I said. "This is a treat!" I admired the single red rose, the scrambled eggs and croissants. I was ravenous.

"You deserve it. Eat it while it's hot."

I spread strawberry jam on a croissant. "Aren't you having any?"

"I'm not hungry. Coffee's fine for me right now. But you, on the other hand, need your strength, so eat while I get dressed."

She left me to it and went into her walk-in closet, which really was another room altogether. Breakfast was delicious, but I still felt a little broken and very, very tired. I thought back to our hours of talk about our plans. I did a quick check for regrets: Did I feel any? No, this had not been idle chatter, or rambling ideas spewing out from my over-emotional, drunken self. I was feeling the excitement of a new voyage about to begin. My life was going to change completely, and that was a very good thing.

I demolished that breakfast, enjoying every mouthful.

"Feeling better?" She was standing at the foot of the bed, looking fabulous as usual.

"Feeling pretty great, actually, thank you for asking."

"That's wonderful, darling, I'm so pleased." She sat beside me on the bed. "We're still on with our little project?"

"We certainly are."

"Fantastic. So the next step here is that I'm going to give you the manuscript—the hard copy."

"I can't wait to read it."

"It's the only copy."

"Seriously?"

"Of course! It's still on my computer. But you need to retype it, on your computer. Then I'll delete mine."

"This is a little cloak-and-dagger, isn't it? Or will I discover state secrets when I read this manuscript?"

"Trust me—it's best we don't take any chances. Any at all."

"If you say so." I pushed the breakfast tray aside. "I should probably go home, sort out my life." I got out of bed.

"But you're all right now?"

"Oh, Beatrice, I can't thank you enough. Yes, I'm all right. And our long talk last night really made me see my options. I just need to go home and deal with it."

"Good for you, darling. You're very brave—remember that, always." She fished something from her pocket and handed it to me. It was a key.

"What's this?"

"Whatever happens, you can always come back here."

"Oh, thank you, but I don't need this."

"I know, but take it anyway." She put the key in my hand.

I started to cry. "Sorry," I said, as she handed me a Kleenex. "I'm a bit fragile."

"I know you are, but you'll be fine—you'll see."

I took a shower, got dressed, and joined her in her office.

"I have the manuscript here"—she tapped a fat envelope on the desk—"but let's get the nitty-gritty stuff done, all right?"

I knew what was going to happen. We'd spoken at length last night about how this was going to work. I would do all the interviews, show up for the events, and promote the novel to the best of my ability. Beatrice told me over and over that there might not be a lot of publicity, so I should lower my expectations and not be disappointed.

As if.

She kept telling me the book might bomb, and I kept telling her I hoped it would. In return for doing my bit, I was to receive 50 percent of the proceeds. We had no idea how much that might be—it could be a few hundred dollars, or even less—but if the book did well, it could go into thousands of dollars.

During the time frame of our project, Beatrice would help me finish my own work; she thought it might take a year or so. That was the part I was most excited about. The other business, being the front woman for her novel, didn't seem real.

Beatrice was to handle the actual publishing deal under the guise of "doing a favor for a friend." She would use her clout to open doors, and get top agents and publishers to consider the manuscript, as a favor to her protégée.

"Don't let that weasel of a husband upset you. You deserve better, all right?" she said as I got into the elevator.

"Thank you for everything, Beatrice, really. And don't worry, I'll be fine. We'll be fine."

She hugged me tight again and I took in her lovely scent, bottled it up so it would last me all day. She released her grip, and held me by my shoulders at arm's length.

"If you and Jim are going to break up, you need a safe place, Emma. Come and stay here any time. Any time at all."

Break up? No, no—nobody is breaking up here. "I'll be fine, there's no need to do that."

"You never know. It can't hurt."

◆　◆　◆

I didn't call Jim, I didn't text him; I didn't leave wailing messages telling him that I loved him so much it had driven me to say such stupid things. I did none of that, but I did spend my day productively. I tracked down that woman.

It wasn't that I'd never thought Jim would find someone better than me, it's just that I'd never thought it would be someone like *her*.

He'd said she was an ex-student, so I looked up the website of the university where he used to work, where they'd met. I'd gotten a good enough look at her the other day: I knew she had copper-colored hair and she was in her early to mid-twenties, give or take; that she was thin, pretty.

I went to the directory section of the website and typed *Allison* in the search bar. I had to start somewhere.

There were over sixty results, but, helpfully, there was a headshot next to each entry, so I scanned through the pages quickly; mostly they were easy to dismiss. Wrong age group, wrong look. A couple of them had a generic avatar instead of a photo, the blue-outline type, so I made a note of those—and then, on page three, bingo! Allison Vickars, still a PhD student.

The sight of her smug face smiling at me from the screen made my stomach churn. For a second I wanted to slap her. There were no personal details, but I figured that Vickars was not such a common name, so I searched for an address or a number for Allison Vickars; no luck.

Next, I called the university, pretending to be Jim's assistant, and they were very helpful. Being a successful product of the university had its perks. They were especially proud of him, and by the time I hung up, I had a phone number and an address.

It took three attempts for me to punch in the number. It was hard to focus—those few glasses of wine for the sake of courage didn't help after all—and when I finally got it right, it went straight to voice mail. I pressed the phone hard against my ear, listening to her cheery, singsong voice: "Hi! Sorry, but I can't get the phone. You know what to do!"

I figured she was too busy fucking my husband to take the call, and I didn't leave a message.

◆ ◆ ◆

By the time Jim called me, I was very pleased that I had managed such self-restraint.

"I miss you," he said. He'd been gone for two days and already I'd been climbing the walls, frightened beyond belief that I might never see him again.

"Do you? I don't miss you at all."

He gave a small chuckle. "I'm coming home tomorrow," he said.

"So soon? Weren't you supposed to be back on Monday?" This little exercise in self-control was making me feel like I had the upper hand. Welcome back to high school.

"I can't wait any more. Screw them—I want to come home and be with my wife."

His words made me dizzy with happiness. I was smiling so much my cheeks hurt. "I can't wait either, my darling. I've missed you more than I can say," I replied, throwing caution to the wind.

◆ ◆ ◆

We had a romantic dinner the night he came home. I made him his favorite, *boeuf en croûte*, a welcome-home surprise.

It was only later, when we were sitting together on the couch, drinking wine, my head resting on his shoulder, that he brought it up.

"I'm not having an affair, Emma. Certainly not with Allison—not with anyone."

"I know," I replied, even though I didn't, not really.

"And I should have explained sooner that the plan had changed. I'm sorry, that was insensitive of me." I was listening to him with my eyes closed. "What did you get up to while I was gone?" he asked.

I hesitated for a second, not wanting to ruin the moment, but I said it anyway, my eyes still shut. "I've started work on my book."

"Good for you," he said, and I let out the breath I'd been holding. "How's it coming along?"

"Very well, actually."

"I'm glad."

So was I.

◆ ◆ ◆

Jim had already left for work when I woke up. There was a note on the kitchen counter: *I love you, see you tonight.* I took the note and put it in my wallet.

I love you too.

I called Jackie, making up some excuse. "I'm not feeling very well," I said. "Can you take over for the day?"

I hadn't had the heart to read the manuscript while Jim was gone— I didn't have the head for it either—but on this sunny, happy day, I retrieved it from its bag, still resting by the front door, chiding myself for being so casual with it. I settled myself comfortably on the couch, and began to read what was about to become my novel.

The day turned to dusk, and when my eyes could no longer make out the words on the page, I turned on the lamp next to me. I didn't want to stop reading. I had become enthralled, a hostage to this story and its characters, and I believed with all my heart that this must be the best work she'd ever done. Eventually I took a break to pour myself a glass of wine and think about what I'd just read. This strange tale could have been ordinary in the hands of most people. There was no murder here, no big romantic entanglement, but there was no shortage of tension to leave you breathless at every turn. It wasn't so much the plot that drew you in, it was that the narrative was so compelling, the layers so detailed that you could touch this world just by reaching out to it.

I didn't hear Jim come in, and I jumped with a start when I saw him right there, standing in front of me.

"You scared me!"

"Sorry. How are you feeling?"

"Very good, thank you." I gathered the pages together—this was not the time for me to finish reading—and I put them back in the envelope.

"What's this?" he asked.

"The novel I'm working on: I told you last night."

"Really?"

"Yes, why?"

"I didn't realize you'd done so much, that's all. Can I read it?"

"Soon, but not yet."

"Okay."

I wanted to call Beatrice right there and then, to tell her that this was something incredible; that I was sorry I'd taken three days to start it, because they were three days that I'd wasted; that she had transported me from my surroundings into a world I'd never known, but that she'd made so familiar I was there, with these characters.

I was in love with the book.

13

We sealed the deal in a bar, as I stared into her face and told her what reading her book had done to me, and I could tell she was pleased, really pleased, that I loved it so much. We wrote our contract on a cocktail napkin, because so many important deals were made that way, she said, and it was in keeping with our crazy project anyway. It was very short, just the title of the book, that she had written it but I would be posing as the author, and that any proceeds were to be split fifty-fifty. We signed, awkwardly, messily, and that was it. We did it twice, one copy for her and one for me.

"Guard it with your life, okay?"

"You bet."

In the days after that, Beatrice and I were consumed with plotting and scheming. I was obsessed with my novel—because that's how I thought of it by then. Mine.

I knew it almost by heart. We had spent countless hours discussing its intricacies. I had retyped the manuscript on my own computer as agreed, and by the time Christmas arrived, we were ready. We burned the original in her fireplace. We made it an occasion, dumping stacks of paper into the flames. I'd spent even more countless hours late at night recreating this work word for word, Jim in the background, being wonderfully supportive of my newfound passion for writing, if a little puzzled. I really thought he was impressed. He kept saying he couldn't wait to read it, and I couldn't wait for him to do so. I even changed a few things, tiny things, undetectable things, a comma here, a word there, so that little by little it became mine. I was a little bit the author.

◆ ◆ ◆

"I'm sorry," Beatrice was saying, "it's going to take longer than I thought." We were sipping coffee at Altitude, almost three weeks after our cocktail napkin evening. I should have been excited when she called to meet up, but she made it sound urgent, and I knew it was not going to be good news.

"I don't understand. This manuscript is wonderful. It's"—I had difficulty finding the right word—"it's remarkable. How can anyone want to pass this up?"

Beatrice had not been able to get an agent interested in the novel. It made no sense to me. What would happen now?

"They all say the same thing: the story is complex, doesn't follow the usual narrative styles." Then she said in a singsong voice, making air quotes, "'The market is not right for this book at the moment.'"

"How many people have you contacted?"

"Four, so far. But they're the best in the business. They're the ones I would trust with this, so if they're not biting, then we just have to wait, Emma."

"I still don't understand why we don't ask Hannah," I said petulantly.

"You know why. Hannah is my agent, and she doesn't normally work with unknown authors. If she represents the book, someone might suspect I wrote it. We need to do this fresh. Please trust me, Emma."

She reached a hand over the table to cover mine.

"It will happen, you'll see."

The irony wasn't lost on me: this was her project, her idea; she'd worked so hard to convince me to do it, and now she was the one taking it in her stride and I was so disappointed I wanted to weep. "Did any of them read it?"

"I don't think so. These people are busy. They may have flicked through it, but even so, who knows?"

She was also annoyed, obviously. This was her experiment, after all, and it seemed to be fizzling out before it had even begun.

Her eyes had left mine; she was studying the tablecloth. I wanted to reach out and shake her. *The answer isn't there,* I wanted to yell at her. *Why aren't you trying harder? How can you give up so easily? You're supposed to be the expert, for Christ's sake!*

I took a deep breath. "It makes no sense to me," I said, finally. "This is a work of art, and if they don't know that, then either they haven't bothered to read it, or they're terrible at their jobs."

She raised her eyes back to me. "It's a matter of time, Emma, I promise."

"But you were supposed to find us an agent. You're supposed to be someone these people listen to, right? Aren't you?"

She made a sharp movement with her head and raised an eyebrow.

"Sorry, I don't know why I said that. That was uncalled for." I sat back in my chair, deflated. "This is such bad news."

"You need to be patient, Emma! Seriously. These things take time. I'll keep prodding. That's how it works, believe me—I do know what I'm talking about."

"How long?"

She studied my face, surprised at how hard I was taking the news. "I don't know. Maybe a few months?"

I slapped my palms on the table. "A few months?"

"Just be patient! Emma! What's the matter with you?"

She was right, of course—I was overreacting. But doubt had gripped me, and I was panicking. I was terrified that she'd give up and the idea would die its own unremarkable death. I steadied myself and took a deep breath, squared my shoulders. "Sorry, again. I just love this book, that's all."

She smiled at me. "I know you do. Leave it to me, okay? We'll get there, you'll see." She took my hand again. "I'll try again in a few weeks."

"A few weeks? But why? Why that long?"

"Because I want to think about how I'm approaching this. Once the best in the business have turned it down, you need to be very careful where you go from there. I don't want to kill this project, you understand? It could be the wrong time."

"Okay." I sighed, giving in. "You know best, I know you do."

"That's right, I do know best. Don't worry, Emma, it'll happen before you know it."

Hardly, not if it's weeks or months or God knows how long from now. But I pretended to go along with her confidence and let go of my bad mood.

◆ ◆ ◆

I dreamed of boats and a wild river. I was alone on a barge, and Beatrice was on a large ship, like a cruise ship, some way off. I desperately wanted to join her. I was waving my arms and shouting, doing everything I could to get her attention, but she didn't notice me. She was drinking pink champagne and laughing her head off at the heart of a little gathering. They were not that far away from me and I couldn't figure out why she couldn't see me.

There were oars in my barge. I picked them up and slapped at the water in a frenzied attempt to go to her, but the barge didn't move an inch. I was doing it all wrong. By the time I looked up, Beatrice's boat had receded to a small triangle in the distance and the terror of being left behind, hopeless and utterly alone, was so real it woke me up, my heart beating fast in my chest and my hair damp with sweat.

It was barely dawn and I didn't want to go back to sleep in case I slipped back into that awful dream.

I got up quietly and went downstairs to make myself a pot of strong black coffee. I was craving it. While it was brewing, I cast my mind back to the previous day's disappointment. I'd had a heavy heart since I heard that the book hadn't been accepted by an agent—not just because it was going to take longer to get it published, but because I was afraid Beatrice would change her mind.

What if she decided to get someone else to be the author? Someone who already had one or two books under their belt? That would be easier, right? And what if she changed her mind completely and decided to use her own name? After all, it was the "unknown" author that was the problem. It was me that was the problem.

I'd decided last night, before the snatches of sleep turned into nightmares, that I needed to take control of this. I *was* the author, after all. I couldn't sit on the sidelines and wait for things to happen. I did that too often, and where did it ever get me?

I started a list in my head of my favorite contemporary writers: That was where I was going to start. I then spent the next hour pulling from the list the ones in a similar genre to Beatrice's new novel. Eventually Jim came into the kitchen, bent down, and kissed me softly on the lips.

"Hard at work already."

"Mmm . . ."

He poured himself a cup of coffee. I could see by his demeanor that he was in a rush this morning, itching to get on with his day. He looked nice, wearing new jeans I'd bought for him. He drained his cup and bent down to kiss the top of my head.

"I'll see you tonight, Em. Have a great day. Watch out for that carpal tunnel syndrome."

"Ha ha!" That was Jim's new joke: he said I was attached to my laptop, and he was going to buy some advertising space on Google to get my attention. Sweet.

It turned out to be a lot easier than I thought, tracking down publishers; most of them had contact names, email addresses, phone numbers on their websites. By lunchtime I had my short list, along with my letter of introduction and a brief bio, in my own words, which I was pretty happy with. I emailed them and the manuscript to seven people from my list.

I was ravenous, even more so than usual. It was a day for beef bourguignon, I decided. I should have been exhausted, but instead I was tingling with excitement, and I whiled away the rest of the day shopping for ingredients and cooking.

◆ ◆ ◆

I was at the hair salon when Jim called me with the big news; he blurted it out quickly. The Department of the Treasury was commissioning the Forum to do some economic modeling about a specific policy area.

"It's only the beginning," he said. "They just want to try out our theories against some of their real data. What happens after that will depend on the results—but we've done it!"

I laughed with him into the phone and told him to stop shouting. He was so excited, he could barely breathe.

"We're going to celebrate," he said. "Come to the Tavern, meet me there. We're having champagne. Lots of it."

I was happy for him, hugely happy, and I quieted the small disappointment I felt in the pit of my stomach each time the phone rang and it wasn't one of the publishers I'd emailed. It had only been two weeks, which I was sure in that world was no time at all, but to me it was a century and a half, and every time I answered the phone I was a little crushed.

My hairdresser shot me a stern look in the mirror; I needed to hang up the phone. *Sorry*, I mouthed, but he was not impressed. He made that clear as he teased and snipped and poked at my hair. They didn't like to be called hairdressers here: this was a work of art, not a haircut. At least I hoped it was a work of art, because it was by far the most expensive haircut I'd ever had.

"I want you to look your best, Emma. When the time comes, you'll thank me for it," Beatrice had said. I'd thanked her already since she was paying for this haircut. My income had taken a bit of a dive lately. I was losing interest in the store, barely going in these days and relying more and more on Jackie, who had been okay with it so far, though I knew it was not what she'd expected when she took the job. As a result, our stock was all over the place, orders weren't being filled because I'd ordered the wrong items from the supplier, and some of my customers were getting a little upset at the slowness of their deliveries.

"You're not pregnant, are you?" Jackie had asked me the other day, after I made yet another excuse about not feeling well enough to go in.

"Why on earth would you say that? I'm just tired, that's all."

"Seriously, you're exhibiting all the symptoms."

"Like what?"

"Like you're tired all the time and you're forgetful, you're mixing up orders, that sort of thing. Go pee on a stick. Seriously."

As if. But I was starting to wonder: What would I do if this book didn't take off? I couldn't even consider that possibility. It was just too scary. And anyway, Beatrice was confident—she'd sent me here, after all. I wasn't concerned about the money. I was still making enough; Jim was earning more than he ever had, and he wasn't resentful about things like that, I'll say that for him. He never minded how much I spent, or what I spent it on.

When I got to the Tavern shortly before 6:00 p.m., it was packed. People were spilling onto the sidewalk. I wove my way through them and just as I reached the front door, I caught something in my line of vision that made my head turn. Allison was leaning against the wall on the other side of the street. I turned around, fully, and she walked away. Maybe I had been mistaken, and it wasn't Allison at all.

Once inside, I didn't need to look for Jim. I could hear his voice booming deep down in the throng.

"Hear hear! To the future! To prosperity!" he cried.

"To efficiency dividends!" someone shouted, to roars of laugher. Clearly an inside joke.

There were only about six of them around the table. I put my hand on Jim's back and kissed him on the cheek.

"Emma! There you are!" He took a moment to take in my new look, and I was trying not to beam because I knew I looked wonderful, and was extremely happy with myself. It felt good.

"You look fantastic!" he said, just as Carol leaned across the table to kiss me hello.

"That's a great look for you, Emma. You look beautiful," she said.

"Thanks, Carol." Jim put his arm around my shoulders. He'd gone back to raving away, his glass held high as he demonstrated some point or another. They were all a little drunk, but he was more so than anyone.

"Here." Terry handed me a glass and filled it with champagne.

They were all so happy, and I wanted to join in the festivities, so I polished off the drink in record time. I wanted to match the mood, to be a part of their success. I was the only spouse there, I noticed. I figured I should be flattered that Jim wanted me there.

Terry obligingly replenished my glass. "Thirsty, I see," he said.

"Parched."

Maybe I should flirt with Terry, I thought. But I didn't think he'd like it, not in front of Jim anyway.

It was too warm in there. As I folded my coat up on a stool, I felt more than heard my phone ring in the pocket. I reached for it and smiled my apologies at Terry, who was telling me something I couldn't quite hear. I turned around to take the call, cupping my other ear with my hand, but it was no use, so I pushed my way back through the crowd to get outside, hoping the caller could hear me when I asked them to wait a moment.

14

"You did what?"

I could smell a whiff of yesterday's alcohol on Beatrice's breath. If only she could have smelled it herself, she'd have stopped drinking immediately and completely. I struggled not to recoil.

"You're not pleased?" I didn't know why I'd asked. She didn't look pleased—it wasn't like I could be mistaken about that. I shifted my gaze sideways, the wayward student before the principal. "Frankie Badosa! It's a major coup, Beatrice," I assured her.

We were having an early lunch. I'd picked the place because it was one of her favorites. *I have news*, I'd told her. *I'll take you out—wait till you hear. I'm bursting to tell you.*

I'd wanted to tell her sooner, last night, immediately after I hung up from the call, of the admiration I'd heard in the voice of Frankie Badosa. I'd wanted to tell her what he'd said: that he wanted to meet me immediately, so we didn't waste any time; that he'd checked whether I was speaking with anyone else, because he would up whatever sum they were offering me. I'd laughed into the phone, told him that he was the first person to contact me, and I'd heard the unmistakable relief in his voice. He'd made me promise not to take any calls until this morning, and when I'd arrived, his assistant had plied me with coffee and croissants and raisin toast and anything to keep me there while he explained everything to me. He wouldn't normally do this, he said. He generally worked only with agents, but he'd take me on, and I thought he had tears in his eyes when he silently gave me a pen and the contract, and we signed, and he called for champagne, and all this had only just happened and I was drunk with joy.

I had wanted it to be a surprise for Beatrice. *Look what I can do: I'm a part of this now. I'm pulling my weight. I found us a publisher. I'm a team player. I did that by myself so I could show you how committed I am to your—our—project.*

"You signed, without speaking to me first?" She was staring at me as if I had two heads.

You couldn't get us a publisher, I wanted to say, *it's been weeks, what have you been doing?* But I didn't. Instead I told her, smugly, that he was the first to publish Solomon Sully, that we were in excellent company.

"Fifteen years ago, Emma, Frankie Badosa published Sully's first two books, yes. They sank. Then Sully was picked up by Random House and his career took off."

"Oh, I'm sorry. I didn't know Random House was banging on the door." I couldn't help myself—her attitude was grating on me.

"Anyway, that's irrelevant," she went on, as if I hadn't spoken. "You *never* go directly to a publisher. You don't know *anything*, Emma. You sign with an *agent* first. They get you a *publisher*. Do you have any idea what could go wrong?"

I could see from the corner of my eye the waiter hovering a respectful distance away. We hadn't ordered yet and he wasn't sure whether to approach us. I mentally shooed him away.

"You should never have done this without discussing it with me first." She said this slowly, as if I were a child and she was deeply disappointed in me.

"Well, it's done now, so . . ." I replied, my eyes again flicking to the side, still the sullen teenager being reprimanded. I crossed my arms for good measure.

"We'll tear up the contract. I'll think of a way out of this," she said.

Oh no, you won't, I thought. "Why? He *loves* the book, Beatrice! He says it's the most excited he's been in years! He's going to give it everything he's got! His whole firm is going to get behind this book. Why on earth wouldn't I go with Frankie Badosa?"

"Excuse me?"

"Why wouldn't we go with him? I don't—"

"Wait, you said 'Why wouldn't *I* . . .'"

"No I didn't. Anyway, what does it matter, I still don't understand what the problem is." I sat back, deflated. This conversation was very different from what I'd imagined. In my head, all night long, it was like a track on repeat, something more like: *That's fantastic, Emma, well done! Taking the initiative, and look what you've achieved! We have a publishing contract! Champagne all around!* So to say I was a little disappointed would be an understatement.

"Of course you don't know what the problem is!" The couple at the next table glanced over at us. She noticed this too and smiled at them briefly. "Because you don't know the publishing world," she said, more softly but with the same steely anger. "Frankie Badosa's going under, he's broke—he hasn't had a good author in years. Of course he'd pick this up. He has nothing to lose. We'll be stuck with him, and the book will get a small print run and languish on the shelves for a little while until it ends up on the remainder tables."

"Or in your storage unit?"

She shook her head, and then, to my horror, she stood up, grabbed her purse, and pushed her chair back in toward the table.

"What are you doing?"

"I've made a mistake," she said. She picked up her coat from the back of the chair.

"What?"

"I should never have asked you to be involved."

"Beatrice, please, wait, sit back down—come on." I was pleading with her. The couple at the next table weren't even pretending not to listen. No doubt they thought they were witnessing a lovers' tiff. I didn't care.

"Please? I'm sorry, please sit down." But I knew it was hopeless. She'd already walked away. I stood up as well, grabbed my own coat, mumbled my apologies to the dumbfounded waiter, and ran outside, but she was gone.

◆ ◆ ◆

I went straight to bed and slept all afternoon, a restless, fitful sleep, but I was so very tired, and so very, very sad. How could I possibly have gotten this so wrong? Would she really find a way to cancel the contract? I was trying desperately not to think about how angry she was with me. I tried to do my little trick to make myself feel better. It's something I used to do when I was a child and my mother was crying at the kitchen table when there was no money for food, no money for bills, no money for hope. I used to pretend it was a movie, but one that I'd seen before, and it had a happy ending, so I could watch the despair of this woman and her child, knowing something they didn't—that it would turn out fine in the end.

I tried this trick again, over and over—*It's going to turn out fine. You've seen the movie already: this is just the part where the author's very angry with the protagonist, but you don't have to feel the despair because in the next scene everything changes for the better, and you know that already*—until Jim opened the door.

"Sweetheart?" he called out quietly, and I pretended to be asleep, but he came closer. "Darling, it's Beatrice on the phone." I opened my eyes and he had my phone in one hand, the other cupped over it. "I told her you're not feeling well but she says it's urgent. Do you want to speak to her?"

Before I had time to think, my arm had shot out and I'd snatched the phone from him, but I waited a moment before saying anything and smiled at him.

"I feel better, thanks." He smiled back, gave me a little nod, and left the room, closing the door behind him.

"Hello?"

"Emma, darling? It's Beatrice."

"Oh. What time is it?"

"Eightish, I think. Why, is this a bad time?" I didn't know if she was being sarcastic. Beatrice had never inquired about whether it was a bad time, ever.

"No, of course not."

"I've been thinking," she said. It came out as *I've been shinking*.

"Yes?"

"I overreacted this afternoon. Let's give it a go with Badosa."

I sat up in the bed. "Seriously?"

"Yes, seriously."

"But you said he was going under, he was nobody, he was a deadweight."

"It's not a bad idea to get someone in that position. I agree with you that he'll give it everything he's got. He might invest a lot in this—it might be his last shot at righting the ship, so to speak."

Sho to shpeak.

"Oh, Beatrice—" I burst into tears. "I'm sorry about—you know—before. You're right, I never should have—I just—"

"I know," she said. "It's all right, darling Emma, I'm sorry too. I needed reminding I'm not doing this on my own now."

"Oh God, I'm so relieved—you have no idea."

"Just don't do it again, please. All right?"

"Yes, no, I mean, I won't. Scout's honor."

"I do think this is a good move, maybe, but we could have discussed it. That would have been appropriate."

"I wanted to surprise you, I really did."

"I know, just don't do it again."

I chuckled through my tears. "Scout's honor," I repeated.

"Well done, Emma."

"I love you," I mumbled.

"I'll talk to you tomorrow, all right?"

I hung up. I didn't know if she'd heard me.

15

It was the happiest day of my life. For the first time since we'd started all this, it was real—physically, undeniably real. It existed outside my own head. That's what I thought as I held the first printed copy of *Long Grass Running* in my hands.

Long Grass Running by Emma Fern.

I could smell its paper, feel the gloss of the cover under my fingers. I thought then that this was the most faithful way to distinguish what was real from what was not: What is real has a weight; what is imaginary does not. The imaginary doesn't fall when you let go; gravity isn't interested in the imaginary. The earth only pulls to her what has substance.

They don't call it substance for nothing.

Long Grass Running by Emma Fern.

It was with an understandably great sense of pride and achievement that I placed the copy in Jim's hands when he came into the kitchen that happy morning, almost six months after signing with Frankie.

"No reason to wait," Frankie had said. "The sooner we get this book out in the world, the better."

Even Beatrice was impressed by how quickly it all happened. "Does Frankie ever sleep?" she'd asked when I told her I'd received it.

"Well, well! Here it is!" Jim said, looking down at its cover.

"Look inside." And he opened the front cover as I stood up to stand next to him, our shoulders touching, both our heads bent down together. I thumbed through a couple of pages and pointed at the dedication.

To my husband, James. Thank you for inspiring me every day. With all my love.

"Are you pleased?"

He looked sideways at me, a small, satisfied smile on his lips. "I'm very happy for you, sweetheart, I really am."

I was beaming. I'd thought a lot about this moment, and I had at one point wondered whether it was a mistake. Jim didn't approve of overt displays of affection—he said that kind of thing was for children—and I wasn't sure whether he'd be embarrassed by my public acknowledgment.

He put his arms around me, still holding the book, and we embraced each other tightly. I let my body deflate, like an old balloon. "I'm very proud of you," he whispered into my hair, and I held him tight for as long as he would let me, basking in the warmth of his body.

"Isn't it absolutely wonderful?" He let me go and I actually twirled in the kitchen, laughing with joy, my heart bursting with it.

"It most certainly is, sweetheart. Well done." He lifted his reading glasses from his shirt pocket and with one hand put them on his nose, but not to start reading the book right there and then, as I'd first thought. Instead he put it down on the kitchen table and gathered the loose sheets of paper that were lying next to it—something he was working on—and started to move toward his study. Was that it? Really?

He must have picked up something of my disappointment because he turned and gave me an apologetic smile as he did so. "We have to go and celebrate. I'll take you somewhere special for dinner. I just really need to get this done right now."

Years of solitary work—that's what he must have believed this book represented for me—and the biggest achievement of my life so far, and yet here I was, standing alone at the kitchen counter. But I managed to smile back through my disappointment and he gave me a little nod, satisfied that he had done what was expected of him and all was well, and he could get back to whatever was on his mind.

To say I felt let down would be an understatement, and as I sat down again, it occurred to me that maybe things between us had been exactly the way Jim liked them: namely that he was the genius, the alpha male, the super-achiever, and that the view, looking down from his lofty perch, was of me, filled with gratitude for the attention he bestowed on me, motivated only by a desire to be worthy of it, secure in the knowledge that I could never do better than him.

Which of course was the truth, but even I had the occasional flash of understanding, even as I strove to manage it, that relationships like this generate a never-ending thirst for approval, and even for a little admiration now and then, which is almost never granted, since the party whose approval is sought is the one who has the most to lose in upsetting the status quo.

Beatrice had balked at the dedication when I first showed her the proofs.

"It's a bit excessive, isn't it?" She meant it to sound lighthearted but I could tell from her tone that she was put out.

"I thought it would cement my role as the author," I offered. "Don't you think it's a good idea?"

"Well, it cements the pretense, certainly." Then she added, with false detachment, "Lots of people know I've been helping you with your writing"—she made air quotes around *your writing*—"so they may be a little surprised that you didn't thank me instead."

"I thought about it," I replied, which was true. My original inscription had thanked Beatrice, for obvious reasons, but then I'd changed my mind. I'd told myself it was because we shouldn't associate Beatrice too much with the novel, so that her anonymity remained safe. We didn't want someone familiar with her books to pick up some stylistic similarities between her work and mine and put two and two together.

When I explained this to her, she could see some value in my thinking and accepted it. But the truth was I just wanted it to be mine, that was all, and I figured that if I was prepared to act the part she had asked me to play, with all the time and effort and trust it represented, I deserved to get something back. I thought that all the people I knew—the people you know are the only people who matter—would assume that she had guided me through every sentence to the point where she just about wrote it for me, because who would believe that little old Emma could have done this by herself?

So instead I had then decided to dedicate the novel to my mother, she who'd felt she was born for a life in pursuit of intellectual stimulation and good taste, but only got close to it by cleaning other people's houses. I wanted to tell her it was all right now, we had arrived, we had made it after all, but at that point I was still fully conscious that this book wasn't really mine, and I knew in my heart she deserved better, so I resolved instead to wait until the next one, the book I knew I would write after this, in which the inscription would read, *To my mother, with all my love.*

In the end, it seemed entirely appropriate to turn my gratitude to my husband, for whom I strove every day to be something that I was not.

It was at least a couple of weeks after that that I returned to my local bookstore, a medium-sized store that always stocked titles I liked. I had been in there twice already in the last few days, but *Long Grass Running* wasn't on the shelves, and this time I'd decided I would ask for a copy. *Let them order a few*, I thought. I wouldn't come back to pick them up: they'd have to put them on the shelves. It was a stupid idea, but as it turned out it didn't matter; it was already there.

I always thought that the first time I spotted the book outside my own house would be when I happened past a bookshop. I imagined myself stopping in my tracks, walking back a couple of steps, and staring at copies of *Long Grass Running* arranged in the window. Instead, I found two copies on the shelves, in the literary fiction section on the back wall, so not quite the same, but still, it made my heart stop.

I picked one up and pretended to flick through it, just a regular customer looking for something to read, and I was going to buy it, but instead I waited until the woman behind the counter was busy helping another customer, and when I was sure she wasn't looking my way, I lifted both copies from the shelf and arranged them in the small display shelf near the front door, the one with the "New Releases" sign above it, reserved for notable authors who were known to sell books, and I covered up Patricia Cornwell's latest thriller.

My phone rang loudly in the quiet bookstore, and I jumped and left quickly, feeling rather sly, without looking back to see whether I had been caught, so it was only when I was outside that I realized how it must have looked, like I'd just stolen something. But I didn't need to worry. When I turned back to glance through the shop window as I pulled my phone from my handbag, the woman behind the counter was still engaged with her customer and seemed to have only barely registered my departure.

"I've booked you for tomorrow morning, NPR. Michael Gusek. Tell me you can be there, because I had to call in a favor."

Just hearing Frankie's voice was enough to give me a thrill. *My publisher's calling, 'scuse me—I must take this.* I was standing in the middle of the sidewalk, phone glued to my ear, oblivious to the annoyed stares of people who had to walk around me. *It's my publisher, you see, I'm a published author and this call is very important.*

"Michael Gusek? You're kidding!"

"Certainly not. You'll be there, right? Ten a.m.? I've emailed you some prep questions."

I could tell he was very pleased with himself—dear Frankie.

I didn't know it then, but I would come to understand that Frankie viewed this book as his probable salvation, that this was likely to be his last shot at reviving his failing business and, as Beatrice had guessed, he would put everything he had behind it.

"Oh, I'll be there," I said, butterflies already forming in my stomach. "But how did you pull this off?" I didn't need to clarify my surprise: Gusek was a big-shot interviewer and everyone I knew listened to his morning radio show.

"Like I told you, I called in a favor."

"But for me? You're sure you're not wasting it on me?"

"Oh, I'm sure. Don't you worry about that." I heard the smile in his voice. "Call me when you've read the email, all right? So we can prepare."

"I'm on my way home now. And, Frankie, thank you—thank you so much." I said this with heartfelt gratitude and I meant it. He made me feel like we were in this together, and I most certainly needed someone on my side at this point. I had no idea what was coming, and I was a little scared.

"You'll be fine," Beatrice said when I told her the news. I'd called her immediately of course. "It's always the same formula: He'll introduce you and the book by summarizing the story, then he'll ask you to read a couple of pages. After that he'll bring up the main characters and you'll have a conversation about them. He'll probably ask about the period the novel is set in, how you got the idea, that sort of thing. It's your first book, and since no one knows anything about you, there'll be questions about your background, etc. Gusek's very good—he'll keep it going seamlessly, you'll see. All very straightforward, I assure you."

"Okay, good, I think." I was already nervous, but a bit gratified that she'd been impressed when I told her.

The traffic was making it hard to hear her, so I turned into a small street and leaned against the wall, trying to calm my nervous excitement, which was gravitating perilously toward anxiety by that stage.

"I admit I underestimated Frankie," she said. *That* was especially nice to hear. *Told you so*, I wanted to say. "Come over now, we'll go over it together. I don't think you should read the very beginning; you won't have enough time to establish the scene. I'll give it some thought while I wait for you."

"I told Frankie I'd go straight home and go over the questions he put together, and then call him."

"Don't worry about the questions. Gusek will do what he wants anyway, and you can call Frankie from here."

I didn't hesitate. I needed all the help I could get, and Beatrice's more than most. Half an hour later we were settled in her study.

She had marked the pages she wanted me to read, and I could see why she'd chosen that passage. It was early in the book, and beautifully conveyed the longing and regret that would later propel the story forward. But I had a different chapter in mind, one of my favorite scenes in the book, and I was sure that because I loved it as a reader, other people would feel the same.

"There won't be enough context, you'll only have a few minutes to read, ten at the most," she said. She handed me the book, open at her selection, and I knew we wouldn't be discussing the alternatives. "Read it for me." She settled back in her armchair. I wasn't very happy about it, but I lifted the book and did as I was told.

"Jesus, Emma! What's the rush?" she interrupted almost immediately. "Take your time, breathe. You're telling a story. You'll hardly inspire the audience to buy the book if you sound like you can't wait for it to be over."

I took a deep breath and started again. She corrected my delivery here and there, but overall it was fine, and we spent the next two hours going over possible questions, discussing the book and everything that Frankie suggested when I got around to calling him, so by the time I left Beatrice, I had relaxed a little bit, feeling as prepared as I could possibly be.

16

The radio studio was way smaller than I'd expected, and I felt a little cramped in it, which didn't help. It was time for the news bulletin, so Gusek was free to show me the ropes, how close I should get to the microphone, the various hand signals to indicate whether we were on or we were wrapping up. We put our respective headsets on, and then he made a gesture with his index finger that we were about to begin.

"*Long Grass Running* tells the story of three sisters during World War One who are left to run the family farm after their brothers leave for the Front. It's a sprawling novel, and much of the action takes place in the struggles of the sisters to keep the farm going while the men are fighting the war. Emma Fern joins me to discuss her fascinating debut novel. Welcome, Emma."

And like the true amateur, incompetent dilettante that I was, I nodded. On the radio.

"It's good to have you on the show," Gusek said, raising an eyebrow in my direction that perfectly conveyed his irritation. It wasn't easy to get a spot on his show, and it was especially difficult for a first-time author. He'd probably decided in that moment that he'd get this interview wrapped up as quickly as possible, and would have to work extra hard in the process.

"It's great to be here." Hearing my own voice in the headphones was odd, unexpected, but not unpleasant. I paused for just a second and, determined to recover myself, continued just as he was about to say something else, and I found myself enjoying the sound of my own voice, literally.

"Thank you for having me, Michael, and thank you for the summary of the novel you just gave, because you nailed it. The heart of this novel lies indeed in the relationship between the three sisters, but I'd add something to that: that the landscape is almost as much a character as they are. The landscape, I think—I hope—provides the tension in the story."

I knew he had the summary in the notes Frankie had provided.

Gusek raised an eyebrow again, one of his mannerisms I decided, but this time he had a little smile, like a punctuation mark to his evident surprise that I might just turn out to be "good talent" after all.

We fell into an easy conversation, peppered by a spot of flirting here and there on my part, all in good fun. It added a little banter between us during the proceedings. He even waved an index finger at me at one point in amused admonition, and I raised an eyebrow at him in return, which made him chuckle silently.

We got to the part of the interview where I was to read a passage, and with the book in my hand already opened at the right page, I changed my mind. I decided to go with my first instinct. This interview was going well and I felt a sense of ownership of it. I figured it would be all right for me to veer a little from the script.

"Now, Emma, it's an ambitious work, this novel, and it doesn't follow a traditional narrative arc. Interspersed in the novel are excerpts from agricultural bills being presented at the time, some that never became law, and there are extracts of bills of sale for wheat exports. It's quite fascinating and very original. Can you talk a little about that?"

"Yes, thank you for asking about that. As you can imagine, I did a lot of research into farming conditions at that time, and the political and economic repercussions, on women particularly, and I wanted to explore different styles of narrative and try something completely different from my previous books. I mean, as a writer of contemporary crime fiction, I follow a more conventional storytelling approach, as you know, so I—"

"I'm sorry, I'm going to stop you there a moment. Your previous books? I was under the impression this was your first novel. But crime fiction, did you say?"

It was as if I had been turned and turned around and released and the world was spinning and I'd lost my balance. What had I said? Did I really get so confused that I'd started to speak as Beatrice rather than myself? My heart was beating, and I felt sweat pearling on my forehead. I stared at Gusek, still as a statue. He was waiting for me to go on, but his eyes registered something of my confusion.

"I'm sorry, I interrupted you," he said. "Please go on."

"No, that's fine," I replied, determined now to repair the damage and regain control. "It's just that this is my first published novel, you see, but there are a few half-finished others languishing in the drawers of my desk, hardly unusual for a writer, but yes—I completely changed my own writing direction in *Long Grass Running*. As I said just now, I wanted to try something different, unconventional, and I figured, why not, since no one will publish me anyway." I laughed.

"Well, that change of direction certainly paid off."

"You know, Michael, I completely agree with you." We both laughed.

We chatted some more about the characters and the settings. I felt fine now, just. I figured that it would make more sense anyway if I already had a body of work, and if it were unfinished and unpublished, all the better. Because let's face it, it would border on the unlikely to lay down a work of the caliber and originality of *Long Grass Running* on a first try.

When we wrapped it up, we had gone over the allotted time. They'd planned to follow my interview with a long-ago-recorded filler of some kind for the second half of the book-review part of the show. The producer who had pulled strings as a favor to Frankie had been quite happy to keep it as short as possible. But in the end, they didn't use it. They let me stay on for the duration instead.

"Well done," Gusek said, as he stood to shake my hand goodbye. "You know, I think I might even read the book," he added with a smile.

I was ecstatic.

◆ ◆ ◆

Frankie was waiting for me in the outer part of the studio, behind a pane of glass. I glanced at him, and he made a gesture to indicate we should meet outside. I felt lightheaded, exhausted, and dizzy with relief, my cheeks burning with pleasure. My face was frozen in place, bright red with a wide grin that I couldn't control no matter how much I wanted to, and when I saw Frankie in the corridor outside, he looked almost as happy as me. We didn't say a word, just walked side by side to the exit, like two children giddy with a secret, hurrying to be by ourselves so that we could dissect this thing that had just happened.

When the doors of the elevator closed behind us and we were alone, Frankie pumped the air with his fist and I burst out laughing.

"It was good, right?" I said, jumping a little on the spot.

"Are you kidding? It was fantastic! You were fantastic!" He turned and grabbed me by the shoulders as he said it and I wrapped my arms around him. We hugged hard, laughing, and jumped with joy some more.

"What now?" I said.

"Let's get a drink," he replied.

"Now? It's not even noon yet!"

"I don't care, I need a drink, and you're having one too." He put his arm around my shoulders and I put mine around his waist, and we walked down the street, and I loved him. He was with me, all the way. He was my friend, he had made this possible for me, and he was proud of me, happy for me and with me, and we were doing this thing together.

He took me to a bar around the corner and we sat on plush couches in a large, elegant room with frescoed cornices and a long semicircular bar against a wall of floor-to-ceiling mirrors. I thought it was perfect. I picked up the lunch menu from the small round table and Frankie asked the waiter for a bottle of champagne.

We went over the interview, repeating certain particularly clever or interesting moments to each other, and Frankie said, "I didn't know you were this funny, Em. How come I didn't know that?"

"What do you mean, funny?"

"You know what I mean. You made Michael laugh out loud, and he's a fairly serious guy. But it was so great; it was interesting and entertaining at the same time."

"I hope I didn't screw it up, then. It's not a funny book," I said.

"Oh, stop it." He slapped my knee gently. "You know you nailed it. Don't be so coy." I smiled, and he paused for a few seconds before adding, "We'll be seeing some good sales from this, you know, and not just from the people who listened this morning. People will talk; download the program. This is great."

I was thinking of what Frankie had just said about my being funny. I didn't let on, but I was a little hurt by his comment. Did he mean to imply that up until that point he'd thought I was dull? But in truth I knew exactly what he meant, and it made me reflect on who I'd become over the last few years, as if looking at myself from the outside. I used to be funny—that is to say, I used to be comfortable enough in my skin to be spontaneous. But somehow, sliver by sliver, life had chipped away at that easy self-confidence, so that now I was always careful, walking on eggshells, to the point that this acquired self-censorship had grown into a second skin over me.

But apparently the small flame had not been irrevocably snuffed out, and my old self had sprung out ready and whole. I felt great about myself.

"Do you think that about me?" I asked.

"Think what?"

"That I'm dull? You said just now that you didn't know I could be funny or something." I didn't say this with any trace of resentment, and I wasn't trying to confront Frankie about it, but I genuinely wanted to know, and since an easy friendship seemed to have materialized between us almost instantaneously, I thought I could ask him that. And anyway, I didn't want to pack the old Emma away just yet, the one who spoke her mind without hesitation.

"I never thought about it," he replied, "but no, I couldn't possibly have thought of you as *dull*, not after reading that manuscript." He smiled warmly. I could have been disappointed by that answer for obvious reasons, but I was gratified by it, without fully understanding why. "But you're a dark horse. What's this about crime novels gathering dust in the attic? You need to bring them out into the fresh air, Em—to me, I mean. I'll dust them off, don't you worry."

"They need a lot more work before they're ready to see the sun, but yes, you'll be the first to see them, when I'm ready."

He rubbed his hands together in mock anticipation. I hadn't gone back in my mind yet to that moment when I'd literally confused myself with Beatrice, and I shuddered a little at the thought. Just as I was wondering what she would make of that, I remembered I hadn't turned my cell phone back on, and I reached for it now to see whether I'd missed any calls or messages.

There was no word from Jim. I wondered whether he'd heard the program; he'd promised he would listen, but who knows, he'd probably forgotten. There was, however, a voice mail from Beatrice.

"Hello, darling, not bad, not bad at all. Call me when you get this, please?" I'd expected a little more gushing, so I ignored it, put the phone back in my handbag, and helped myself to another glass of bubbly.

We spent the next hour making exciting plans for more publicity, and each time Frankie brought up numbers and sales that seemed in the realm of the fantastic to me, I hushed him, at one point going as far as putting my hand over his mouth as he continued to talk nonsense through it, and we laughed. It was wonderful.

◆ ◆ ◆

The brightness of the day made my eyes water when we left the bar, and Frankie put me in a taxi, but instead of going home I decided to go to Beatrice's apartment instead, on the spur of the moment.

"Darling Emma, congratulations," she greeted me, as warmly as ever, and planted a kiss on each cheek.

"Not bad, hey?" I said, dropping my bag on the narrow table in the hall. I hooked my arm through hers and we walked down the corridor.

"Not bad at all," she replied, tapping my arm gently with her hand, but I sensed a slight reluctance in her gesture, as if she were going through the motions only because she had decided to do so.

"Is everything all right?" We sat down.

"Everything's wonderful, but I must say . . ." She hesitated. So there was something after all.

"Yes?"

"I thought we'd decided on that other passage," she said, finally.

I shrugged. "I just went with the moment. It felt right to read that one. Does it matter?"

She shook her head. "No, not at all." But I wondered whether she was disappointed. I had hoped she'd be pleased, impressed even, and would agree with me that it was a good choice after all.

I let it go. "I'm glad," I said, leaning forward and putting my hand on her knee so she would look at me, "because I really appreciate the trust you've put in me, and I intend to do my very best to live up to it. I want to make you proud, I really do, Beatrice."

She smiled, took my hand into her own, and nodded. "I know you do, and I'm thrilled with how it went today, I really am. You did a brilliant job, darling."

"I did, didn't I!" I exclaimed happily, clapping my hands once, like a child. I gave Beatrice a recap of what Frankie and I had discussed earlier, analyzing everything. I'd almost forgotten about my little slip-up when she said, "So what was that about? That business about your earlier books and all that?"

"I thought of it on the spur of the moment," I said. "Let's face it, the novel's structure is fairly complex; the whole thing is really accomplished. Was anyone really going to buy it? That I could pull something like that out of thin air? On a first try? And I have been writing, you know that."

She looked at me, her head slightly tilted, one corner of her mouth raised in a kind of amused condescension.

I continued, undeterred. "So it made sense, right? To draw on my own experience. Isn't that what they say? To make a lie as believable as possible, keep it as close to the truth as it can be? So to say that this novel is unlike anything I have written before injected a sort of truth in the proceedings; that's what I thought."

She shot her head back and burst out laughing. "Emma, my dear, that's so clever of you! But the crime fiction part? That could get confusing, you know. You'll be asked about this again."

"Like I said, stick to the truth as closely as possible." And we both laughed.

"Well, since imitation is the best form of flattery, I'm all for it," she said warmly.

But I thought back to that moment when Gusek had stopped short my ravings about my process as a crime fiction writer, and I knew I hadn't meant to imitate her. I hadn't meant to pretend I was talking about my own body of work, obviously. No, it was more complicated than that: in that moment back there, I'd forgotten that I *wasn't* her.

She gave me a couple of notes, as she called it, but I was barely paying attention. I just wanted to go home. I'd done great; I knew that. I was excited and I wanted to see Jim, to hear what he thought. I couldn't wait to hear the pride in his voice.

17

It was nagging at me, this thing, this slight annoyance I felt toward her. It was creeping under the surface of my skin like an itch. She could have been more appreciative. I'd done a good job out there. I'd chosen a good passage to read, better than what she'd suggested, and anyway, it was up to me now, surely. I replayed in my mind the moment when she asked about my slip-up—except she didn't know it was a slip-up, of course. Was she annoyed that I'd put myself out there as a crime writer, or a potential one anyway? I tried to remember her tone, her eyes. She was all right about it once I'd explained; that was the main thing.

On the way home, I decided I was going to sit down right away and work on my own novel. I was going to need a follow-up to this, we had both agreed, and the sooner the better.

If I started now, then by the time the circus of *Long Grass Running* had left town—which is to say when the publicity opportunities had dried up and the sales started to dwindle—I'd be ready. Beatrice herself had pointed out early on that it would be so much easier the second time around. I wouldn't be a first-time author anymore.

I had my own little study at home—more of a nook, really—that extended from our bedroom upstairs, but I'd never used it. I'd meant it to be a space for me to catch up on paperwork when I was away from the store, but I did most of that sort of thing at work, and if I really needed to go over orders or invoices, I did that from my laptop at the kitchen table. It was all computerized; I didn't even own a filing cabinet.

But I now had a dedicated desk where I could spread out my index cards and my notes—only the last part of writing should be on a screen, I had decided. All the work that came before needed to be tangible for my brain to make sense of it. And I'd purchased a small stack of beautiful notebooks, bound in soft velvety leather, the ruled pages just waiting for my unwritten stories. I'd upgraded my laptop, and traded my small modern desk for a beautiful model that I sold in the store. It was made from reclaimed hardwood and had a variety of grains and patinas, with thin legs that tapered at the bottom.

I sat down, all ready to go, and spent the next half hour organizing my nook. I could use a large corkboard too, I decided. I could pin tidbits of ideas and inspirational quotes on it.

Jim was still at the office, so I had an opportunity to work uninterrupted, although considering how much time he spent in his own study, it wouldn't have made much difference if he were here. He had seen me hunched over my laptop for hours at a time, typing frantically what he thought was my first novel as if guided by divine inspiration, without needing to pause for reflection, so this time it was better to get started without him around. He'd have made me feel self-conscious. And, anyway, I was feeling a little miffed that he still hadn't called to congratulate me on the interview.

There was nothing languishing, gathering dust in drawers, for me to pull up and revisit. Obviously, I'd long since thrown away the few scraps of ideas from years ago, and I couldn't possibly start on the story that Beatrice had so thoroughly dismissed—just the thought of those lines of red ink made me cringe—so I set out to write something brand new. Something fresh—yes, that was it, something exciting.

I opened the first notebook to the first blank page and cleared my thoughts, willing myself into a state of inspiration.

Two hours later, I had written approximately half a page of notes, all of which I'd subsequently crossed out, so this was going to take more time than I'd thought. I'd been sure when I first sat down that a novel would spring forth on the page, whole and perfectly formed, as if it were simply a matter of taking dictation from an unknown source, so when no such thing happened in the first half hour, I'd decided to take a more pragmatic approach and write a storyline in one or two sentences. Some of those scribbled attempts were ridiculously close to the plot of *Long Grass Running*, and everything else I'd come up with—all two ideas—had come across as insipid and ordinary when I read them back to myself.

I told myself that it was silly for me to attempt this now, after everything that had happened today, with my mind understandably bloated with Beatrice's novel, so it was with a somewhat guilty relief that I heard the door open downstairs and Jim walk in.

"Hello! Anyone home?" he sang out.

"Coming down!" I closed the notebook and the laptop—not much point in keeping going—and joined him downstairs.

"Sweetheart, there you are! How did it go?" He was standing at the bottom of the stairs, his arms open in greeting and a happy expression on his face, holding a bottle of champagne with a big red bow. "How's my favorite author?"

I jumped from the bottom step, threw my arms around his neck, and laughed in his hair. "It was great! Did you hear it? What did you think?"

"Not yet, but Jenny came in to tell me all about it."

"Jenny? From Admin?"

"Yep, everyone heard it down there, and I'm told you were terrific! Here, let's celebrate!" He lifted the bottle, and we walked together arm in arm into the kitchen.

"Well, I wasn't bad, even if I do say so myself." He gave my shoulders a squeeze and I knew I'd be able to write the next day. It would be fine. One should always write when one is happy, I decided. It was so simple: how we judge the work we do is bound to be affected by how we feel about ourselves, by our mood. That little tinge of annoyance I'd felt toward Beatrice had stolen the afternoon from me. I needed to be careful not to let these things get to me.

◆　◆　◆

Days later I was still walking on air, thinking about my interview with Gusek. I had been transformed from the reluctant, accidental author into a confident, talented professional. I felt great. No, I felt *fantastic*. Beatrice started to take me shopping, to places I used to only dream about, in neighborhoods I'd never had any reason to visit, with price tags that once would have given me a coughing fit. "It's my treat," she would invariably say. It was embarrassing. "Let me, please. Think of it as an investment on my part. That's what it is, after all," Beatrice would argue.

It was amazing how quickly I got used to it. There was something about wearing soft fabrics elegantly draped on your body, and once I started, it became impossible to go back. I caught Jackie staring at me one day; one of those rare occasions when we both happened to be at the store.

"What's wrong? Do I have something on my face?"

"No, it's just, I don't know, you look different."

"Different how?"

"I don't know, just different."

I wanted to say, *Of course I do, I'm wearing hundreds of dollars' worth of fashion. My haircut costs more than your handbag.* But I didn't, of course.

I joined a gym—something I'd never even contemplated in my entire existence—and I became obsessed with getting my body into shape. I would do it all, I decided, a regimen of weights, yoga, Pilates, treadmills, trainers, whatever it took. I booked a manicure and made a regular weekly appointment, and had a session with a professional makeup artist to learn what worked best for me.

I looked so amazing, I even wondered if I should get Frankie to redo my jacket photo, but who knew whether there would be another print run.

Jim noticed the change in me, thank the Lord, because if he hadn't, we would have had an even bigger problem than I'd imagined. I noticed how if we happened to be out together, he'd touch me more often, be more attentive.

The one thing he objected to, however, was the color of my hair. I'd changed it from its original unremarkable hue—what people called light brown or "mousy" and I called "the color of compost"—to its current dark, almost jet-black shade.

"It makes you look like her," he said.

"Who?"

"Your friend, what's her name."

As if he didn't know.

"Beatrice?"

"Yes, you're starting to look like her, same haircut, same hair color. Same, I don't know, demeanor."

"Thank you."

"It's creepy, Em."

18

As Frankie had predicted, the book was selling reasonably well, all things considered, and thanks to the Gusek interview, at this point the novel was enjoying a little buzz of minor success.

I had done a handful of radio and online interviews, and a couple of reviews had been published in slightly more notable publications. One morning, as I engaged in my twice-daily routine of checking rankings and reviews on Amazon, I was pleased to find out the novel had broken through the ten-thousand ranking barrier and was sitting at a respectable 8,788 in the literary fiction category.

Beatrice, too, had been delighted, and a little surprised at this modicum of success. We talked regularly, we compared notes, we brainstormed ideas to push it a little further, but by this point—only a couple of months after the launch of the novel—things had started to level off. Sales were still respectable, but slowing down; Frankie was struggling to generate more interest in the press; and I was beginning to wonder if maybe we had reached the peak, and this was the start of our slow descent into eventual oblivion.

I was a little disappointed by that prospect, obviously, and while anyone would be forgiven for thinking this was because I was reluctant to give up my place in the sun, the truth was I loved this book. I could recite my favorite passages by heart; I thought of the sisters as if they were real people, I knew every bend and every loop in the intricate path of their lives over the decade that was covered in the novel, and I thought they deserved better than to be forgotten, relegated to the remainders heap.

Beatrice was just as anxious to keep the momentum going, and why wouldn't she be? It was her book. The sisters and their lives, as I had to remind myself regularly, were after all the product of Beatrice's wonderful imagination, so if I was attached to them, it was hardly surprising that she was as well, and I strove to put aside the disagreeable feeling that she was encroaching on my emotional territory.

But what puzzled me was the fact that in all our discussions when we'd first begun this duplicity, she had insisted that she didn't expect the novel to do very well, that it was more of an experiment to see whether she could write something other than crime fiction, and that she was happy to release it into my arms and let it have its own life.

"It will be all yours, Emma. Do with it what you feel is right, but don't get your hopes up. If we sell a few hundred copies I'll be over the moon, and you should as well."

But then she started to fret all the time, calling me almost daily: Had I talked to Frankie? What was he doing about it? Why wasn't I doing more book signings? Did I engage with readers on Amazon? I pointed out to her during one of these increasingly annoying phone calls that she was the one with all the contacts, so why didn't she send a review copy to so-and-so? After all, it was no secret that we were friends, and it would not be unusual for someone like her to help out someone like me if she believed the novel was good enough.

"No no no, I can't do that. People might get suspicious if I'm associated with it in that way."

I found it hard to believe anyone could reach that conclusion just because she made a phone call or two on my behalf, as a favor to a friend.

"Anyway," she countered, "the whole point is to see whether the novel can stand on its own two feet, without my name attached to it, so let's not go there."

"So there it is then. This is the best that it can do on its own two feet. I guess you've got the results of your experiment now. I'm not sure what else you want me to do," I replied. She was getting on my nerves.

It was a bit malicious on my part to say that—I too believed that *Long Grass Running* had more life in it and I wasn't ready to declare defeat—but it made me feel a little satisfied when she'd get agitated in reply, oblivious to my goading, rising to the bait and defending the novel, carrying on about the years that she had toiled at it, etc., etc., etc., until finally I'd release her from her state of panic and say, "All right, I'll give it another push," or, "Don't worry about it, I'll talk to Frankie, I'm sure he has something else up his sleeve," and I'd promise to report back the next day, with no intention of doing so.

Needless to say, I didn't have the faintest idea of what to do to push the novel further into the world. I didn't have any experience in self-promotion, mailing lists, social media. I'd left all that to Frankie, who I knew was doing his very best and had more to lose than anyone if the novel didn't succeed, really succeed. He didn't have the time or the resources to try again with another book. His creditors, his bank manager, and probably his partner wouldn't allow it. *Long Grass Running* was going to be either his salvation or his swan song.

And then something extraordinary happened.

Terry was giving a small dinner for a respected economist who was in town for a conference, and of course Jim was invited, as was Carol—and me too, as Jim's wife, obviously.

"I'm not sure why I'm invited," I said to Jim as we were getting ready that evening. "I'll be the only non-economist at the table—I'll be bored to tears. Why don't you go without me?"

"He brought his wife with him," Jim said, arranging his tie in front of the mirror.

"Who, the famous professor?"

"Yes."

"Oh, I see."

So I went along, and she was nice—Véronique was her name—and we quickly broke away from the dinner-table conversation about debts and deficits and micro-this and macro-that into our own little party.

Véronique had relocated from France fifteen years earlier to take up a position as a theater director in a now-defunct ensemble, which was around the time she and Marc, her husband, first met, and we spent the first hour talking about French furniture, the French countryside, and French food of course. She seemed pleased by my knowledge of—and passion for—the country of her birth.

"Do you miss it?"

She thought about that for a moment. "At this time of year, yes, I do. Summer in France—you know how it is. We go on vacation: by the sea, to the country . . . Here, it's business as usual. Americans, you work too hard."

We laughed.

"Speaking of which, what is it you do here? For work, I mean?"

"I'm a journalist now."

Marc, who was sitting next to his wife and must have had one ear to our conversation, put an arm around her shoulders and said proudly, "Véro writes for the *Book Review*," squeezing her shoulders in a sweet, proud way.

"What's that?" Terry asked. "The *Book Review*, I mean." But I already knew, of course, that Marc was talking about the *New York*

Times Book Review, the dedicated literary supplement the paper published on Sundays, and I had stopped breathing.

"God, your life sounds *so* interesting," Carol said when Véronique had explained what she did and who for, and the conversation turned to, "Have you met such-and-such?" and, "What did you think of so-and-so's novel?" With a mock sigh, Carol turned to Jim. "Do you ever wonder, Jim, why we chose this dry, dull career path? Do you feel like maybe we're stuck in a lab like a bunch of rats, while everyone else is having a great time over in the arts? Because I do," she concluded wistfully.

"I don't," Jim replied. "What we do at the Millennium Forum is at least as important to humanity as the arts, don't worry about that." He said this a little pompously, I thought, and I caught Carol winking at him, as if to say, *I know, I'm just humoring them*, although maybe I was reading too much into it.

I sat there, waiting for one of them, Jim preferably, to say something like, *What a coincidence! Emma here, who happens to be sitting opposite you, has just published a novel.*

"Have you read Emma's novel?" Terry asked suddenly, and I wanted to kiss him, Lord love him.

"No?" she replied, looking at me quizzically. It was more of a question than an answer, which she then expanded upon. "You didn't mention it, Emma. Are you a writer?"

"It didn't really come up." I shrugged, smiling. "But yes, I've just published my first novel." I said this almost trembling from excitement at the discussion we were about to have, and an equal amount of anxiety that if I pushed too hard I might frighten her away.

Terry got up from the table and returned with the book. "Here," he said, giving it to her, "take a look. It's very good—better than that, it's terrific." He said this while looking at me, and I smiled gratefully, though I was a little embarrassed.

125

Véronique took the book from him and said, "I'm sorry, I haven't heard of this novel yet. I'd love to find out more though."

"I'm surprised you have a copy, Terry," I said. "You should have told me—I'd have gladly given you one."

"Why don't you, so Véronique can keep this one? I think you'll find it fascinating," he said to her. And it struck me that he knew how important this was to me, to give Véronique an opportunity to get to know the novel and perhaps review it for the *New York Times*, and I loved him with all my heart at that moment.

"Thank you," Véronique said, "I would love to read it. When was this published, Emma?"

So I told her, and she wanted to know a bit more about it, but I explained that I'd prefer it if she read it fresh, without knowing anything about the story.

In days to come I would not be able to recall anything else about that evening beyond that point, no matter how much I tried. We all stayed for a long while more, but in my memory it was a complete blank, because even though I engaged in conversation—attentive, responsive, witty, inquisitive—my mind was stuck on the fact that Véronique was taking my book away with her, and that if she read it and she liked it, she'd maybe review it, and if she did—well, I couldn't bear to even think about that.

We all exchanged business cards that night, but I didn't call her to find out what she thought. That would have been too eager, and I figured that if she didn't like it she wouldn't tell me anyway. But after one week I began to think that she'd forgotten about me completely—that she had left the book on a pile with others—and my nervous excitement started to wane.

It took only another week before I heard from her again, but to me it seemed like an eternity. I was working at the store when she called, and when she did, she introduced herself—"Emma, it's Véronique

Hillyard, we met at dinner"—as if I had to be reminded of the circumstances. My heart leaped in my chest.

"Véronique, it's nice to hear from you. How are you?" I made a hand gesture to Jackie that signified I had to go into the office at the back, and she nodded at me and took over at the counter.

We exchanged the obligatory pleasantries and she came right to the point.

"I love it, Emma, I really do. Terry wasn't lying: it's wonderful. Congratulations."

A wave of joy engulfed me then. I opened my mouth to say something, I don't know what, but nothing came out.

"I just got off the phone with Frankie Badosa," she continued. "I thought he should know, since it wasn't reviewed by us yet, that I took the liberty of doing so, and I think you'll be pleased. The review will be in this week's issue."

19

When Sunday came, I woke up feeling very ill. I was terrified. I was about to be exposed, judged, and hanged, because for one thing, no one would believe that an unknown thirty-two-year-old shopkeeper could possibly churn out a book this good. My schoolteachers would come out of the woodwork announcing that I'd never written anything remotely memorable in all my school years and questioning how this could possibly be my work. I should never have agreed to this charade.

And then there was the possibility that Véronique didn't really like it. Could that happen? Or was she stringing me along to be polite, only for me to find out there was no review this week, only excuses?

Of course not. I was being paranoid again. I stared at the ceiling at three o'clock in the morning. I felt as if I were in a nightmare, except I was awake. *Why is it always 3:00 a.m.*, I wondered, *when the dark, silent world of naked truth slides in beside us in bed, keeping us from the relief of sleep?* I'd read that line somewhere, a long time ago. How appropriate to think of it now. What on earth had I been thinking? I'd never pull this off, and even if I managed to muddle through, I'd be found out. No one in their right mind was going to believe that I, little old me, just woke up one day and spewed this masterpiece out of nowhere.

My phone buzzed and lit up on the night table. I picked it up. I knew before I read it that it was a text from Beatrice.

You're awake? it said.

What do you think? I replied.

Go to sleep, she texted back.

I laughed silently. *Right back at you :)*

Tomorrow is the beginning of the rest of our lives.

That's what I'm afraid of, I replied.

She sent back a smiley face, and I lay staring at the ceiling.

"You'll be famous after this," she'd said when I told her. She had more confidence than me about the contents, although Véronique had said she liked it, so what was I so worried about?

There were three more hours until I could read a copy of the review online, and my thoughts were swinging wildly between despair and disbelief, excitement and pride.

Jim was snoring softly next to me, lying on his side with his arm flung across my chest, the contact of his skin soothing me, and I rubbed his forearm gently. He made a soft noise of pleasure in his sleep, and I wondered if I'd entered his dream.

He had no idea what this day meant to me, but he had tried hard and been surprisingly supportive and attentive. That made me so very happy, so the thought of my subterfuge being discovered sent me into a deep, dark despair about what that would do to my relationship, in the highly unlikely event that it should survive.

At a little after 5:00 a.m., I knew I wouldn't get any more sleep. I gently moved Jim's arm and got up quietly, grabbing my phone from the night table and my bathrobe from its hook behind the door, trying to remember where I'd left my slippers, and finding them in the bathroom. I padded my way down the stairs, softly, silently, into the kitchen, where I turned on the coffeemaker.

It was rare for me to be up this early, but I liked it, this quiet hour before dawn. There was room for thought, and I suspected that the creative tap would flow well at this time. I decided to give it a go, to try to write my novel in the early hours, and see how it worked.

I poured myself a cup of coffee, my taste buds rejoicing. Everything was amplified: all my senses were heightened, and my body was vibrating. I'd barely slept, but I felt no tiredness. I hoped that was a good thing as I sat at the kitchen table, where my laptop lay shut.

I looked up at the ceiling and I prayed with all my might. I promised to be a better person, a better friend, a better partner. I promised to donate money to charities. I'd help Mrs. Williams next door with her grocery shopping once a week, something I kept meaning to do but only achieved very rarely. I promised all sorts of things—I'd invite friends and Jim's colleagues for dinner more often. I'd rescue a dog from the pound.

Finally, at the appointed time, I opened the browser and looked, one hand over one eye.

How best to describe this remarkable novel by Emma Fern?

Words jumped off the page and hit me in the face, muddled together: *enthralling, powerful, self-assured, a new talent.* The breath that had been locked inside my chest escaped in a long, whistling, deflating motion. *A tour de force. A new voice in the literary landscape that will change the way people write novels from now on.*

I burst into tears.

My phone buzzed and I knew it was a text from Beatrice even before I picked it up.

Emma darling! We did it! She LOVES my book!

What? "*My* book"? What did she mean "*my* book"? Of course, yes, technically it was hers, once, but not anymore—which was the point, wasn't it?

Was it just a slip on her part? Yes, of course, it must have been. She probably meant "*the* book." Or "*our* book," even.

130

But I did feel a small shiver of anxiety. It made me realize how vulnerable I was in all this, and I made a promise to myself that I would bring this up with Beatrice at an appropriate time. If this was going to work, we needed to treat this novel as *mine* at all times. Otherwise, how could I pull this off?

20

I came to think of the novel's trajectory in terms of Before the Review and After the Review. After Véronique published her glowing critique, everything changed, almost overnight. The sales went through the roof, the reviews came fast, and I was run ragged doing publicity, book signings, festival circuits—especially since we said yes to everything, Frankie and I, and everyone wanted a piece of me. It was exhausting, and exhilarating.

I was under no illusions: had I not met Véronique, or had she not liked the novel, of course, it would have plodded on for a little while, and after a few short weeks dwindled to oblivion. Instead, we were already on the first reprint, in much larger numbers than the original print run, and still could barely keep up with the demand.

It made me wonder about the many books that must have been out there that didn't get the benefit of a glowing review in the *New York Times*, simply because their authors didn't happen to sit opposite one of the most respected literary journalists in the country at a dinner party. Could literary success really be so . . . random?

I didn't let that train of thought bother me. Since I was on the right side of said randomness, what did I care?

All this activity had the added and not unwelcome benefit of paying me substantial royalties. Frankie had only been able to afford a small advance, and at the time I hadn't cared, but by this point, we were starting to make some significant profits, he and I.

Beatrice and I spoke regularly, but we hadn't seen each other much over the last two months, partly because I was crisscrossing the country doing my bit, partly because she had her own busy schedule to contend with. I missed her, and decided on the spur of the moment to invite her to lunch, at L'Ambroisie, of course. I also wanted to talk to her about my own book. I needed her advice on how to make headway with it. Some nights, I would wake up with a start, as if from a bad dream, in a state of panic that I hadn't written a single word yet.

◆ ◆ ◆

I'd been there myself recently, at L'Ambroisie, without Beatrice. In fact, I'd been there a few times. It had become my restaurant of choice for any sort of casual business lunch, such as the meeting Frankie and I had with a film producer who wanted to acquire the movie rights to *Long Grass Running*.

As a result, I was no longer Madame Johnson Greene's guest; instead, Alain the maître d', the sommelier Monsieur Raymond, and the floor staff all knew me and greeted me by name: "Madame Fern. How wonderful to see you again. Come this way, please, your party is waiting."

Beatrice was sitting at our table, breaking off small morsels from a crusty roll. Looking bored.

"Darling!" I exclaimed, arms wide, imitating the way she normally greeted me.

"You're late," she said dully.

This must have been the first and only time since we'd met that Beatrice had had to wait for me, a fact that clearly had not occurred to her.

"No, you're early," I replied, sitting down opposite her. I meant it as a joke but she didn't laugh.

A middle-aged couple at the table near us smiled in our direction and gave a little nod in greeting. I looked at Beatrice, waiting for her to nod back, and then realized it was me they were looking at. I couldn't stop my heart from doing a little leap of pride, and I stole a glance at Beatrice to see if she'd noticed, but it was hard to tell.

"So! You're unusually quiet today. Everything all right?" I asked. She was looking down at the menu, seemingly choosing something to eat, but really avoiding looking at me, for some reason I didn't understand.

I tried again.

"I've had some thoughts about my novel I want to ask you about. I think I should get a little recording device—do you use one of those? They even make pens like that, I think. See, the thing is, whenever I have a brilliant idea, I'm invariably in the shower"—I chuckled—"but also I could use it to record our writing sessions. I'm sure my brain always bubbles over with ideas when I talk to you." I was rambling, but she was still studying the menu as if it were the most fascinating piece of literature she'd ever read in her life.

"You need to bring me some pages—some real ones, Emma. I need to see something," she said finally, still not looking up.

"Yes, I know. It's been hard to concentrate but I've got it now. I've started and it's going well," I lied.

So we decided that I'd bring over some pages, that there was no need for us to do anything else until I did. I reluctantly agreed to this, knowing that I had been promising to do so for weeks. Neither of us mentioned that.

"Let's talk about something else then. No more work—that's all we talk about," she said, finally letting go of the menu and sitting up in her chair. "How's the store going?"

The store. I couldn't even remember the last time I went there. "It's ticking along nicely. Jackie has it all under control, you know? I'm not really needed there anymore. Lord knows, I'm so busy, I hardly have time to sleep. And anyway, selling my wares, I don't know, I feel like I've moved on."

Because why were we talking about the store anyway? Surely my life was more exciting than that these days? I changed the subject.

"Did you see my piece in the *Globe*?"

"Your profile? Yes, of course."

"What did you think?"

Before she could reply, the waiter came to get our orders.

"No champagne today?" I asked. This was different and disappointing. I wanted us to joke and laugh and celebrate and carry on, like we normally did.

"No, I have work to do after this. I need a clear head."

"Oh."

Which was also different, but maybe she was busy and had things on her mind. It deflated me somewhat. We hadn't seen each other for weeks. Couldn't she have said today wasn't ideal? That she'd rather we got together on another day? When she was more available?

I found myself irritated with her again. I was working so hard for her—surely I deserved a little more than being slotted into her schedule.

"So you didn't like it?" I asked, trying to match her bored tone.

"Like what?"

"The *Globe*!"

"Oh, I liked it." She hesitated a little. "It's just that—I don't know."

"Tell me."

"I don't think you should be so—now, how shall I put it—forthcoming?"

That made me recoil slightly. I took a short audible breath. "What on earth does that mean?"

"You make it sound as if you've earned it, this success. You wax lyrical about how *hard* you've worked for it." She was shaking her head in disbelief as she said this.

"What else am I supposed to do? This is my role, isn't it? I can't exactly say I popped it out of a cereal box, can I?"

"No, but I think you should tone it down a notch. The 'tortured writer' life, the years of toiling at your craft. It's a little, I don't know—jarring."

"Jarring?" I said that very loudly, felt my face go crimson. I put my napkin down on the table and glared at her, waiting for her to enlighten me some more.

Jarring?

"Oh, darling, don't be upset. I'm guiding you, you know that. Readers don't want to hear the author ramble on about how special they are. It's a turnoff. They'll leave you in droves if you keep this up."

"In the first place, I don't ramble on about how special I am, but I need to project a persona—we discussed this. I need to give some history, some context to my novel, and that's what I'm doing."

"'*My* novel'?" She raised an eyebrow.

"You know what I mean." I looked away. "Anyway, we've discussed this a million times. It's my job. I bring life to the novel so that people will buy it. I construct an aura around it. I know what I'm doing, I promise. I know what this novel needs."

"You think you know this book better than I do?"

This was an interesting question. I leaned back and thought about it before replying.

"I know it sounds strange, Beatrice"—I leaned forward then—"but it's as if I've transcended it, do you understand that? It's as if *I* was meant to write it, and now it's as if I have, so yes, I do know this book better than you do."

She looked at me as if I had two heads. "That's the most ridiculous thing I've ever heard."

I shrugged.

"Don't let this go to your head, Emma, and I'm saying this for your own good, because you're starting to sound a little crazy, my dear."

"You know what I think, Beatrice?"

"No, but I suspect you're going to tell me."

"I think you're a little jealous."

She snapped her head up, her lips pursed together tightly. It deepened the wrinkles around her mouth—not a good look for her.

"I think you're forgetting who you're talking to, Emma." Her voice was dripping with that snobbish haughtiness I'd heard her use on other people, but never with me, until this moment. I was about to say something cutting in reply, but then I caught myself. What was wrong with me? What on earth was I thinking? I couldn't get on the wrong side of Beatrice, for God's sake.

I made a show of staring at her with narrowed eyes, as if I was about to shoot burning embers from them, and then I broke and hooted with laughter, banging both my hands on the table. "Oh, Beatrice, I was only joking! You should see your face!" The couple at the table beside us looked up and smiled. "Beatrice, come on! I was putting you on!"

She blinked a couple of times and lifted a hand to rub the base of her neck, and her features started to relax a little. She was going to give me the benefit of the doubt. I knew her. After all, she'd done the same to me, many times. Making me cringe with embarrassment, telling me I'd made the ultimate blunder, only to laugh in my face.

"Very funny," she said, her mouth now in a little pout. I'd offended her, of course, and she couldn't have been enjoying the attention lavished onto me, her "protégée," even if we both knew it was a charade. But to the people there, in that restaurant, I was the more interesting of the two of us. I was the one they had noticed. And Beatrice was going to have to get used to it.

I sighed.

"Look, you're right. Of course you are. I don't really know how to do this and I do need your guidance. You know how it is. It's a circus, a whirlwind—it's insane." I shook my head. "Thank the Lord you're here to set me straight. Thank you, really. I'll take your advice to heart."

She raised an eyebrow, as if trying to decide whether I was mocking her or not, but her mood shifted and she smiled a little.

"How's your lovely George anyway?" I asked, desperate to change the subject. "You should bring him along to one of our lunches sometime. It would be nice to see him."

She shrugged. "George always eats at his desk. He's not really a lunch person."

"Really? What—like you pack yesterday's leftovers for him in a little lunchbox?"

"Smoked salmon and cream cheese on a bagel from the deli around the corner, and coffee from Starbucks. Always the same. When he's at his office downtown, anyway. He thinks going out for lunch is a waste of his time. He prefers to be working."

My phone rang. I fumbled through my handbag. "I'm sorry. I should have turned it off."

"That's all right." She flapped a hand in the air. "Take it, really. It's fine."

I looked at the screen. "It's Frankie—I'll just be a second," I said.

I took the call. I was about to ask him to call me later, explain I couldn't talk right now, but the urgency in his voice stopped me, so I listened to him, and it suddenly felt too warm in there.

When he had finished, I thanked him, told him I'd call him later, and hung up.

"Everything all right?"

I was staring at her, but it was difficult to focus.

"I've been shortlisted for the Poulton Prize."

Beatrice was as excited as I was at the news, and as shocked.

"This is wonderful. It couldn't be better. What good news, Emma! What absolutely wonderful news."

I was relieved she was so positive about it, and why wouldn't she be?

"I have to go, but come over later, will you?" She stood up and was signaling for the check.

"Really? You don't want to have your lunch?"

"Sorry, my dear, but I couldn't eat anything right now. This is such wonderful news. I need to dash, but will you come over this evening? We'll go to Craig's. It'll be fun, just like old times."

"Sure!" I said, a bit puzzled, but yes, it would be fun, it would be loads of fun, especially when I told them—her friends, our friends. Was I allowed to tell? I wondered. I hadn't checked with Frankie. Yes, probably, surely.

Oh, I wished Beatrice hadn't dashed off like that, I wished she'd stayed with me. We should have been celebrating! Pink champagne!

◆ ◆ ◆

That evening I took a taxi to Beatrice's apartment, and my mood was restored as soon as I saw her. She was beaming with joy and flushed with excitement in greeting me.

"I keep thinking I'll wake up and find that none of this ever happened," I said in her embrace.

She pinched me hard on the arm.

"Hey, that hurt!"

"You're awake then," she laughed. "Have a cocktail with me before we go." We walked over to the bar. She was a little unsteady on her feet: this clearly wasn't her first cocktail of the evening.

"I haven't eaten anything yet. I'm not sure I should be drinking."

She waved a hand in the air. "Oh, don't worry about that—there'll be food at Craig's party."

I didn't take much convincing and accepted the glass she offered.

"Can you believe this? In your wildest dreams?" she said, her eyes wide, sparkling.

"Maybe in my wildest dreams, yes, probably."

She laughed. "We need to do more plotting and scheming, you and me, to keep the momentum up."

"And you need to do some real mentoring. I'm starting to get terrified that I won't have anything to follow this up with."

"Don't worry, we will. We'll start soon, all right? We'll do some *real* plotting and scheming. Let's talk about that tomorrow." This was great news. First thing tomorrow, I decided, I'd start on the new outline. We downed our drinks quickly and left.

◆ ◆ ◆

"The protégée! There she is, everyone!" I laughed into the noise, the heat, as Craig kissed me warmly on both cheeks, then took my hand and bowed to kiss it. "Congratulations, Emma," he said, very genuinely.

"Thank you, Craig, very much. I assume you mean *The New York Times* review?"

"Oh, everyone knows about your review, darling. But the prize! The prize! You're the toast of the town!" He handed me a glass of champagne. People were coming over to say hello to me, some of whom had never done so before. In fact, it wasn't that long ago that I'd felt I was perpetually reintroducing myself to most of them.

A woman I vaguely recognized, but had never spoken to, made her way through the crowd to join us. She put a hand out to me and I shook it. "Emma, we've never been introduced." She turned to Beatrice as she said this. "Hello, Bea," she said, kissing Beatrice on the cheek, still holding my hand.

"Hello, Natasha. This is Emma Fern," Beatrice said.

"I know who you are, although until today I didn't know your name. Everyone seems to call you 'Bea's little protégée,' but I don't think that's going to happen anymore."

Beatrice's body stiffened a little.

"I wanted to congratulate you, Emma. I confess I had no idea we had such a talent in our midst." She was speaking to me, but looking at Beatrice when she said it. "You've been keeping her very close, Bea."

Craig put an arm around my shoulders. "I must say, success suits you!" He looked down at my outfit, then up at my hair. "The dowdy peasant housewife look was never for you. I'm pleased to see you gave it up."

I laughed. Had it been that long since I'd seen him?

Craig turned to Beatrice. "So, Bea, it looks like your little protégée has outclassed you. Congratulations to you too—you must be an excellent tutor."

"Are you working on anything new, Bea? A sweet little cozy mystery, perhaps?" Natasha asked.

Beatrice tried to smile at her and failed, so it came out more like a grimace. "I'm writing the perfect murder, in fact, Natasha."

"Then I won't stay on your radar any longer, lest I get hit by a stray bullet." Natasha gave my hand a squeeze and walked away.

It all sounded like genial banter on the surface, but I knew Beatrice, and I could tell she was tense. Something was off. It occurred to me that she had brought me here to show me off, her little protégée who had done so well under her tutelage. She had expected to bask in my glory as much as I did, and it wasn't turning out that way.

She got very drunk that evening, even more than usual, so much so that when I put her in a taxi, I wondered if she'd remember that we had plans the next day to work on my own novel.

◆ ◆ ◆

The next morning I found myself being whipsawed by my emotions. In one moment I was elated, floating on a cloud, thinking that no one could possibly be happier than me, ever. In the next moment, I became paralyzed with fear, consumed with paranoia, vibrating with anxiety.

The most important thing I needed to do was write my own novel, and Beatrice absolutely had to help me do that: it was imperative. Did I really believe that I could follow this success with something comparable? Did it matter? After all, there must be plenty of people who only ever write one book. There was nothing wrong with that, surely.

But the fact was, I'd become affected with that most modern of diseases, an addiction to myself. I knew that in a year or two the interest in me would wane; and that even if I made enough money from this to invest and live off later—it was out of the question that I'd go back to work in the store. I'd already decided to sell it—I'd still need my fix of fame and unbridled admiration: the way people wanted to know what I thought on any given topic, the way they looked up to me. I was almost famous, and for all the right reasons. And to cap it off, Jim loved it, loved me, even more. He was so proud of me. We had become such a good match. I loved how proud he looked when we went out to various functions and conferences; he insisted all the time now that I join him, whenever my schedule allowed it.

There had been no mention of Allison, no phone calls, no sudden dashing off to conferences somewhere or other, and no young women on the doorstep. Whatever had been going on between those two, I was pretty sure it was over.

George greeted me when I arrived at Beatrice's house for our writing session. "Darling George, how are you?" I kissed him on both cheeks.

"Oh, you know, ticking along, but what about you, more to the point? Are you enjoying fame?"

I laughed heartily. *Who, me?* "It has its moments," I replied.

He nodded thoughtfully, as if he knew exactly what I meant. "Beatrice is upstairs in her office."

"Lovely, I'll go up then. You're well?"

"Just fine, thank you. I'll leave you to it then."

This was a little unusual for George. I was used to his being attentive to me; he even called me his little friend. "My little friend Emma, who is Beatrice's big friend." It was a funny thing to say, but I liked it.

Maybe he had things on his mind. After all, his work was very demanding. Beatrice said that often enough.

"Darling George barely knows I exist today. I might as well be a chair. But what can I do? He has things on his mind, and when he does, I'm a chair. I just hope I'm a Louis Quatorze–style chair. I always wanted one of those," she'd say.

I went upstairs to meet her in her office. She was typing at her desk, clearly concentrating, so I trod softly and sat in my usual spot on the large couch.

"Oh, here you are, darling. How are you?"

"Mighty fine. You're busy?"

"No rest for the wicked." She turned to me then, put her hands on her knees. "So, what have you brought me?"

She wasn't unfriendly exactly, but there was something in her tone that made me think she was annoyed with me. Was it about the prize? The party?

I bent down to my bag to pull out the folder with my pages; I'd brought my laptop also. I stood up and put the folder on the desk.

"Let me see that." She took it and flicked quickly through its contents. "This is the outline?"

"Lord, no, it's the outline of the first couple of chapters. The life of the successful writer is a little more demanding than I'd expected." I laughed, hoping for some lighthearted banter between us—*Don't I know it! Tell me about it!* Something like that. We were equals now, right?

"So why did you come?" she asked instead.

"What do you mean? You know why I came."

"We keep making plans, Emma. You want me to help you and I am. Now, so far, all I can see is basically nothing. What have you been doing? Other than photo shoots?"

"Hey, Beatrice, are you joking? Do you have any idea what's been happening here? I don't have the time to catch my breath! If I have to wait a little before doing some more work on the novel, then so be it. I don't really have a choice here, do I?"

She snorted. "Some *more* work? Emma, please! This"—she threw the contents of the folder on the floor—"is not work!"

The back of my eyes hurt from the prickles of tears. "Don't say that."

"The only person who's done any work so far is me."

"Are you kidding me? You don't think what I've been doing is work? I am literally being run ragged. Everyone wants a piece of me—there's hardly anything left for me to give!" I was crying now. Tears of frustration and exhaustion were finally escaping, and I couldn't stop them.

"Well, you can relax, Emma. It'll be over soon."

"You think so? Doesn't seem very likely, Beatrice. The buzz around the Poulton Prize has already started, and it's only the shortlist. Can you imagine if I win?"

She studied me, her head very still, then she drew herself up.

"This changes everything, the Poulton. You do realize that, don't you?"

Boom!

"What are you saying, Beatrice?"

"We have to come clean, Emma. *I* have to come clean."

"You're not suggesting—"

"I'm not suggesting anything, I'm *telling* you that now that the novel is nominated for the Poulton Prize, we must explain to the world that I wrote it, not you. It would be a deception otherwise. Probably fraud even."

The room began to sway. I felt faint. "That's not possible now, Beatrice. You know that," I managed to say, but my voice was trembling.

"It's already in motion, Emma. I've spoken to Hannah—"

"What? Your agent, Hannah?"

"I've spoken to Hannah and told her that you and I have a big announcement to make. She's going to schedule an appearance on *Books and Letters*. She'll talk to Frankie first of course."

Frankie. Hearing his name made my heart flutter. *What will Frankie think?*

"When did you do that?"

"This morning. Before you got here."

"You *told* her?"

"Only what I just told you. She doesn't know what the announcement is about. I think it will be more effective if we do that on the show, don't you?"

"And you didn't think you should discuss this with me first?"

"No, not really, and anyway, I'm discussing it now, aren't I?"

I was shaking; from anger, from fear, from watching my world collapse, from hanging on desperately to the tendrils of hope that maybe I could make her see we had come too far for that. "I can't believe you've talked to Hannah."

"I told you, I haven't told her why, just that we want to make an appearance on *Books and Letters*. You don't have to come if you don't want to. I'm only asking out of courtesy."

"Courtesy?"

"You can keep all the proceeds so far. Don't worry about my half."

I sat back down silently, watching her. Why was she being like this? My darling Beatrice, my friend, my very dear friend. What was going on?

She was busying herself with papers on her desk, not looking at me. The skin I was gnawing at on the side of my thumb had started to bleed.

"Is that it? We don't have anything to discuss?" I asked, although I wasn't expecting the situation to improve much.

"No."

"You know this can't happen, right?" I tried again, clinging to whatever sliver of hope I'd gotten hold of. "It's too late now, Beatrice. You can't back out of the deal now."

"Oh, shut up, Emma. I think you should leave."

This was truly awful. I was crushed. Why was she so angry with me? She was the one who was doing wrong by me, and yet she was making me feel like I'd screwed up.

"And take your trash with you." She gestured to the papers on the floor. I got up from the couch and bent down to pick them up.

"Can I still go with you to the interview?" I asked in a small voice.

"Just go, Emma."

I went home. I was devastated. I was due at a book reading later that afternoon, which, obviously, I needed to cancel. I'd tell Frankie I was too ill. He'd be sympathetic. Dear Frankie, he always accompanied me to these events even though I didn't need his moral support anymore. I was no longer terrified of public speaking, but he still came, to be there for me, and I'd never bailed on him before.

I went upstairs and lay on my bed, trying to silence the panic that gripped me. *What will they think of me now?* I imagined Jim's reaction to the news that it was never me, the talented Emma, whose soul was so rich in humanity that she had penned this masterpiece, and with no great effort either. I could picture his shock, but also I feared the small, smug smile on his lips, the unmistakable look in his eyes that would say *I knew it.*

I thought of how hurt Frankie would be on discovering that I was a liar and had lied to him all along. Our friendship was not going to survive this. I had no illusions about that. Would Beatrice even keep him on as the publisher? Or would she transfer it to her own? Poor Frankie—just when he was about to hit the jackpot, the rug would be pulled out from under him.

Oh, how I wished I had never met Véronique. None of this would have happened. The novel would have enjoyed a respectable life, but no more, and Beatrice and I would have laughed in years to come about the deception we'd performed, and how lucky we were that we'd gotten away with it.

The betrayal I felt was making it impossible for me to breathe properly. After everything I'd done, all of which had led us to exactly where we were today. None of this would have happened without me, and now I was to be discarded, scorned, and humiliated. Surely I was the one who should be angry, for God's sake, but instead she was angry with *me*? That old trick.

I sat up—I needed to go back and see Beatrice, right away. Make her see the cruelty of her suggestion; beg like I had never begged anyone before. Call upon her kindness, her generosity, impress upon her that the Poulton shortlist was because of me. Because of *me*. Make her see that she was about to ruin my life.

Just write another one, I would tell her. *You can—you truly are a great writer, and you did find out how successful you can be at this. You can just write another, and the Poulton will be yours, next time.*

I would go to the book reading after all, I decided. I needed to keep everything going as normally as possible and make Beatrice see sense.

◆　◆　◆

"So! What are you two up to?" Frankie wore a little grin when he greeted me at the bookstore.

"Who?" I pretended to be casual.

"You and Beatrice? Hannah called me."

"What did she say?"

"That we're talking with *Books and Letters* for some sort of joint appearance by you and Beatrice?" He said this as a question, as if I were supposed to know what he was talking about.

I'd been hoping Hannah hadn't spoken to him yet, but no such luck. Oh Lord, I was dreading this conversation. I wasn't ready for it.

"I didn't realize Beatrice had a book coming out," he continued.

"Neither did I—well, I don't think she does." He gave me a puzzled look. "She's working on one, I know that, but it's still at the draft stage."

"I see, so just a straight interview then?"

"Hannah didn't say?"

"No, she asked me if I knew. So I'm asking you."

This was getting ridiculous. "I don't know either, Frankie, just that Beatrice wants us both to go on *Books and Letters*. That's all."

"Oh, come on, Emma, don't make me wiggle it out of you. What's the angle?"

"You know—mentor and mentored, I think." I sighed a little. "I think Beatrice wants to talk about the process of teaching me how to write, how she took me from a complete unknown to Poulton Prize shortlist."

He raised both hands up, palms toward me, as if to ward me off. "Whoa, Emma, please! I don't know if that's a good idea."

Thank the Lord. "Well, you know"—I pretended to think about this—"she has a point. She did encourage me enormously. She gave me the confidence I needed." I figured a little generosity of spirit wouldn't hurt.

"It's your novel, Emma. That's all that matters."

"I know. To be honest I'm not crazy about the idea either, but Beatrice is, well, she's adamant we should do this." I looked at him. "What do you think I should do?"

"Leaving aside the fact that I, not Hannah or Beatrice, handle your publicity"—*Good point*, I thought—"it's going to come across as a little desperate on her part," he said finally.

"I've had those thoughts exactly," I replied, watching the room filling up fast. A staff member motioned for me to take my place on the stage. "To be honest, Frankie, and I hate to say this, I really do, but

I think Beatrice is a little—I don't know—put out, I guess. She'd like some of this success for herself somehow, or to be associated with it."

Now he looked really confused.

"I don't know Beatrice very well, certainly not like you do, but that doesn't sound like her."

I was overplaying it. *Go back, careful, tread carefully.*

I shrugged. "Maybe I'm imagining it." I began to walk away from him toward the armchair that had been set up for me. "But she's been saying things lately," I continued, reluctantly, "like that without her help, her guidance, none of this would have happened to me, something along those lines."

Someone was introducing me onstage.

He shook his head. "You'd better go. I'll talk to Hannah."

I turned and put a hand on his arm. "Don't tell Hannah what I just said, please. I may be completely off the mark."

"Don't worry. I'll ask her to wait before scheduling anything. Anyway, there's no great rush—Beatrice is away until the end of next week."

"What?"

"Los Angeles. The Crime and Thriller Writers of America conference."

That's right, I'd forgotten about that. I wouldn't be able to see Beatrice again until she got back. Maybe that was a good thing. Maybe she'd take time to think about what she'd said; about the consequences.

And then something twinkled in me. The merest germ of a thought, barely an idea yet, flickered on the very edge of my mind.

I reached the stage and the applause lasted a long time. It's difficult to explain the effect of adoration of complete strangers to people who have never experienced it, but it's the closest thing to feeling like you're blessed.

Finally, the host of the event managed to calm everyone down and I began my sixth book reading in as many days.

21

It was cold on the day I went crazy. I remember because it meant I could wear my hooded parka, and no one would see that as unusual or suspicious. I did all the things one reads about in novels. I called Beatrice's apartment that morning, and I let it ring until it cut out, which took twenty-one rings. When I arrived at her apartment building, I called again from my cell phone. Still no answer.

I went in through the basement parking garage, and from there I buzzed her three times. I was about to punch in the code on the keypad—the code that opened the door, the door that would let me get upstairs—when a young woman came out. She barely looked at me, her head down. She wore one of those navy duffel coats. I saw the slightly pilled cuffs when she held the door open for me. I figured it wasn't likely she lived there, and I noticed the garbage bag she was taking out.

Beatrice's apartment door still had the old-fashioned type of doorbell, a brass circle with a small button protruding from its center. I pressed on that twice, although I did wonder if anyone else in the building could hear its shrill sound and, thinking that I shouldn't bring attention to myself, I kept that short.

Finally satisfied that no one was home, I took the key from my pocket and opened the door.

Houses are strange beasts, I thought, not for the first time. They're permeated by the energy of their inhabitants, and Beatrice's apartment was no exception. I had never been there on my own before, and it was a very different experience. The silence I found myself in was slightly uncomfortable, certainly not welcoming, and not just because I was there uninvited. It felt more empty and cold than it should, slightly accusatory even. It made me shiver, and I had no intention of lingering.

I went upstairs immediately to proceed with the purpose of my visit. I was fairly sure that was where I should start. I intended to complete my task as quickly as possible and get out of there pronto.

Talking to Frankie the previous day had given me the idea. I still held out hope that I could convince Beatrice that her intentions were completely dishonorable toward me, and might not do her any favors either, but now I had a fallback position. I decided that, should she go ahead with her betrayal, all I had to do was deny everything. It was so simple: unable to graciously accept her protégée's success, Beatrice had been eaten from within with jealousy. In her seething, deranged state, she became obsessed with being nominated for the Poulton, and the fastest, surest way to achieve that was to claim to be the actual author of *Long Grass Running*. Brilliant.

I'd even planted that seed the day before, talking to Frankie, without grasping the full potential of my words. But I did now.

The only piece of evidence that tied us together to this book was the stupid cocktail napkin on which Beatrice had drawn up our agreement. There was no trace of the manuscript she'd given me, and I knew she hadn't kept a copy on her own computer. She had been so careful to cover her tracks. So all I had to do was retrieve the napkin and destroy that, and all would be right with the world.

The stars had aligned beautifully for my quest: Beatrice was away for a week, George was at work as usual, and I had a key. To top it off, it was a beautiful, if cold, sunny day, and I'd even booked a last-minute appointment with my hair salon, around the corner from here, so should anyone spot me in the neighborhood, I had an explanation.

I started with her office. That's where we had gone when we returned from our drinks and our signing ceremony, and I vaguely remembered her putting it on top of her desk. With any luck it would still be there, but if not, it probably wasn't very far—in one of the drawers; somewhere like that.

Her desk was neat. There were only a couple of letters stacked on the top, a pen, a photo of George.

Her drawers were equally tidy; a couple of flash drives in a little wire basket, a few pens, an unopened pack of white envelopes, along with a few more equally dull items of stationery. Definitely no cocktail napkin.

I scanned the bookshelves on the wall—plenty of places there to store the napkin—but then I thought of the bedroom. The *sulking room*. That was a more personal place for Beatrice. Lord knows we'd spent a lot of time there, chatting, laughing, getting drunk. So I went in there and started rifling through her (much less tidy) nightstand.

"What on earth are you doing?"

I jumped. I really did. I straightened up and turned around in one single movement and felt my heart explode in my chest. Beatrice was standing in the doorway, staring at me with a mixture of disbelief and anger, her eyes narrowed, a thin pale line where her lips should have been.

"Oh! You're here! Thank God! I was so worried!"

"What are you talking about?"

"I've been trying to reach you—you were so upset yesterday . . ." I walked, arms open, toward her, and she actually took a few steps back, as if she were slightly repelled by me. "I must have called a hundred times, Beatrice! I didn't want to leave things like this between us! It's only a book, right? Why would we fight like this over a stupid book, you and me? But I couldn't reach you, and . . ."

I sat on the end of the bed, shaking my head.

"I was so worried, Beatrice, when I couldn't reach you. I had to come and see you were okay. I just had to."

"How did you get in?"

"With my key—you know, the one you gave me months ago, when I stayed here with you one night, remember?"

She put a hand out to me. "Can I have it back, please?" she said sternly.

"You did say I could use it anytime. I only did to see if you were here. To make sure you were okay."

"You thought you might find me curled up in my night table?"

"Ha ha ha!" I laughed gaily, for quite a while actually, scrambling to come up with an appropriate response. She still had her hand out, waiting for me to give her the key.

"It's downstairs, the key, on the table in the hall," I said finally, wiping my eyes as if from the hilarity of her earlier joke.

"Can you leave, please?" She turned to her side to make room for me to walk past her, the arm previously extended toward me now pointing in the exact opposite direction, outside the room. "Now?" she added, presumably in case I had misunderstood the directive and assumed she meant for us to have tea and cake first.

But I had come with a specific task in mind, which was not yet completed, and as anyone who knew me would agree, when I started something, I liked to finish it.

"Beatrice, don't be like that, what's wrong with you?" I stood up again.

"What are you really doing, Emma? You're not here to check up on me. You know very well I'm supposed to be in LA, so what, exactly, are you doing here?"

"I forgot you were going away. Why aren't you there, anyway?"

"My session got moved, if you must know. You still haven't answered me, Emma. What do you want?"

I sighed. "Let's talk, please. I really don't want to fight with you. Let's go and sit down and talk."

She snorted. She was starting to do that a lot with me, which was a bit off-putting, certainly, but also not terribly attractive, especially in someone so particular about her appearance.

"Talk about what?" she pretended to wonder, eyes raised to the sky, an index finger resting on her lips. "I know! Let's talk about how you want me to keep my mouth shut, while you continue to be the celebrated author of a bestseller you never wrote in the first place! Am I getting warm?"

She said this in a mocking, singsong voice, as if talking to a child. It was especially nasty.

"It will ruin my life," I said somberly, appealing to her kinder self. "I will be humiliated, Beatrice. I'll be a joke, a fool. We never worked on my own book, so I don't even have that to fall back on." I kept my head bent down, but raised a sad eye at her when I said this, hoping to make her feel guilty that even though she had promised to help me write, nothing had ever come of that.

"Oh, don't worry, you'll recover. A little humiliation never killed anyone. They'll forget about you. You've made a lot of money out of this, and it's all yours. I never claimed my half and I won't. Keep it— every cent you made out of me so far."

"It's not about money, Beatrice." Now I was matching her own angry tone. "If I'd known, I would *never* have agreed to this!" I shouted.

"Which is why I never mentioned it," she said calmly.

"What do you mean?"

We were inches from each other now. We could spit at each other with complete confidence of reaching our target.

She narrowed her eyes at me, her body even more taut with spite, if that were possible.

"That book," she hissed, "is my life's work. It's the novel I was born to write. I put my heart and soul into that novel. I took ten years to write it, and I wasn't going to take any chances with it. You said to me once that you would never have given it up if you'd written it. Did you really believe I gave it up?" She laughed in a somewhat insane way, then stopped just as quickly as she'd started. "Do you know what they said about me when I published a novel that wasn't in the style I've been 'categorized' into?" She made helpful air quotes with her fingers.

She took a deep breath, and I said nothing, knowing a rhetorical question when I heard one.

"I wrote another book, years ago, that also was not"—helpful air quotes again—"a 'crime novel.' It was a serious work, a truly literary tour de force. Do you know what they said? 'If only female crime writers like Ms. Johnson Greene would stick to the genre their readers enjoy so much, literature would be grateful.'" She waited for my reaction, which was shock of course. In terms of nasty reviews, that one did seem a bit over the top.

"Was that the book you told me about? The one lining the walls of your storage unit?"

She ignored me. "They demolished me. They called me pretentious. They wrote that it was excruciating that writers like me should pretend to pen a masterpiece that was at best a poor imitation of better novels. Whatever that means."

She looked like a witch, her face distorted in anger, her eyes filled with fury. *Go back to snorting*, I thought, *I take it all back.*

"What was the book?" I asked again. I'd read everything she'd written and I didn't remember *that*.

She deflated, shook her head, lost a little of her composure. "I took it out of circulation. It sank without a trace and I couldn't bear it. I recalled every copy, and it's never been mentioned in any of my bios or my backlist. It doesn't matter anymore." She waved a hand in the air, then turned to me sharply.

"I wasn't going to let that happen with this one. Middle-aged men who had failed to write anything more worthy than a hack job, turning on me like that because I was rich, successful, and achieved a million times more than they ever would in their entire pathetic lives."

She stood up straight. "I needed to show them. I was going to write a masterpiece, yes! A masterpiece! But publish it as someone else, someone with no history. Let those critics wax lyrical in their praises and then, bang! Hello, boys! Guess who's back?" And from the full height of her superiority, she looked down at me and said, "I needed a stand-in. You were perfect."

◆ ◆ ◆

I sat back down on the edge of the bed. I felt lightheaded and couldn't breathe properly.

"You set me up like that?"

"You really were gold, Emma. I couldn't have found anyone better if I'd tried. I mean, from the moment I met you, you've wanted to be *me*. You copied me; you followed me around; you wanted to write a book, although by now we both know that's not likely to ever happen; you dressed like me; you talked like me. You were perfect."

"Oh my God. And all this time I thought you *liked* me." It was as if the bottom of the world had fallen out, and I was spinning down into space.

"Oh, I did a bit. It was sweet having you around, your little puppy eyes on me all the time." She laughed.

"They'll hang you out to dry, Beatrice. No one should do that to another human being—it's too cruel."

"No. Of course they won't. Because you'll say you were in on it. You knew the whole time I would come out at some point as the real author."

"Why would I do that?"

"Because you'll look like a complete idiot if you don't, with your interviews, your photo shoots, your deluded monologues about your writing efforts. How do you think that'll work out for you now?"

I had of course thought of that eventuality before, but it hadn't occurred to me to pretend to the world that it was all a front on my part. I even contemplated that possibility just then, to see how it tasted.

"What if the book had flopped? Would you have still come out and owned it?"

"What do you think?" She snorted again. "Anyway, it's all decided now. You do as you please, but if I were you, I'd definitely take the route that this was always part of the plan as far as you're concerned. At least you'll be remembered as an excellent actor."

She walked out of the bedroom then, and left me there, sitting on the bed, feeling crushed. I had been used right from the beginning. There was no friendship, no mentoring; she didn't even like me, for God's sake.

I wish I could say I don't remember what happened next, but I do, unfortunately, in hyperrealistic detail.

I remember hearing a great big sob come out of me; I remember shaking; and I remember that as I watched her leave the room, a wave of violent fury rose inside me. I wanted her to turn around and look at me. I wanted to smash that haughty face of hers with the lamp conveniently within my arm's reach. I imagined blinding her, strangling her, and I saw myself as if from above, standing up suddenly like a spring that's been released. I walked toward her in great strides. Her back was to me. She was strolling toward the staircase as if she didn't even remember that I was in the bedroom anymore, or if she did, she no longer cared. I heard growling, shouting, and realized it was coming from my throat. I started to call her names, my arms extended in front of me to grab at her hair, to pull her back, stop her from discarding me like this, and throughout all this she completely ignored me. She was at the top of the stairs when I reached her and she turned her head to me. She was actually smiling. Instead of clawing at her, grabbing her, closing my hands around her neck as I'd intended to, I pushed her. Violently, with all the force of my wrath.

She screamed and tumbled, and not at all like a rag doll. It was more like a full-body roll, but the violence of my action had given her such momentum that she literally bounced down the stairs. I heard her head crack at one point, or was it her neck? Every part of her was getting smashed on those steps. Her back, her shoulders, her head, her knees— she was flinging her arms around a bit, but her fall was unstoppable.

I watched it all, frozen on the top landing, my mind completely blank, unable to comprehend what was happening in front of me, until, after what seemed an awfully long time, she landed hard at the bottom with a thud, and then I screamed. Then I stifled that scream.

I ran down to her, wobbling with shock, calling out to her, "Beatrice! Beatrice!" I wanted to touch her, to lift her up, but I couldn't bring myself to do it, I was so frightened of breaking her even more. I tried to feel for a pulse, but I was shaking so violently I couldn't hold her wrist steady for long enough. And then I saw the blood, dark and thick and oily, seeping out of the side of her head, and I thought, *She's dead.*

It ran out of her so fast it was like a horror movie. The blood would not stop oozing, and I thought it would fill the floor and then rise up against the walls and I'd be trying to keep myself above it, until it reached the ceiling and there was nowhere to go to breathe anymore, and it would drown me. I was about to stand up to get out of the way when I heard a noise—a deep growling moan that didn't sound human at all—coming from her. I saw that she was trying to move her head, and I didn't know what to do, how to help her. I turned around for the phone I knew was standing in its base on the low bookshelf nearby, and I scrambled up to get it, but then I stopped. I might survive the humiliation of being outed as a fraud, barely, but I would not survive this, if she lived.

So I went back to her. She was still moaning—it was more like a guttural bubbling sound now. She'd probably die shortly, but I put one hand on her mouth anyway, the other on her nose as I crouched beside her, and I waited, sobbing, begging for her forgiveness, her eyes wide, staring at me, until I saw the light go out of them and I was sure that she was really, really dead.

When I stood up, I saw that the tip of my shoe had left a small imprint in the pool of her blood. I took my shoes off and was about to run out the door, but decided to do one last thing first. I stepped over her body and ran to the very top of the stairs, where that bit of carpet had never been glued down properly, and clutching my shoes under my arm, I pulled hard at it, really hard, so that it was gaping up slightly, dislodged from where the brass bars held it down on either side of the step.

I gave the room downstairs one last check; the blood had pooled where my toe had previously left its mark. I ran the hell out of there, barefoot, not even stopping to put my shoes back on until I'd reached the basement parking garage exit.

22

"You never said it was a complete manuscript," Frankie says to me when I walk out of the studio. *It's over*, I keep telling myself. *I did the show. I survived it. I survived it because Beatrice wasn't there to ruin my life.*

After a few false starts, *Books and Letters* went extremely well and now we're having coffee, as usual. It's what we do after any event or interview: we "deconstruct" what has taken place, as Frankie calls it. I don't know why, considering how much effort we put into constructing it in the first place. "You did say you'd started a few times but never finished, and even threw it out."

"Which is what I meant. I know it didn't come out like that, but it's what I meant to say. There is no 'other' manuscript."

God, I feel better. No. I feel great! This is the first time in I don't know how long that the threat of Beatrice isn't engulfing me in a total panic. That weight has truly lifted from me. I feel so light I could grow wings.

There's nothing quite as confidence-boosting as killing someone, I now realize. Especially someone who plans to ruin your life.

"Of course," Frankie says, pulling me out of my reverie, "but just so we're clear, that manuscript that isn't there? I'm the first to not see it, okay? Will you promise me that?"

"I promise you solemnly," I say, nodding.

"Good. Because we need something to follow this with, you know? And I'm being serious here, Emma. Your fans—"

I snort so hard, I spray coffee all over the table.

"Don't kid yourself. That's the business you're in now. You have fans, and they need something from you. That's the transaction you've entered into."

Again, I nod solemnly.

"So? Are you working on something?"

"Don't, Frankie, please."

"I'll cut you some slack, Emma, for now, because I know there's a lot going on here for you, and you're doing a terrific job, you really are." He takes my hand above the table. He makes me feel loved.

"Thank you, Frankie, for understanding. Give me a little time and then we'll talk about that again."

"Fine."

"And what about you? You're okay now?" I'm changing the subject. "Things are more . . . secure for you? Financially, I mean?"

"They sure are, and thank you for asking." He takes my hand and raises it to his lips, kisses it, and puts it back down. "Thanks to you." He smiles. I love him. I really do.

"I'm glad, Frankie. You deserve it."

"We both do! And I have a couple of prospects I'm about to sign up." He grins, clearly pleased with himself.

"Do you! Now, that's interesting! Anyone who's going to take the wind out from beneath my wings?"

"Certainly not. I wouldn't allow it." We both laugh.

"Does this mean you'll be able to afford a publicist now? You won't have to accompany me everywhere and hold my hand?" I ask.

"I'll always come with you to these sorts of things Emma. I don't care how successful we become."

"Good. Just checking." I smile.

I'm about to suggest we have another cup of coffee—Frankie is like me in that regard: we drink coffee like it's water—when my phone vibrates on the table.

"Take it." He stands. "I'll be right back," he says, and moves toward the restroom at the far end of the café.

I glance at the screen but it's not a number I recognize.

"Hello?"

"Emma? It's Hannah. Hannah Beal."

"Hannah! How *are* you?" I exclaim, as if she's a dear friend I've been longing to hear from. I don't know why, since I don't particularly want to speak to Hannah.

"Oh, you know," she sighs, and I remind myself that we have both lost someone very dear to us, and I need to tone it down a notch. So I sigh also.

"I do, I do. Lord, I do. So, how are you holding up, Hannah?"

"Same as you, probably." She laughs bitterly. "But let's not go there."

No. Let's not.

"How did the taping go today?"

She means *Books and Letters* of course.

"Oh, you know, it was sad. I couldn't stop thinking that Beatrice should be there with me, by my side. I didn't want to do it, you know, but Jim convinced me I should. You know what husbands are like," I chuckle.

"Not really, no, but I'm sure he meant well. That's—" She pauses a moment. "That's actually what I wanted to talk to you about. Can you explain what that was all about? The two of you going on the show? Beatrice never told me. It sounded big, but I can't for the life of me guess. It's been bothering me a lot," she says.

"Oh please! Don't I know it! It's been bothering me hugely too! I've been racking my brain, but I've come up blank. I was going to call you to ask the exact same thing. So she never said anything to you either?"

"Oh." I can hear how disappointed she is. I bet she's been stopping herself from making this call until it was appropriate. Like after the *Books and Letters* interview. "No," she says. "It was very odd though. It's a strange thing to suggest, an interview like this, without discussing why."

"I'm with you. To be honest, it worried me a little, but she promised she'd tell me the morning of the show. Well, she would have had to, if we were to be joint guests. I suspected she had the idea that we write a book together."

"Really?" She makes the word draw out—*reeaaaalllyy?*—then pauses again, pondering what I've said, probably. "That doesn't sound like her at all," she says finally.

"I guess we'll never know now." I wish she'd go away. I'm tired of this conversation. "Hannah, I'm sorry, but I'm with Frankie now, so I should probably let you go," I say regretfully.

"Of course, I'm sorry."

"No, I'm the one who's sorry. I wish I could help, but unfortunately, I'm as much in the dark as you are. If I ever think of something, I'll let you know, and you do the same, okay?"

"Before you go, there was another reason I called."

"Yes?"

"I've started going through her papers—God, it's awful to have to do this, it's so depressing. But it's important. She was a great writer and a great person—oh dear, sorry, I'm rambling now."

Yes, you are.

"No, that's okay, I understand." I wonder if she wants to give me something of Beatrice's. George hasn't mentioned anything about a will, although it's early days. Anyway, I doubt she'd have made any sort of bequest to me, considering.

"Well, as I was saying, I'm going through her papers." Hannah hesitates again. She's repeating herself; she's clearly emotional.

163

If she wants to give me something, maybe an original manuscript of one of Beatrice's books—and I'm sure she thinks that would be appropriate, considerate even—then I will accept it gratefully, with a voice trembling with emotion, moved by the prospect of owning something so personal and so quintessentially Beatrice. I can always use extra scrap paper to write my shopping lists on anyway. Recycling makes me feel virtuous.

"And I found something . . . odd. I wanted to ask you about it."

I stiffen and sit still, like a dog that's picked up a scent. "Ask away."

"It's an outline—not even that, it's very rough, a couple of scribbled pages really. I don't even know why it's in the office. She never submitted it to me properly, but she must have given it to me to read, to give her feedback, that sort of thing." I can hear from the repeated intakes of breath that she's about to cry, if she isn't already. "We used to do that you know, discuss her ideas, talk over her plots . . ." She sniffs.

A week ago I would have believed that, without question. But now that I know who Beatrice really was, the very idea that narcissistic, snobbish, patronizing Beatrice would consult Hannah about plot or narrative style makes me want to burst out in hoots of laughter. If there's a stage of denial after the death of a loved one, then Hannah is well and truly in the grip of it.

"Anyway, it's just that, I don't know how to say this—"

Oh, spit it out, Hannah.

"—but it's awfully close to *Long Grass Running.*"

23

I am petrified into silence. "I don't know why these notes are in your possession," I blurt out once I've recovered myself. Frankie has returned and is sitting down. "But I know what they are."

"You do?"

"Of course—she was helping me, remember? Lord, it feels like such a long time ago now." I let out a little sob for good measure. "I used to go to her house; we'd work together. I gave her my outline. Is it my handwriting?"

"Definitely hers, definitely."

"She took notes with me. She showed me how to put a story together, in bullet-point form. Can you imagine? What she did for me? Oh, I will never get over her passing away, Hannah. Just hearing about those notes takes me back."

"Oh. I see. It's just that . . ."

"Yes?"

"Well, they were in an old folder, with some other tidbits, scraps of paper of hers, part of an old file. I'm surprised to find them there if they're that recent."

"I don't know what to tell you, but that's exactly what they are. Notes from the teacher." I giggle at the memory. "You should hang on to them—they'll be valuable one day," I add.

"No no, they're yours. I'll return them to you."

What a good idea.

"I'm sorry to have brought all that up then. I can see it's upsetting."

"Yes, it is, of course. But that's all right, Hannah. I would like to have them, as a keepsake. If you could pop them in the mail for me, I'd be grateful."

"Of course. Well, I'll leave you to it then. It's good to talk to you, Emma."

"It's good to talk to you too, Hannah, let's do it again soon."

Not.

◆ ◆ ◆

I don't think too much about my conversation with Hannah after that. It's only been a few days and I figure she'll send me the papers as we discussed, and that will be that. So I'm feeling pretty relaxed about everything—thinking about what to wear at the Poulton ceremony; looking at real estate online, because it's high time we moved—when my phone buzzes a familiar chime. It's a text from Frankie:

Turn on the news, now!

I reach for the remote and turn on the TV in the kitchen.

"—in relation to the death of the celebrated writer Beatrice Johnson Greene. We spoke with Deputy Superintendent Price earlier this morning. Deputy Superintendent, can you tell us why George Greene is being interrogated by the police as we speak?"

Sweet Jesus! George? I reach for the remote again and turn up the volume. My scalp prickles and feels cold.

"To be very clear, Mr. Greene is assisting us with our inquiries; nothing more at this stage."

"Do you have reason to suspect there's more to Mrs. Johnson Greene's death than originally thought? It's been widely reported as an accident. Has there been new evidence now to the contrary?"

"Look, I'm not going into any of the details right now. Mr. Greene is helping us with our inquiries and that's all I have to say. Thank you."

"Thank you, Deputy Superintendent Price."

They cut from the interview to the anchor. "We have more from Juanita Sanchez. Juanita, you have some details for us, is that right?"

"Yes, John, it seems that a neighbor who lived in the apartment below Beatrice Johnson Greene's was about to leave on a trip overseas, and this person heard someone enter the apartment above. We understand this person was getting luggage out of their apartment at the time and heard distinctly— and I quote here: 'distinctly'—someone open the door and go in. Now, up until now it has been understood that Mrs. Johnson Greene was alone in the apartment when she fell, so this puts that theory in jeopardy."

No no no no no—there was no neighbor. I was very careful, no one could have heard me. She's lying. *She's lying!*

"So this person who went inside Mrs. Johnson Greene's apartment had a key, is that what you're saying, Juanita?"

"Yes, John, that's what seems to be the case. Someone allegedly let themselves inside Mrs. Johnson Greene's apartment with a key. The neighbor in question didn't think much of it. They left their own apartment and met Mrs. Johnson Greene downstairs, as she was waiting for the elevator to go upstairs."

"Do we know who that person is? Who entered Mrs. Johnson Greene's apartment prior to her arrival?"

"No, John, that's the mystery. George Greene has always maintained he found his wife dead when he returned from work that evening, but it seems the story is more complicated now."

"Did the neighbor identify George Greene as being the person who entered the apartment?"

"I don't believe so, John, not at this stage. There has not been any definite identification of that person, but we believe that they had a key, from what we've been told. George Greene is at the station right now, speaking to the police. But that's all we know for now."

"Thank you, Juanita. We will keep you updated on this developing story."

I turn off the television and throw the remote against the wall. I sit on the couch and slam the coffee table with both palms. Then I do it again, louder, then again, harder still. I put my hands on my face and stifle a scream in them, gritting my teeth and tightening my whole body in frustration and fear.

I screwed up. Did I screw up? No, they're lying, they can't have heard me come in. I was so careful. They're just trying to get attention for themselves. That's what people are like, they want to insert themselves into the story, there's no way the neighbor heard me. I was so careful. I was so careful. What am I going to do?

Okay, wait, they think it's George. No one knows I had a key. Does George know Beatrice gave me a key? I don't think so. They didn't speak of little things like that. I don't think he knows, and if he does, who cares. Why would anyone think I went to her apartment and killed her? They think it's George. Let them think that. They've got him in custody. That's what "helping us with our inquiries" means, doesn't it? It means an arrest is imminent. They've probably arrested him already, he's at the station—

He's at the police station.

I need to get into that apartment again and find that stupid stupid stupid cocktail napkin.

I want to rush out the door, but how can I do that when I have to run around for my stuff and I'm shaking so much I can't keep things together? I finally get my bag. Beatrice's key is safely tucked into the zipped pocket, where it's always been. I grab my own keys, my phone, my coat, and now I'm finally out the door.

I drive like a crazy person through midday traffic; I almost run over a woman and her stroller. I park the car one block away, and I run; I trip on the curb and graze my knee; the contents of my bag tumble into the gutter; I pick them up quickly, wave off the people who try to help me; I hope I have everything; I shove everything back in my bag; my knee hurts. I hobble over to the building where George lives, where Beatrice used to live.

I'm at the street door when it opens. A man gives me a surprised look but he doesn't stop me from coming in. The doorman is talking animatedly to someone; there are a few people in the lobby and he doesn't notice me as I take the elevator to the apartment. The elevator door opens, and I stand on the landing. I'm holding the door key and just as I reach to open it, something stops me. There are sounds inside. I quickly put the key back into my bag just before the door opens and a woman stands before me, and I gasp audibly.

She does not, however, and if she's surprised to see someone standing there in front of the door, she doesn't show it.

She looks me up and down, and I do the same to her. She's wearing what I'd describe as office attire: white shirt buttoned up to the collar, dark blue jacket and pants. It looks cheap.

"Mrs. Fern?"

"How do you know who I am?"

"What are you doing here, Mrs. Fern?"

"I've come to see George. He's a friend of mine. Is that all right with you?" I have recovered my composure and I'm petulant now. I crane my neck sideways and step forward to show I intend to come in, but she doesn't budge. I can see the edges of people milling about in the living room. "What's going on?"

"He's not here right now."

"What are you doing in his apartment then?" I sound almost shrill now. I know exactly who these people are, of course, they're the police, here to poke around the place.

"Mrs. Fern—"

"How do you know my name?"

"I'm Detective Massoud. We're speaking to a number of friends and acquaintances of Mrs. Johnson Greene. We need to speak to you also, and since you're here—"

Again I make a move to walk inside. I can't bear that the police are searching the place, because that's what they're doing, I know that already, and I need to watch them. They can't find that fucking napkin before I do.

"Should I go inside then?"

"No, ma'am, there are detectives working in the apartment." She turns around and looks behind her, pulls the door almost shut so that we're both standing on the landing now. "We will come to your home shortly to ask you a few questions, Mrs. Fern. Why don't you wait for us there?"

"Questions about what? What do I have to do with this?"

"It's just a few questions, Mrs. Fern. My colleague and I will be over in about an hour. Does that work for you?"

"I don't understand what's happening!"

There's a quick spark of frustration in her eyes, but it's gone in a flash. She's a professional.

I need to calm down. My fists are closed and in my coat pockets. I'm trying to keep myself from trembling. I want to go inside now, but I accept that I can't.

"All right. I'll be home. You know where to go?"

"Yes, we do, Mrs. Fern. We will see you in an hour."

I turn back to the elevator and press the button.

"Mrs. Fern?"

She's inside the apartment now, holding the door ajar.

"Yes?"

"How did you get into the building?"

"What?"

"The doorman didn't buzz you up. How did you get in?"

"Someone was coming out as I came in. The doorman didn't see me."

She gives a little nod. "All right. We'll be over shortly, Mrs. Fern." She shuts the door.

I could have told her: *The doorman always lets me come up. Beatrice was my friend—she adored me, and if you did your homework you would know that. I was welcome in her home any time of the day or night.*

24

"So? How can I help you?"

We're standing in my living room, the three of us. Detective Massoud has brought along a colleague, whom she introduced as Detective Carr. A big man, fair and freckled, as badly dressed as she.

"Mind if we sit down?"

"Sure." I indicate the low couch for them while I sit on the very edge of the armchair, prim as a schoolteacher. "Would you like some coffee?" I ask suddenly. I feel off-kilter, here in my living room. I need a few more minutes to collect myself.

"That's okay, Mrs. Fern, this won't take long."

I sigh inwardly. I push myself back into the chair to show I'm willing to get on with this, whatever this is. Detective Carr retrieves a notebook from his pocket and pulls a pen from its pages. I hear it click. A signal between them that he's ready to commence, I suspect.

"Did you know Beatrice Johnson Greene?" Detective Massoud asks.

"Of course I did! She was my friend, you know that already!" She gives me a surprised look. I guess she didn't expect me to be defensive. I try to quiet the dread that's rising inside me. I remind myself that everything I do or say is going to be noted in that little book. I need to act as normal as possible.

"So you knew her well?"

"Yes, extremely well. We've been close friends for, let me see, a year maybe. We always spent a lot of time together. What is this about?"

"We're looking into the circumstances of her death."

"Why? It was an accident!"

"There have been some new developments recently that have prompted us to take another look."

"Oh, I heard that—the neighbor, right? Surely you don't listen to every conspiracy theory spun by bored, nosy neighbors?"

She looks at me askance again. I don't know how I am supposed to behave, but clearly this is not what she expects.

"We listen to everyone who has valid concerns, Mrs. Fern—that's our job. Did you go to Mrs. Johnson Greene's apartment on the day she died?"

This comes very suddenly, no doubt to put me off balance, but I don't hesitate, not for a second. "No! Of course not!"

I have prepared myself for this question ever since that day. Not because I thought the police would come and ask, but as a precaution. Specifically, I wanted to be ready if the question ever came.

I kept my eyes peeled that day, looking for the merest indication that someone was watching. I didn't care if someone thought they saw a woman with a warm coat and her hood up buzz the apartment from the garage, but when I punched the code on the panel to the right of that door, the security code that would let me into the building, I really made sure that no one was watching me. I walked up the stairs instead of taking the elevator. I did not pass anyone on the stairs. The landing on the third floor—Beatrice's floor—has two doors, one facing the stairs and one to the right of the landing, both of which lead to her apartment. Of course, I was in shock when I left, but because of that I was even more careful. I did not see anyone and no one saw me. I am completely sure of that. They may have seen a woman in a parka coming out of the building, but no one would have known it was me.

"How can you be sure?" She lifts an eyebrow, as if she's genuinely curious. "It's been a few weeks now. Do you know what you did every day since then?"

The gall of that woman. If I said I didn't remember, she'd no doubt ask me how I could forget what I did the day my close friend died tragically.

"I know what I did that day because I got the news that evening that Beatrice had died. It was not a day like any other."

"How did you find out?"

"Mark Boswell called me. He's the family lawyer."

"Not Mr. Greene then?"

"He was too distressed. He found her, you know."

She nodded. "So you definitely did not visit Mrs. Johnson Greene on the day she died?"

I wish I knew if the neighbor was able to describe me or say if it was a man or a woman.

"Beatrice was supposed to be away for a few days. I didn't think she was home anyway. I couldn't have visited her if I'd wanted."

"Except she didn't go away."

I sigh. "But I didn't know that at the time."

Did I leave something behind? No, I know I didn't, and anyway, even if I had, so what, I spent a lot of time there. If they're taking fingerprints, then mine are everywhere. In her study, in the bathrooms, in the kitchen—I even slept in her bedroom, for God's sake.

"Are you saying it may not have been an accident?" I ask.

"We're saying nothing of the sort, ma'am. Just tying up a couple loose ends, that's all."

"But she's been buried! Surely it's too late for that!"

Something in her eyes snaps and she looks straight into mine. "Why would you say that?"

God, these people are wired to see the worst in everyone.

"You wouldn't exhume . . . Beatrice"—I have to say her name; I was going to say *the body* but that would be callous—"surely? That would be too awful for words! It would be horrendous for George and for every one of her friends!"

"For an autopsy, you mean? There's already been an autopsy, ma'am. No, we won't do that, unless we have a very good reason."

That's something then. There isn't a good reason to look too deep, pardon the pun.

"Why did you come to see Mr. Greene today? Didn't you think he'd be at work?"

"I heard the terrible news, on the TV. I went to see him right away, to see if he was all right, if there was anything I could do to help."

"What did you want to speak to him about?"

"I told you! He was being questioned! Harassed probably! He's a friend of mine—I wanted to help."

Detective Massoud looks at her colleague. "If you knew he was at the police station being questioned, why would you come to his apartment?"

"Oh, for Christ's sake! I didn't know he was still at the police station!"

"Did you call him to find out?"

"I didn't think, Detective Massoud. I just left to go to him. Is that all right with you?" She ignores my tone of outrage. "Is he still there? Are you arresting him? Can I go and see him? Is he home now?"

"Not right now, Mrs. Fern."

"When will he be home?"

"We're still searching the apartment. I can't tell you how long that will take."

Oh God. They're going to find it, I know it. If they do, I don't think they'll think anything of it—they won't know what it is—but what if they show it to George?

"One more question, Mrs. Fern. Did you speak to Mr. Greene on that day? Around the middle of the day?"

"No, I did not." Massoud gives Detective Carr a nod. He clicks his pen and closes the notebook. They both stand up.

And then it comes to me, and I take a gamble.

"But I saw him."

They snap their heads toward me, in unison.

"You saw him on that day? Where?" They both sit down again and Carr opens the notebook.

"I went downtown for some shopping, near the building where he works. I was on the other side of the street, and he was standing outside, with what looked like a lunch bag, a sandwich, and coffee in a paper cup. I called out to him but he didn't hear me and he went inside."

"What time was that?"

"Oh, about twelve thirty, I'd say." The exact time that Beatrice died.

"Are you absolutely sure?"

"Yes, I am. I was about to take the subway to my hair appointment at one o'clock."

"We'll need to take a formal statement, Mrs. Fern. When can you come into the station?"

"What about right now?"

They stand up again. "That's fine." She hands me a card with the address. "Join us whenever you're ready."

We're at the door now. I open it, and watch them leave and get into their car. I close the front door and let out a deep, long breath that I have been holding for what felt like the entire time.

Shit.

That spike of fear that has been lurking in the bottom of my stomach, ever ready to poke my heart, has gone. They've been driving me crazy, these loose ends. I couldn't care less about the police. They could come and interrogate me all day if they like, handcuff me to the wall, beat me senseless with thick telephone books, and I would not care. I know nothing, I have nothing to reproach myself for, I have nothing to fear.

I don't know where the cocktail napkin is, but I know it's in Beatrice's apartment, and I need to go there and find it before anyone else does. And to do that, I need to get the police out of the place. I need to get George back in there.

The statement takes no more than twenty minutes. I know exactly what I need to say and I say it in a square, bland, pale room, with both detectives sitting on one side of the cheap table and me on the other side.

Massoud wants to know what George was wearing.

"A dark suit of some kind. I'm not sure what color, so don't bother asking," I reply petulantly.

"You said he was carrying"—she flips through her notes—"a lunch bag? How could you tell that's what it was, from the other side of the street?"

"I guess I assumed it was lunch. It was a brown paper bag, and he had a cup of coffee, one of those paper cups of coffee."

"Could you tell what brand? Starbucks? McDonald's? Dunkin' Donuts?"

What had Beatrice said again? He always gets the same thing, a sandwich, a bagel I think, and coffee from . . . was it Starbucks?

"How could I possibly tell that? I was standing on the other side of the street," I say, and smirk at her.

She puts down her pen and looks at me. "Is there a problem, Mrs. Fern?"

"You mean apart from being dragged into the police station like a common criminal?"

"I'd have thought you of all people would want to assist us in determining exactly what happened to Mrs. Johnson Greene."

"We know what happened, Detective—she fell and she died!" I'm shaking, almost shouting now. "It was a terrible tragedy and we're all trying to come to terms with it! What good does it do to sully her husband's name like this? To drag us all here like we're—like we're common criminals! Is it because of who we are? Because Beatrice was rich and famous? Because her husband is rich? Does it ensure your name gets in the papers, Detective Massoud?"

She's glaring at me. If her eyes could shoot bullets, I would be Swiss cheese by now. She picks up her pen again, and her tone is almost distracted when she asks, "Mrs. Fern, do you have a key to the apartment?"

Here it is. The question I have been dreading ever since I heard the news this morning. But I'm prepared. I match her tone of near boredom.

"I used to. Beatrice gave me a key once, a long time ago, but I gave it back to her."

"Why did she give you a key?"

"I was going through a rough patch in my personal life. I came to stay with her, just once, overnight. She gave me a key then, in case I wanted to come back. We were friends, we were very close, we did things like that for each other."

"Did she ask for it back?"

"No, but I didn't need it anymore. I was at her house, we were doing some work together, and I saw the key in my bag and gave it back to her. She wanted me to keep it, but I had no need for it."

I never used to lie. I don't think I told a single deliberate lie in my entire life until I met Beatrice. I'm impressed with myself at how good I have become at it. A grain of truth, self-control in my body language, and a clear gaze at the questioner. It's actually not that hard if you put your mind to it. Having everything to lose also helps.

"What did you buy on that day, when you went shopping downtown and saw Mr. Greene?"

"Nothing in the end. I was looking for an outfit for an upcoming television interview. I browsed, then I realized the time and I needed to get to my hair appointment, so I didn't buy anything."

Massoud wraps it up. They don't seem to be bothered that I had a key.

"Did anyone see you?"

"Lots of people saw me. Whether they registered it is another question."

She tears a piece of paper from her notebook and slides it across the table, with a pencil. "Could you list the stores you went to on that day, please? And we would like the phone number of the hair salon too."

I find the business card for the hair salon and I list two stores that I frequent regularly downtown. I'm hoping they won't be able to pin the exact date but they will be able to say I was there around that time.

25

You'd never guess the police had been here, unless you lived here, I guess. Then you might notice that a pile of letters had been moved to the other side of that vase, or that books had been replaced in the wrong order on the shelves. But unless, like me, you knew the details of the house, you would not see any signs that a search had taken place here.

I rushed over as soon as I left the station. We're in the living room, and I stare at the spot at the bottom of the stairs, where so much blood pooled, where I cradled her head at first, and then I—never mind, let's not go there.

It's hard to believe, but there's no sign of what happened here. Only the narrow carpet on the stairs has been removed, leaving behind a very faint line on either side of it, a slight change in the coloring of the pale stone. I never thought that carpet looked good there anyway. The color was all wrong.

There's a tall, wide shelving unit on one wall of this room, that has a mixture of shelves and small cabinets with doors. While I've been staring and taking a trip down memory lane, George has opened one of the cabinets and is busy tapping numbers on a keypad.

I stand very still. "I didn't know you had a safe."

"Why should you?" The door releases with a soft click.

"We're thinking of getting one ourselves. This one looks good." I move closer to him so I can peer inside. George reaches inside his jacket pocket and retrieves an envelope. He doesn't seem bothered by my presence next to him, or that I'm staring at his most precious belongings.

It's a small safe with only one shelf. I can make out a couple of large, thick envelopes and a black, velvety box on the bottom—jewelry, I guess.

"I think they're pretty much all the same, to be honest. I'm not sure there's anything special about this one." He says this with a tired voice, like he couldn't care less about safes right now. He deposits the envelope on the shelf and pushes the door closed, then locks the outer cabinet door and turns to me. For a split second he seems surprised to see me there, then he shakes his head and runs his hands through his thick, greying hair. "What a nightmare, Emma. What a horrible nightmare!"

I move to comfort him but he raises a palm and shakes his head. "I'm all right."

"It's that stupid neighbor," I say, "inserting herself or himself into your story. Why would they come up with that now, anyway? She's been dead for weeks, for God's sake."

George snaps his head up to look at me. I raise a finger to wipe an imaginary tear from the corner of my eye.

"Can't they leave her in peace? Hasn't she suffered enough? Haven't we all suffered enough?" I wail.

"They've only just returned from overseas apparently."

"What, they don't have newspapers or the Internet wherever they were?"

"He'd heard but didn't realize the significance of the date until he got back."

So the neighbor was a man.

"Do you believe it?" I ask.

"Believe what?"

"That someone was here, when Beatrice—passed away."

"The police didn't tell you then? Maxine, the young woman who does the cleaning for us. She was here that morning. She left not very long before Beatrice got back. She confirmed the exact times and where she went after that: her next client, I gather." He sighs. "So, it seems that what our neighbor heard was Maxine leaving."

Oh. My. Lord. It never occurred to me someone else might have come in, with a key to boot. I remember the young woman who held the door for me downstairs. The thought crosses my mind that she might have come in later, when we were . . . when I was . . . I banish that thought instantly.

"But I thought, I told them—"

"I know. There was no need to lie for me, Emma."

"It wasn't a lie. I did see you."

"I didn't get my sandwich and coffee that day." He looks at me sideways. "I never do—my assistant does that for me."

But his tone is nonchalant, like he doesn't really care. There's no point in insisting.

"Did you tell the police?"

"That you lied for me? No."

"I meant well, George."

"I know you did, and I'm touched, I really am." He gives me a small, grateful smile and gestures toward the kitchen. "Do you want some coffee? I could do with some."

"I'll make it," I offer.

"No, let me, I need to busy myself with mundane things like this." His smile is sadder now.

"George?"

He turns back to me. "Yes?"

"Do you mind if—would it be all right with you . . ."

"What is it?"

"If I went upstairs? To her office? I just—the last time I was there with her, we had such—"

"I understand. Of course, that's fine."

"Thank you, George."

He leaves the living room and I make my way up the stairs, looking straight ahead.

I know it's likely the cocktail napkin is in the safe, maybe inside one of those thick envelopes. But I still have hope that she left it somewhere in her room or her office. I'm here now, anyway; I have nothing to lose by looking. I don't know what I'll do if it's in the safe. I didn't catch the numbers George typed in.

I experience a strong sensation of déjà vu as I quietly open drawers and rifle through notepads in her office, scan the shelves and open folders, and again, as before, it's not here. Or if it is, I can't find it. I take the opportunity however to deposit the key Beatrice gave me, which I have stashed in my pocket, into the small porcelain dish on the desk, among the paper clips and rubber bands.

I walk into the bedroom and the first thing I notice is that it doesn't smell like her anymore. Her scent has gone, and it's as if she really has left this house behind. Amazing. *Even the sulking room doesn't miss you, Beatrice.*

George has left everything just the way it was on the night table on her side of the bed. Beatrice is looking out from a picture frame—who keeps a picture of themselves on their night stand? I run a finger softly over the glass. A little of bit of dust sticks to the tip. I'm thinking of spitting on her picture.

"That's what she was reading before she died." I turn around and stare at George. We're in almost precisely the same position Beatrice and I were in on that fateful day, in this room. He's leaning against the doorjamb, his arms crossed against his chest. Just like she was. I'm standing; that's the only difference.

He comes over to where I am and we both stare at the pile of books he thought I was looking at.

"*The Red Sweater* by G. K. Austerin," he muses. The book is among the other bits: a magazine; the messy little things that she kept within easy reach—a used package of headache pills, a small notepad, some crumpled tissues.

I touch the book.

"It's one of her favorites," he says. "She was reading it again. You'd like it, I think. Here." He picks it up and hands it to me. "Have it. It really was one of her favorites."

"Oh, George, no. I couldn't."

"Please. I'd like you to, and she would have liked you to have it, I'm sure of it."

I take it from him. *Whatever*, I think as I caress the cover in a gesture I hope displays something like nostalgia. I pat a finger under each eye. "Mascara," I quip. "Whoever invented it never shed a tear in their life."

He gently puts a hand on my shoulder. "Come downstairs, let's have some coffee."

26

After putting in hours of commiseration, endless gentle reminiscences of *dear Beatrice*, and even shedding a couple of shared tears, it's with great relief that I leave George behind in that gloomy apartment. God, it's so depressing being around him, his pained silences, his vacant stares and trembling chin. I found myself doing the same just to pass the time until I could get out of there in good conscience.

"Thank you, Emma, for being here. For everything. It means the world to me," he said when I finally judged that I'd fulfilled my role as the best friend and announced that I *really* should go home.

Jim's already here. Not only that but he has returned with containers of takeout food from the local Vietnamese restaurant; something we haven't done in years. "I know how hard this is for you, sweetheart," he says. "Let me look after you, for a change." He calls getting takeout "looking after me." God bless him. Not.

He has to work anyway, he says, and he locks himself in his study as usual, leaving me to clean up after dinner. I'll give that to him, he works hard. Maybe if I had worked a bit harder myself, I'd have my own book. Beatrice would have helped me, I know she would have, and I wouldn't be here, tense, anxious, paranoid, thinking about the police. Thank God that George didn't contradict me. I could always say it was another businessman with a dark suit. They all look like clones in that part of town.

I go to bed alone, but my thoughts are swirling around, stopping me from sleeping. I wish Jim would come to bed. I get up slowly, pull my bathrobe from the back of the door, and walk softly downstairs to make myself a cup of herb tea.

Poor Jim, still hard at work. I can see the light seeping from beneath the closed door of his office. I'm about to knock on the door to ask him if he too needs a cup of tea when I hear something inside.

I open the door, but there's something odd about his posture. He's almost huddled on his chair, at his desk, with the phone in the crook of his arm.

"Yes yes yes! Of course it's going to happen . . ." He's whispering, but it's more like a hiss. "Don't do that again. Please, I know you—"

I rap my knuckles on the door to signal I'm here, and he jumps up with a start.

"I have to go," he says into the phone, but in a normal voice this time, and ends the call.

"Is everything all right?" I ask.

"Yes, no, sort of. Just some work stuff I need to sort out."

"Who was that on the phone?"

"That was Terry. He's been on my back about something."

"It's a bit late, isn't it?"

"I thought you were asleep." He's shuffling papers on his desk now, pretending to tidy up.

"Not anymore. I'm getting a cup of tea. Do you want one?"

"No, I'm fine. Still work to do."

"Okay, I'll leave you to it then." I doubt very much that was Terry on the line, and I don't understand why he's lying to me, but my instinct tells me not to push it. I don't know what to make of this, but at least it's taken my mind off things.

As I make my tea, I spot the book that George gave me on the kitchen table. I take it with me when I go back upstairs with my tea—let's see what "Beatrice's favorite book" is about—but there's something odd. It's a slim volume, but its thickness feels uneven. I put my tea on the table by the bed, sit down, and open it. Something falls to the floor and I recognize its texture immediately. It's a couple of tissues, or a paper towel maybe, folded in half but not neatly, slightly crooked.

I pick it up quickly and open it flat, stare at it, and then I close my eyes and put my hand on my chest to try to still my beating heart. I look again, throw my head back, and let out a deep groan of relief. This isn't just any old Kleenex used as a bookmark. It's *the* cocktail napkin.

27

Isn't it amazing how everything can change in a flash? It's incredible how things turn out. I wake up late, having slept like a baby, although as Jackie likes to point out, people who say they slept like a baby obviously have never had one. Before going back to bed last night, I took that stupid cocktail napkin and tore it up into as many little pieces as I could manage, and flushed it all down the toilet. Today—*Hello world!*—I'm a celebrated author, contender for the Poulton, if you please, and I have just one teeny little loose end to tie up.

The Hannah situation.

I haven't wanted to think of Hannah, considering everything that's been going on, especially with the police. The thought of our last conversation makes me shudder. For a horrible moment, it felt like the walls were closing in on me, when she said that she had in her hands an outline of *Long Grass Running*, stuck among Beatrice's papers. But I hadn't come this far to be taken in by the likes of Hannah.

I'm sure she bought it, my little explanation. I could see why it was still confusing to her, but she had no other explanation for it anyway, and mine was perfectly reasonable. A good fit even, considering the facts of our friendship.

I figure once I receive the outline, I'll be sure to get rid of it immediately. Or maybe I'll rewrite it in my own handwriting first, see if I can match the paper even. If this ever comes up again, I'll have it at hand, but this time it will be undeniably mine.

Except that I have not received it yet and it's been long enough, in spite of Hannah's assurances that she'd return it to me immediately. That's the problem with trusting people to do the right thing—they rarely ever do. The moment they make the promise, it's as if the deed itself is done and no further work is required.

I give her a call at the office. She's not there and I don't leave a message. But then the phone rings right back—not my cell, but the home telephone, which is highly unusual in our house. I'm not sure I ever gave out the number to anyone. Anyway, it must be Hannah, calling me back, somehow.

I pick it up.

"Hello?" But it's silence at the other end. Not silence as in the connection was never established, but silence like someone's there, but won't speak.

"Hello?" I say again, then I hang up. People are so rude. Wrong number, I guess, sure, but still, wouldn't kill them to say so, would it?

I go back to the couch and proceed to mentally plan my morning's activities. I have a book reading later this afternoon—I love saying things like that—so maybe first I'll catch up on emails and then, let me see, do I have time for a manicure? Probably not, but I could—

The phone rings again.

"Yes?"

This time I get a reply: a woman's voice asks for Jim. Nothing else, just, "Is Jim there?" No *please*, no *hello*, no *excuse me for bothering you*.

"No, he's not, who is this?" *I'm not his secretary, and you're calling my home. Show me some manners.*

"Where is he?" she asks.

"I'm sorry, who is this?" Did I say *I'm sorry*?

I can hear her sigh, this rude person, as if this were rather inconvenient.

"Hello? Are you still there?"

"Where can I reach him?" she asks.

"At his office, where you should have called to begin with. This is his home. Who is this?"

"He's not at work, I tried there already, three times. Tell him Allison called." Then she adds a belated, perfunctory "Thank you."

"What's this about?" I ask, but she's gone.

Allison. The little bitch hanging out outside our house with Jim. I was sure I caught sight of her that time, months ago, when I went to meet him at the bar. I told him afterward, asked him, "Was Allison waiting for you?" but he'd stiffened and said, "No, don't be silly, Emma." But now I think it was Allison, waiting for Jim, always waiting for Jim. So they were having an affair; I can feel it. What's she up to now? Are they still involved? This is who Jim was talking to last night, I'm sure of it. I knew it wasn't Terry—that was a stupid lie, unworthy of Jim, really.

God, I never picked him for the type, the bastard. The professor who screws his young ex-student. Please.

My stomach's churning. What's he up to? How can he do this to me? I do everything for him; I'd do anything for him. I can't lose him: that's simply not an option. I have worked so hard to make our marriage a success. We're in love, we're happy, we're perfect together. Two very successful people who love each other. We are the envy of everyone who knows us. But maybe he's not having an affair. When I think back to the phone call, his tone, he didn't sound enamored, he sounded hassled. Maybe he doesn't want to be with her—maybe she won't let go. Yes, that sounds more like it. Didn't Allison just say she'd called him three times at work and hadn't heard back from him? That makes me chuckle. If you think that's the way to get to my husband, you're sadly mistaken, little girl. Jim hates being harassed.

I call the office, ostensibly to pass on the message. Jenny, the receptionist, puts me through immediately. Good.

"Em, sweetheart."

"Hello, darling. How's your day going so far?"

"Excellent. Couldn't be better. Things are rocking around here, let me tell you."

I laugh. "That's great, Jim, good to hear."

"Everything okay?"

"Oh yes, but I got a strange call just now—well, you did. Allison called. She was rather insistent so I thought I'd tell you right away."

Silence.

"She said she called you three times at work but you weren't there."

"Oh, I was here all right. Jesus, what a—sorry, sweetheart, she shouldn't interrupt you at home like this. I'll take care of it. I'm sorry. The stupid woman."

I give a mental fist pump. *Yes!*

"What does she want?"

"She wants a job. She was a student. I told you all this already."

"Okay. As long as everything is all right."

"It is, really. One moment, sweetheart."

I hear muffled sounds. Someone's speaking; his hand must be cupped over the phone.

"I have to go, sweetheart. Terry says hello, and he's looking forward to tonight."

Oh God, I completely forgot.

"Say hello to Terry. And that I'm looking forward to seeing him also."

"Will do. I really have to go, Em."

"I know. I love you."

"I love you, sweetheart."

My heart sings.

◆ ◆ ◆

I'm having too good a day to let the likes of Allison ruin it for me. Whatever was going on between them, he's over it, that's clear. I banish her from my mind and get to work on the laptop. I check the Amazon ranking—twenty-seven, thank you very much—and read through emails. Frankie's planning all sorts of events for me, and it takes a while to go through it all.

I'm surprised at the time, which has just caught my eye from the corner of my screen. I need to get ready for that book signing. It's exhausting being me, really. I stretch my arms above my head. I need to get changed, freshen up. I'm about to shut the computer but something on the Amazon page, which is still up, catches my eye and I glance at this new review that has just appeared in the sidebar.

The room moves. It's as if the house is tilting on its axis but without taking me with it. I can't breathe properly; there's something pressing against my chest and the air won't go in. I try to make sense of the latest comment, but I'm having great difficulty focusing and the letters keep getting jumbled up.

One star – Great story, with a great twist! But…

I cannot begin to say how much I enjoyed this book. The story of its provenance, however, is a lot less, shall we say, uplifting, and the real mystery here is who wrote it. Now, I don't want to give anything away . . . Oh, never mind, SPOILER ALERT, it's not Emma Fern.

Published 4 minutes ago by Beatrice_777

My whole body trembles. I have to delete this review, now. It's my page. I should be able to delete this right now. I click around the screen without knowing what to do, but it doesn't go away, I can't delete it, I don't know how, my heart hurts, my chest hurts. I click the "Report Abuse" link next to the review because damn right this is *abuse*, and no, this review was not *helpful*, but it won't go away.

I click on the link for *Beatrice_777*. He or she has only just joined and written one single review. Of course.

A sharp pain in my thumb makes me realize I've bitten it so hard it's bleeding. I don't know what to do. I should call Frankie—he'll know what to do. No, of course I can't tell Frankie. My hand's shaking so much, I have trouble keeping my finger steady on the trackpad as I search for a contact listing for Amazon, but all I find are email addresses to register a complaint, and I fire off emails to every single one I can find.

I have to talk to somebody over there right now. I need to explain to them who I am, and that they must remove this review immediately. Finally, I locate a phone number and a robot answers telling me to press a number to choose my selection, but funnily enough, there's no "To discuss trolls, threatening reviews, and other general nut-job bully behavior, please press any key."

I get sent back to the main menu because I'm not making a selection quickly enough, and I go around in circles. I'm crying, as much from fear as from frustration, so I just press a random number, and I'm told a bunch of stuff about international shipping policies and still no one comes on the line, and I'm sent back to the beginning and I scream into the phone and slam it down hard.

I go back to the book page, hoping they've removed it already, that my reporting of the review has worked immediately, but it's still there. No, wait, it's another one, a different one, at the top of the "Most Recent Customer Reviews" list, above the first one.

One star – More to this one than meets the eye!

If you enjoy a good theft story, you won't want to miss *Long Grass Running*! Congratulations to Emma Fern for pulling it off!

Published 3 minutes ago by Beatrice_1234

Once again I frantically click on the "Report" button, and I check the page for *Beatrice_1234*, knowing full well what I will see, that he/she has only just signed up and written one single review. My head's swimming, and I wonder for a second if this is just a nightmare. It's hard to focus on anything. I send more emails. This is worse than abuse, this is slander, it's malicious and cruel. I could sue for this. I will sue for this. I write all this in the emails. They know, whoever they are, about Beatrice. But what do they know exactly? That she wrote the book? I can't bear to think what else they know.

I can't go out, I can't go to the book signing, I should be there now but I can't leave. I have to sort this out. I have to call Frankie and make an excuse I—

Breathe, I tell myself, *breathe, Emma. Figure this out. You have come this far. It's a troll, yes—isn't that what they're called?* The loonies who trawl through the Internet, looking for anyone who's achieving something, looking for success so that they can take it down, one nasty, cruel comment at a time.

I must not call attention to this. Don't give it any air. Do not tell anyone, just get Amazon to take these comments down, now. *There is no proof. Remember that, Emma. There is no proof anymore.*

Nothing happens. I just stare at the book page and slowly pull myself together. I will go to the book signing at Barnes & Noble. I have to be normal. There are a hundred or so people patiently waiting for me, and I'm already dreading how many of these so-called reviews I will find when I get home.

◆　◆　◆

Frankie, who's always watching over me, Lord love him, is a little surprised at my state of mind this afternoon. I give a terrible reading. My attention isn't on the task at hand and I read a chapter with as much enthusiasm as if it were a notice from the IRS.

But people are generous, and after the applause I move over to the table that has been set up for me with piles of *Long Grass Running*, ready for their dedication.

Frankie can tell something's wrong and is looking at me with his eyebrows knotted in genuine concern. I want to tell him that I'm ill—something I ate, I think. I have to go home. Please let me go home.

"What's the matter with you?" he asks, not unkindly.

"Nothing, really, I'm fine."

I take the book from the young woman at the front of the line.

"I so love your books, Emma. They're really wonderful!"

She can't love them that much, or she'd know there's only one.

"Who should I make it out to?" I ask her, as if it's a check I'm handing out.

"If you could make it to—"

My pen's poised on the flyleaf, ready and waiting.

"—Beatrice—"

I snap my head up.

"—please, or even to *Dear Beatrice*? If that's all right, that would be wonderful. It's not—"

"Is it you?"

"What?"

"Is. It. You."

I've stood up and knocked over the table. The piles of books have toppled over, and I am pointing at this woman with a trembling arm. "*What do you want from me?*" I'm shouting, shaking. It's awful, I can't help it. Frankie places himself between me and the woman, who now looks utterly terrified. Everyone in the store has stopped talking and is looking at me. "*Why are you doing this to me?*" I'm like a crazy woman, pushing Frankie out of the way, but he has taken hold of my shoulders with both hands and now he's putting an arm around me and dragging me away.

"What's going on? Emma, get a hold of yourself! What's the matter with you?"

I glance back at the woman, who's on the verge of tears, being consoled by a friend of hers, who's glaring at me. I don't think it's her now. I think that really was her name.

"Emma! Talk to me!"

I don't want to tell him, but he might find out anyway. Better that he hears my version. I take a deep breath.

"I think I'm being stalked." I burst into tears.

He takes me into the ladies' room, having first made sure that there's no one in there, and holds me tight, with compassion and tenderness. "What do you mean, stalked?"

"Just that," I manage to say between sobs. "Anonymous calls, weird emails, that sort of thing." I don't really want to send Frankie to the Amazon book page.

"Did you tell the police?"

"Not yet, do you think I should?"

"Yes, definitely. Right away." His features are set in concentration. He's trying to come up with something to fix it, I can tell. I look at him pleadingly. He smiles gently. "Well, you know what they say: you're not anybody till you've been stalked."

"Very funny," I reply, blowing my nose into the Kleenex he's given me.

"Listen to me, darling, it happens all the time. You're on the bestseller list. I'm sure it's nothing at all, just a fan. Forward the emails to me and I'll look into it, but I really wouldn't worry too much."

I don't say anything. How would he know anyway? No doubt police murder files are riddled with cases of *I wouldn't worry too much—it's probably nothing.*

He pulls out a pen from his shirt pocket, checks a number on his phone, and jots it down on the back of my hand.

"Make an appointment. Dr. Craven. He's the best. He'll take good care of you."

"I'm not sure a doctor can help me, Frankie."

"Emma, you look terrible. You're stressed. He'll give you something to manage the anxiety. Whatever's happening, you need to look after yourself."

"Maybe."

"Trust me."

He pops his head out the door.

"Coast is clear. I'll make excuses for you, I'll think of something."

He takes hold of my elbow and leads me out quickly. There are still many people lingering around, confused about what happens next. I don't see the woman I shouted at earlier.

The table has been put back upright, but the books are nowhere to be seen. I guess management decided there wouldn't be any more book signing today.

Frankie deftly leads me through the store, and in no time we're outside and he has hailed me a taxi.

"Go home and rest, darling. Publisher's orders. Call me tonight and let me know how you are."

"Thank you, Frankie. I'm really sorry."

"And call that doctor," he adds before shutting the door.

First thing I do in the taxi is check my Amazon page from my cell phone, and the two comments are still there. Then, once I'm home, I check again. There are no new ones. Thank God for small mercies. I feel ill. I email Amazon again; I'll spam them into action if I have to. I try the number, but I can't get through to anyone.

It's the middle of the afternoon, and I go upstairs to lie down because I don't know what else to do. I have crazy dreams of falling. I'm standing on top of a ridge, and I need to get to the other side. Everyone around me is doing it easily but I can't. To get to the other side, I have to step on the top of a very tall, very precarious ladder that's balanced on the bottom of the ravine. I don't understand how everyone else is making it look so easy when it's likely that I will lose my balance and drop to the bottom, so I stay behind on my side. Then I lean forward to look down into the ravine, and see Beatrice's broken body lying there in a pool of blood.

I'm sweating when I wake up, my hands on my face, groaning with relief that it was all an awful nightmare, and for a moment life is wonderful again, until I remember.

Oh God, what's going to happen to me?

The light has dimmed; it must be getting late. Jim will be home soon and I should be going downstairs and preparing dinner for our guests.

I'm so tired. I tell myself to get up and finally swing my legs out of the bed and sit for a while, feeling dizzy. The phone rings, and I jump up, hoping Amazon's about to tell me they've sorted this out, but it's the home telephone again. The number I never use, I never give out. The number I don't even remember. Allison? Who else?

I pick it up, ready to explode and tell the stupid girl to leave us alone, but there's silence when I say hello—no, not silence exactly, more like the distorted sound of someone breathing. Later, when I feel calm enough to think about this call, I will think that they were very close to the mouthpiece. Such a vintage word, *mouthpiece*; do we call them that still? I listen to the sound of someone determined to frighten me. I can only hear my own heart beating loudly, and just as I'm about to hang up, those awful words—"*I know what you did*"—hissed right in my ear, and I quickly put the phone down.

I scream, a lonely scream of frustration as much as fear. I'm going to faint. I don't understand why someone's trying to frighten me so. I couldn't tell whether the whisper was a man or woman, but I'm leaning toward female. Is someone out there seriously trying to convince me that Beatrice is back from the dead? Leaving reviews on Amazon? Or am I going completely crazy?

I put my head in my hands, my elbows on my knees, and tears well up, as much from the pain in my head as from the fear that has lodged itself in my stomach.

I need to make sense of this. There's a person behind these phone calls, and there's a person behind those reviews, and it's highly likely they're one and the same. I need to find out who that is, and why they're doing this to me.

And then I remember Jim's calls, the late-night, hushed calls that he lies to me about. Could they be related? Allison's the only person to have called on the home telephone recently; is this her? Could this be about a stupid affair, with a stupid ex-student, gone wrong? Is it remotely possible that Jim knows I didn't write the novel and told her? Maybe Beatrice told Jim at the time, but I can't quite see it. She couldn't stand him, and she was adamant we should keep this a secret to the grave. Ha! Only as long as it suited her, obviously.

Think, Emma, think. Can Allison and therefore Jim be somehow connected to all this?

I unplug the base of the phone from the wall outlet and make a mental note to do the same to the other unit downstairs, then I hear the front door open and the sound of Jim's keys being dropped in the bowl on the table in the hall. I hear all this just as I wonder whether Jim's trying to hurt me.

I grab my cell phone, call the number Frankie wrote for me, and leave a message.

28

After I've splashed water on my face, I remind myself yet again that the only thing that tied Beatrice and me together to this book was our contract, and that contract is gone. I took that cocktail napkin, shredded it, and flushed it down the toilet. I have these thoughts on a loop. My copy of the contract was destroyed a long time ago. So no matter what happens now, even if Beatrice told somebody, they couldn't prove it. Oh—facepalm—Beatrice is dead.

It's making me feel a little better, this train of thought.

"Anyone home?" Jim shouts from downstairs.

"Give me a minute, I'll be down in a sec," I reply.

I return to the bedroom, grab my cell from the bedside table, sit on my bed, and dial.

"Hello?"

"Hi, Hannah, it's Emma."

"Oh, Emma, hello. Nice to hear from you. How are you?"

"I'm well, thank you. A little run-down, but otherwise good."

"Aren't we all!" She laughs a little. "I have my calendar right here. Would you like to catch up sometime?"

"I was thinking this Thursday would be good for me. How about five?"

"Mmm, no. This Thursday I have a function I can't get out of, as much as I'd like to, but the next one's fine. Would that work?"

I can't wait that long. I really need that outline now. The one loose end.

"Ah, no. My husband's taking me away for a few days."

"Nice! For Thanksgiving?"

"No, not exactly, but he has a conference coming up, and we thought it would be good to spend some time together. He travels a lot, and now that I'm busier than ever, it becomes important, you know, to make time."

I made that up. I just want to get her moving.

"That sounds lovely. You're so lucky. So what do you think? Should we wait till you get back? I'm awfully tied up for the next couple weeks, unfortunately."

"Of course. Call me then if you like. Sounds like you're busier than I am."

She giggles. "I'm sure that's not possible."

"Oh, I almost forgot. I wanted to run something past you. I'm thinking of writing something about my friendship with Beatrice—I'd love to know what you think. I thought I could take all my notes from that time I spent working with her on my novel, along with the notes you have—I think it's the old outline I did—and we could put it all together. It would be very interesting to students, I think."

"It's brilliant, Emma. I think it's a terrific idea. Maybe there's even a book in it, have you thought of that? Part memoir, part the craft of putting a story together, from the point of view of both you and Beatrice?"

"Oh my Lord, Hannah! What a wonderful idea!"

"Great! We should talk about it sometime: you, me, and Frankie. Maybe the three of us should get together."

"You have just inspired me so much, Hannah, I don't know how to thank you. Would you pop the notes in the mail for me? If you haven't done it already? I want to get started immediately. This is a wonderful suggestion."

"Sure. I'll wait till the police are done first, then I'll mail them to you."

"The police?"

"Oh, you know, that drab detective, the woman."

"Massoud?"

"That's it. They're trawling through Beatrice's papers. I don't know why."

"I thought that was all sorted out. I talked to George. He said—"

"Is it? Oh, it's fine then, they haven't told me yet. I'll check with her. They wanted to see if there were any, you know, threats, anonymous threats she kept." I heard her take a little breath through her nose. "Just the thought, Emma. That something . . ." She lets it trail, that thought.

"No no, Hannah, really, it's fine, they made—the neighbor, they made a mistake. The police have sorted it out, George told me."

"Oh, thank God."

"Indeed. Anyway, those notes are not exactly a threat, right? What's the big deal?" I mean it to be a joke, but it comes out off-key.

"Are you okay?" she asks after a short pause.

"Sure I am, why?"

"I don't know. You sound a little stressed, maybe."

I sigh. "I need to slow down. I really am being run ragged these days. Frankie's driving me a bit too hard, to be honest."

"You need to talk to him then, really. *Long Grass Running* is doing really great, Emma. You can slow down a notch. You need to take care of yourself."

Her words are surprisingly genuine and my attitude toward her softens a little. "Yes, you're right. Thank you."

"Take a break, then let's work on this memoir. It will be a fitting tribute, I think."

"It most certainly will, and thank you so much for thinking of it. It's important to me to acknowledge Beatrice, both her talent and our friendship. Your idea is very thoughtful. Thank you, Hannah."

She giggles. "Oh, you're welcome. Us girls have to stick together, don't we? It's nice to talk to you, Emma. See you in a couple of weeks."

"Yes, and don't forget to send the papers, will you? I really can't wait to get started. If the police say it's okay, of course."

"Will do!"

◆ ◆ ◆

"Emma, darling! Hello!"

Our guests arrive at the appointed hour with a bunch of flowers and a bottle of wine. I'm already halfway through a bottle myself in a futile attempt to soothe my nerves, so I'm slightly unsteady when we greet them.

"I just need to put on the finishing touches and then I'll join you." I want to go back to the kitchen and leave Jim to take care of the guests. They're his guests anyway, and I've been cooking for two hours, being the good wife, the perfect wife, the Betty Crocker wife that I am—don't worry about me, I'm not busy, I don't have a career, I'm not incredibly intelligent or changing the world, so what if a troll or two wants to scare me half to death, there's dinner to be made and guests to be greeted, for fuck's sake.

"I'll just—" I make helpful gestures toward the kitchen.

"Come and warm up, you look like you're freezing!" Jim leads them to the living room, and I can hear the clink of glasses as he's preparing them an aperitif. I've already set up some canapés, to keep everyone happy. Good times.

I sip on my third glass of Riesling, half listening to their chatter. I never used to like Riesling, but Beatrice taught me a lot about wine. I sure know how to pick them now. I'm standing at the stove, stirring the gravy that has already been stirred to within an inch of its life, trying to figure out the puzzle of those reviews in my head. My cell phone is behind me on the table within easy reach, because I'm checking it, every minute.

"Can I do anything?"

I jump and gasp audibly, and spill a little wine.

"Oh, Emma, I'm sorry, I didn't mean to scare you."

"It's fine, Carol, don't mind me, I'm just—" I resume stirring because I have no idea what else to do. Entertaining guests suddenly seems terribly complicated and totally beyond my capabilities.

She leans against the kitchen table, her martini in hand, the other palm down on the table behind her. I'm still stirring away, my back to her.

"Are you all right?" she asks.

"Of course! Why?"

"You look a little tired, that's all."

"I'm fine, really, just, you know, busy busy busy! Just like you guys!"

"Oh please, I need a vacation. We're incredibly swamped at work. I'm sure you know that already." She grimaces and rolls her eyes.

"I did notice, yes. Poor Jim. Honestly, late-night work calls and all that."

"You must be running around like crazy. You're everywhere at the moment. I can't open a newspaper or a magazine without reading about your book. Which is so wonderful, by the way, that it's going so well, but still, it takes its toll, I guess."

"My Lord, yes, it's been a hard slog. It's not just you guys who work hard, you know." I'm saying these things in a singsong voice almost, like I'm doing an ad for *Good Housekeeping*. *It's not just you professional people holding down important world-improving jobs who get to work hard. Running a home is no picnic, let me tell you.*

But I'm being unfair. Carol's genuinely interested. I know that.

"Actually, *Long Grass Running* was a mammoth project in the end. And you know, I'm still getting used to the schedule. I thought being a writer was just about writing a book." I punctuate that with a cynical little laugh.

"Jim says you wrote it in no time. One minute you were running your store, next minute you're publishing a novel."

I snap my head around.

"Why would you say that?"

I must have said this more forcefully than I intended because her head jolts a little in surprise.

"Just that, it's amazing how creative you are, how talented you are, that you can do that. I envy you. I wish I were creative like you."

I make myself relax, force my shoulders to come down, my muscles to unclench. I have to keep it together, but I just don't know how right this minute.

"Actually, you can help," I tell her, transferring the contents of a casserole into a large serving dish. "Can you take this to the table for me?"

"Sure!" she says brightly, clearly relieved that she can get away from here, from weird me, and takes hold of the heavy dish.

I follow her with more dishes. "Come on, everyone, let's eat!"

"I have to say, Emma, you look great. Success really suits you," Terry says as he sits down next to me at the dining table, and I'm more grateful than I can say, because I know I look like shit.

"Thank you, dear Terry." I pat his hand. He beams at that.

"Now now, Terry, stop flirting with my wife."

"Stop? Not a chance, especially not now that I've tasted her cooking. All bets are off, buddy."

Everyone laughs, me included. If I were more myself I'd have found a way to correct that compliment that's not actually a compliment, but I don't have the energy right now.

"And about time too," Jim says. "My famous wife has been too busy to cook lately. I'll need to hire someone if this keeps up." Gentle chuckles all around. Jim looks at me from across the table and says, "But who cares. I couldn't be more proud of you, my darling," and he raises his glass to me. I'm so pleased, my cheeks hurt from grinning. I'm like a mechanical toy, I decide. I'm either grinning madly or crying, but nothing in between.

I don't really follow the conversation, I'm deep in my own thoughts, so after some initial attempts by Terry and Carol to steer the topic away from work, they accept, with some relief I'm sure, that I don't need to be entertained.

"Hey, Jim, someone called—Allison? Anyway, some person called and left me a very odd message, but I think it was for you." My ears prick up at what Terry just said.

"I don't know any Allison," says Jim, and before I've registered that his jaw is set, that his hand has flattened on the table, I pipe up, "You do know: Allison who wants a job at the Forum?"

Jim has gone pale now. I wonder if Terry has noticed. "Oh, right, she's from my old job, at the university, that's where she's from, I know who she is now."

"She called you here earlier today." I know how uncomfortable he's feeling, but I can't help it. It's like picking at a scab. I too want to know more about this Allison, and why Jim would pretend not to know her.

He throws me a hard look. "Yes, I remember. You told me," he says in a slow, deliberate tone.

So make up your mind, I want to say, *you're the one embarrassing yourself.*

I can see that both Terry and Carol's curiosity is piqued. They're too polite to push it, however, no matter how tempting it is.

"Allison's an old student of Jim's who wants to work at the Forum, apparently," I say, since Jim clearly won't. He looks positively constipated by now.

"Does she?" Terry turns to Jim. "She said she wants to show me some of your work, at least that's the message Jenny passed on, but maybe she misunderstood, because it didn't make a lot of sense to me."

"Jenny never gets it wrong," asserts Carol. She's addressing Terry, but she turns to me. "You know Jenny. We're lucky to have her. She's the one who knows what's going on better than anyone."

"I think Allison's the one with her wires crossed," Jim says. "She must have meant to show you some of her own work. I'll talk to her. Don't worry about the message. I'll deal with it."

"We're not hiring though, are we?" Terry asks.

"Nah. She's just persistent, don't worry about it. Who wants dessert?" Jim says, brightly now, but I can see how agitated he really is. The pain that has lodged between my eyes all day starts to flare up again and I rub the ridge above my nose. Allison. Again. It's all swimming in my head, the phone calls, the reviews, Jim's strange behavior, and my stomach lurches, because while I don't understand anything that's happening, I wonder, again, if Jim has something to do with it.

I hear my name. "What? Sorry, I was miles away."

Carol's looking at me expectantly. "I was just saying I went by your store, Emma. I was in the neighborhood. I popped in on the off chance you might be there."

"Oh Lord, you must be joking, I haven't been there for weeks. Jackie, my assistant, takes care of it all."

"Of course, it was silly of me."

"In fact, I've decided to sell it."

"You can't be serious!" Jim exclaims.

"Why not? I have hardly anything to do with it now, and anyway, I'm rather busy with other things these days, in case you hadn't noticed."

"I'm surprised, that's all. That shop's been such a big part of you, of your heart. I'd have thought it would be hard for you to give it up. That's what I meant."

"I know what you meant. But you know, this is so incredible, what's happened to me, and it's true, I can't do both. I can't do everything. Being a writer is so much better, don't you think?" *If I last long enough to enjoy it, that is.*

207

"Sure, if that's what you want to do," Jim says, "but think about the future. Will you want to write all the time? What if the next one isn't a big success? Isn't it better to have a fallback position?"

He doesn't want me to be successful in my own right. He prefers me to be in awe of him and his accomplishments, me as his supportive companion who will look after his every need, but I shake that unpleasant thought off, like an insect that's crawled up my neck. I know he's proud of me. I remind myself how proud and happy he looks when we're in public, holding my arm, never letting me go very far.

29

"What's this about selling the store?" Jim's loading the dishwasher and I'm pretending to put things away, but I'm constantly glancing at my phone, to see whether Amazon has removed the reviews.

"Why not? I'm too busy. I want to sell it to Jackie—I'll give her a good price."

"But it's your life, Em. You're sure about this?"

"It *was* my life, Jim, but I'm a writer now. I can't do both—haven't you noticed?" I say this with a knot in my stomach. Hopefully, I will remain a writer.

"Well, it's up to you."

Still nothing from Amazon. I put the phone down. "Speaking of being busy, I think we should get some help—at home, I mean."

"Help how?"

Jim really is doing a terrible job of loading the dishwasher. He keeps taking things out to make them fit. I'll be redoing the whole thing as soon as he leaves it alone.

"Cooking, shopping, dry cleaning, that sort of thing."

"We have Julie," he says. Julie is our cleaner. She's been coming once every two weeks.

"Julie doesn't cook, shop, iron your shirts—and I don't have the time anymore. I'm exhausted, Jim."

He straightens up and turns to me. "You do look tired, sweetheart. You should take a break from all this writing business."

"Bit late for that, don't you think?"

He sighs, as if I'm being deliberately difficult. "Of course, you're right. You're doing far too much. I'm sorry, sweetheart. I should take better care of you."

There are tears behind my eyes hearing this. I want to put my head on his chest and forget everything for a moment.

"I wanted to talk to you about something. It's important," he says.

Oh God, what now—something to do with Allison? "What is it?"

"Don't look so worried. I want to talk about money." He's hesitating.

"We have plenty of money. That's one thing you don't need to worry about."

"Exactly, and I want us to invest some of that money."

"Darling, you look after all that. You don't need to discuss it with me. I don't have the head for it, to be honest. Not right now."

"I want to invest your money."

"Invest in what?"

"The Forum." He's concentrating very hard on the cutlery, organizing it in its drawer. "We're so close to our goal. It's going to be big, huge, incredible. But we need some capital."

"And?"

"We have money in the bank, thanks to you. I want to use it for a little while. Not long, just a few months. Then I'll put it back."

"What, all of it?" The money has been piling up—the book's selling fantastically well—and we haven't done anything with it yet. We haven't needed to.

"I have plans for that money, Jim. I think we should move, for one thing."

He's looking at me again. "Move where?"

"Somewhere in Manhattan. You could be closer to work. You'd like that, right? You've talked about that often enough. We can afford it now."

He makes a sweeping gesture. "What's wrong with this?"

Amazing. A year ago, Jim would have sold this house and moved in a flash. And now we've completely reversed our positions.

"It's miles away from everywhere, from your work, from my commitments. Other than that, nothing I guess, but we can afford better now," I say.

There's a pause between us. A silence hanging in the air.

"Just for a couple months, Em. Once I close the deal, you'll get it back."

"What if you don't close the deal?"

"The only way I won't close the deal is if I don't have the cash up front to demonstrate we're in for the long haul."

He leaves the dishwasher alone, finally, stands up and looks at me.

"What's about to happen is enormous, sweetheart. I'm not supposed to tell you, but you're my wife, and I trust you. So I will tell you this: we are in the process of signing up with the most important federal government department. We're this close"—he brings his index finger and thumb close together—"to signing. And then, I really will change the world, Em, really. You have no idea how big this is."

"But I don't understand why you need this money."

"Because I need to show them I can afford the salaries, the overheads, the research, for at least two years. That's part of the contract."

"Can't you?"

"Some, but I need the extra cash."

"How much are we talking about?"

He turns around and bends down again. That dishwasher's being loaded to within an inch of its life.

"One million dollars."

"What?"

"To top up what we already have. That's what it will take."

"Wow! Changing the world isn't cheap."

"I'll put it back, Em."

"With a lot of interest, I hope. Anyway, that's academic. We don't have a million dollars."

"We can take out a second mortgage on the house. With your money, we can come up with a million dollars."

"You want to take out a second mortgage?"

"It's for us too, you know, not just me."

I can't quite see that part, but I let it slide. He comes to me now. Puts his hands on my shoulders and looks me in the eyes.

"That's what it will take, Em. But it's going to be big. It's ambitious to want to change the world. And look at what you've achieved! We're on a roll here. Do this with me, please. Be my partner in this. It's going to be incredible, Em."

Him and me. Changing the world. My heart melts. I've fantasized about Jim saying things like that to me. He takes me in his arms, enveloping me. I love his smell, his touch, his strength.

"You and me, Em," he whispers into my hair. "This is what we've been working for."

The warmth of his embrace releases all the tension that was locked inside, and I start to sob.

"Hey!" He pulls back. "What's this about? Oh, sweetheart, you need a break—you're so tired! I'm going to talk to Frankie, get him to lay off for a while and allow you a vacation." He draws me back into him. I'm crying onto his shirt.

"No," I say between sobs. "I'm fine, really. Just getting used to all this, that's all. I can't—I don't want a break right now."

"Once it's done, you can take all the vacations you like. You can sell the store. We'll move to an English castle somewhere if you want, or a twenty-room farmhouse in the south of France. We'll hire a huge staff, and you can sleep all day if you like."

"Every day?"

"Every day."

"Tell me." I'm nestled against his chest, talking into it.

"I told you."

"Tell me again. Tell me more."

"We're going to be hired by the government. All their economic and social policies will be based on our model. The money's going to be huge, beyond anything you can imagine."

"And you'll be making the world a better place?"

"Much, much better."

I hiccup a little, pull out a crumpled Kleenex from my pocket, and blow my nose.

"Okay, I'm in."

He hugs me tighter. "Thank you, my love." His breath is warm against my ear. We stay like this for a little while until he releases his grip. "I love you," he says. I look into his eyes and I can see he means it. I know Jim—every inch of him, every look, every twitch—and I believe him.

"What does Allison really want?" I ask.

He pushes me away, looks sideways, like he's trying to decide something, then he says, "I told you. She wants a job. She's a pain in the proverbial, believe me."

And because I know him so well, I can see he's lying to me. Although, to be fair, it's not that hard. Jim is a terrible liar.

"You're going to give her a job, then?"

"Seriously? No! Absolutely not! There's no job to offer, and even if there was, the last person I'd give it to is Allison. She's a pain, Em! I'll sort her out, believe me!"

"Have you talked to her about me?"

"No! Why would I?"

"Are you sure? About my novel? About Beatrice?"

"Don't be silly! Why would I talk to her about you?" He lifts a corner of his mouth. "You weren't worried, were you? About Allison?" he asks.

"A little, yes."

"Sweetheart, no! Allison is no one you should worry about, I promise you." He brings me back into his embrace.

I can forgive him this, I decide. I *have* forgiven him.

"I'll go and write some emails. This is just wonderful." He walks out of the kitchen, smiling at me all the way.

Half the dirty dishes are still piled up next to the sink, so I proceed to reload the dishwasher.

When it's all done, I decide to relax, put my feet up, go and watch something mindless on television with a Scotch in hand. I grab my phone on the way, and as usual glance at the Amazon page on the screen.

There's a new one, nestled among the praise, right up at the top.

One star – A rocking good read, especially between the lines!

Enjoying this, Emma? No, I didn't think so. Good news! You can make this go away. Stay tuned.

Published 33 minutes ago by Beatrice_isdead

I scroll down the page and sure enough, the other reviews are still there. Who on earth would choose the user name *Beatrice_isdead*? What kind of sick joke is this? What kind of twisted individual would do this?

I go through the whole rigmarole all over again: I click the "Report" button, I send more emails, and this time I tell them that my life's now in danger, all because they couldn't sort this out quickly enough. This is a threat, for God's sake.

You can make this go away.

What on earth does this mean? Do they want me to reveal myself? Publicly? I shudder.

I sit on the couch with my laptop, staring at the screen, waiting for another review to tell me how I can make this go away, but there are only new genuine reader comments coming through, burying the crazy ones farther down the page, thank God. No one seems to pay attention to the deranged comments, which is a mild relief.

30

"You ready for breakfast? I'm making pancakes." I'm determined this morning to not let these reviews get the better of me. I've made a little mental list I can refer to whenever I find myself getting anxious again: (a) there's no proof—well, not anymore, anyway; (b) there haven't been any new ones since last night, although that doesn't mean much, but still; and (c) why would *anyone* believe nasty reviews like these? The web is full of nutjobs; everyone knows that. People will feel sorry for me that I'm a target—me, the celebrated author of a wonderful novel that has touched so many hearts. So fuck off, *Beatrice_whatever*. I have not come this far to be beaten. There's a lot more fight left in me yet.

We're going to spend a lovely weekend together, Jim and I. I have no appointments/book readings/radio or TV interviews, which is a great relief, as much as I usually enjoy these things. Or used to. I suspect Frankie has been canceling things, paring back my schedule until I'm more myself again.

I've got the Saturday papers spread all over the kitchen table. It's already a lovely day, sunshine streaming through the window. I've been up for a while.

"Pancakes? No, thank you," Jim says.

"Really? But you love pancakes for breakfast."

"I'm watching my figure." He smiles and demonstrates this help-fully by patting his stomach. I take a better look at him.

"What on earth are you wearing?" I can safely say I have never seen Jim in a getup such as this. It's some kind of . . . activewear? A tracksuit of some description.

"I'm going for a run."

I burst out laughing. "You are not!" At least it's not velour. Thank God for small mercies.

"I am so. Do we have fruit or something? Or yogurt? I could have that when I get back."

I look down at gleaming white sneakers that I have never seen before. "Oh my Lord, okay. I wish you'd told me; we could have gone running together."

He smiles. "Let me warm up for a month or two, see how I manage first." He does a little run on the spot, like he's waiting for the lights to change, or to get going.

"Off you go then. I'll see you in a mile or two. Stay away from anything that sparks, because that thing"—I point at his outfit—"looks highly flammable." I wave him off.

He gives a little chuckle and sort of trots out of the house. I shake my head, amused. It's kind of sweet, really. I can't help thinking a little of this newfound vanity is for me. I've upped my game. I look great—well, not lately, but still.

I make pancakes for myself anyway, but replace the maple syrup with lemon and a little honey to make myself feel virtuous, and it works.

The doorbell rings and I laugh to myself. Only half a mile at the most then, and of course Jim didn't take his keys.

"I haven't—oh crap, now what?" Detective Massoud and the other one—what's his name? Carr—are standing there. I wrap my robe tighter around my chest. "I guess I should ask you to come in?"

"You don't have to, Mrs. Fern, but we thought this was better than bringing you to the station, in view of your—public profile. But it's up to you." She says this deadpan, like it's genuine enough, but it sounds sarcastic to me.

"Can I get dressed first?"

I'm being sarcastic, but she says, "You can get dressed. We'll wait out here."

I rush to the bedroom and quickly get changed into more suitable clothes. I hope I can get this, whatever this is, over with before Jim gets back.

When I'm ready, I lead them to the living room.

"So, what can I do for you?"

Carr pulls out his little notebook again, lets Massoud lead.

"We need to clarify something about your movements on the day Mrs. Johnson Greene died."

"Why? What difference does it make?"

"You stated that around 12:30 p.m. you were in the vicinity of Mr. Greene's office."

"So?"

"Do you still maintain that?"

"Why?"

Massoud lets out a sigh. "Mrs. Fern. As we previously explained to you, we're trying to find out exactly what happened to Mrs. Johnson Greene. If you could please answer my questions. I repeat, do you maintain that on the day in question you were in the vicinity of Mr. Greene's office, and that you saw Mr. Greene at that time?"

"I think it was that day, but maybe I was mistaken."

She raises an eyebrow. "You were very sure in your statement."

"I believe that's the day I saw George, yes, but I can't guarantee it one hundred percent."

"I see."

"You didn't answer *my* question. What is this about? I thought you'd cleared that up. George said it was cleared up. You're not still suspecting him, are you? I'm sure he can account for his whereabouts. He works in a busy office after all; his alibi's bound to be—what do you call it? Ironclad?"

"It's not Mr. Greene's whereabouts we're concerned about, Mrs. Fern."

"What then?"

"It's yours."

I explode into loud guffaws. It goes on longer than it should and threatens to turn into hysterics if I don't pull myself together.

"Me?" I manage to say once I've recovered myself, wiping tears of laughter from my eyes. "*My* whereabouts? That's priceless. What do my whereabouts have to do with anything?"

"We're not suggesting anything, Mrs. Fern, but we would like to eliminate the possibility that someone was in Mrs. Johnson Greene's apartment the day she died."

"I see. Things must be quiet out there then, if you have nothing better to do than to listen to gossip from the neighbors and harass Beatrice's family and friends like this. You should be ashamed of yourselves. Beatrice has the right to rest in peace and her loved ones need to grieve in private, not put up with these outrageous, scurrilous stories spread in the media like cheap tabloid fodder. Do you get a kickback for that? Do you have a little arrangement with the tabloids to supply them with nasty gossip about successful, respectable people? Don't they pay enough in the police force?"

I'm starting to hyperventilate, and my cheeks feel hot. I know how shrill I sound, but they say a good offense is the best defense, and I sure hope that's true.

The detectives look at each other. Clearly they're not used to being spoken to like this.

"If that's all, then I'd like you to leave now."

"We were able to confirm your hair appointment that afternoon, Mrs. Fern. But none of the stores you supplied us the names of were able to confirm seeing you prior to that. If you could provide a receipt? Something like that?"

"I can't provide a receipt when I didn't buy anything."

"Because you see, Mrs. Fern, we also checked the CCTV cameras for both stores, and we couldn't find you."

That makes my heart skip a beat. "So? Maybe it was a different day. I thought it was that day—I got confused."

Detective Carr speaks for the first time. His voice surprises me: it's pitched higher than I expected, than his looks suggest.

"Mrs. Fern, the cleaner was in the building that morning and—"

"That's right! She was! George told me that! Oh my Lord!" I clasp a hand over my mouth.

"What is it?" Detective Massoud asks.

"Are you saying she—the cleaner?"

"No, we're not saying that at all. We know Miss O'Brien, the cleaner, left before Mrs. Johnson Greene came home."

"Well, that's a relief then."

Carr speaks again. "Mrs. Fern, Miss O'Brien remembers a woman entering the building when she left: she held the door open for her. The time frame fits. We're trying to establish who that woman was and who she visited on that day."

"Maybe she lives there?"

They look at me like I'm a child with learning difficulties.

"It's not one of the residents, no," Carr offers finally.

"Was it you?" Massoud asks, and at the same time, the phone rings. The home telephone. I stand up and lift an index finger as if to say, *Hold that thought, I'll be right back*, and pick it up in the hall. I'm pretty sure it's my troll/Amazon-stalker, but I need the distraction right now.

"Hello?"

The sound of breathing. Thank you, stalker caller, your timing is impeccable.

"Hello? Who is this?" I say this very loudly, almost shouting. "What do you want? Who are you?" My voice escalates. I sound completely panicked now, and the detectives materialize right next to me. I hand the receiver to Massoud, my eyes wide in terror, or so I hope, just after the loud whisper at the other end. "*I know what you did.*" Like last time.

"This is Detective Massoud," she says sternly. "Who is this?" She looks at me. "They hung up." She presses buttons, star sixty-nine or whatever it is; shakes her head; and puts the phone down. "What's going on?" she asks.

I start to shake a little. "I've been getting threatening calls all week. I'm scared, Detective. Do you think this has anything to do with what happened to Beatrice?"

"What do they say?"

"Nothing! They breathe loudly into the phone, then they whisper something to frighten me! Am I in danger, Detectives? Am I next?"

"Did you report this?"

"No! I thought it was kids at first, but this is the third time this week!" I shake my head. "What should I do?"

"You could change your phone number. Is your number listed?"

"Yes, I never thought to have it unlisted, but now, of course, I will. Do you think this is related?"

"We'll file a report." Carr looks at his watch and makes a note. "We'll follow up on this." I do a fair amount of hand-wringing and jump at the sound of a key being inserted in the door behind me. We all look at Jim, who's sweaty and red in the face.

"What's going on?" he manages between gasps for breath.

I throw my arms around him. "Oh, Jim, these are the police. I've been getting threatening phone calls. Thank God you're home!"

The detectives introduce themselves.

"What do you mean, threatening phone calls?"

"What does this person say, Mrs. Fern?" Massoud asks. "How do they threaten you?"

"I told you, heavy breathing and demented whispers, something like 'What have you done?' or something."

"Did you do something?"

"Don't be silly, Detective. I don't even know what the question means."

She purses her lips a little. She doesn't like to be called silly. "That doesn't constitute a threat exactly."

"Really? What do you call it? Someone's trying to terrify me, Detective. I feel *exactly* threatened."

"You should change your number and have it unlisted. That's the first thing you should do."

Jim looks baffled. "When did this start?"

"All week! It's the third time!"

"Why didn't you tell me?"

"You've been so busy. I didn't think it was serious. I thought it was kids or something. I didn't want to worry you!"

"Is it a woman?"

"I don't know. I can't be sure. I think it's a woman, but it could be a man making his voice higher. They're whispering—hissing! Or something. I told you, it's hard to tell."

Jim rubs his hand over his forehead. He looks surprisingly uncomfortable.

"But yes, I'm pretty sure it's a woman." Just to watch him squirm.

"We can look into it," Massoud replies. Then she turns to me. "We still need to clarify your state—"

"Yes, I know," I interrupt. "Let me get back to you on that. I can't think straight right now. Oh God."

No one says anything for a moment, then Carr breaks the silence.

"If you could get back to us, Mrs. Fern, with as much detail as possible, that would be helpful." He closes his notebook and puts it away in his pocket.

"You'll follow up on the calls?"

"Yes, we will. We'll try to trace this one, see what comes up."

Jim steps in front of the door and puts an arm around my shoulders. "There's no need, Detective."

We all look at him.

"Jim, I've been frightened out of my wits. Of course we need the police to follow up on this."

"Are you saying you know who the caller is, Mr. Fern?"

"My wife has been under enormous stress, Detectives. She has a public profile now. It hasn't been easy for her."

What an odd thing to say. His arm is a little too tight around my shoulders. I'm not sure if he's trying to tell me something, or just very uncomfortable.

"All the more reason to track down this lunatic, wouldn't you say?"

Jim doesn't look at me. He opens the door with his other hand, his eyes still fixed on Massoud. "Leave it to me. If there's anything to be concerned about, I'll be in touch, Detectives."

So he knows something, I'm sure of it.

I nod. "Maybe I'm overreacting. Thank you, Detectives."

Their eyebrows are raised. Massoud is about to say something, but lets it go.

"All right. We'll be in touch anyway, Mrs. Fern," she says finally, walking out the door, Carr behind her.

Carr bends down and picks up something from the front step. He turns and gives me a small envelope.

"Thank you." I take the envelope and close the door. There's no postmark, no address, nothing.

Jim looks at me with concern. "Sweetheart, you should have told me. Are you all right?"

"What was that about?"

"You said yourself, it could be some kids' prank."

"That's pretty unlikely, don't you think?"

He shrugs.

"You think it's Allison." This isn't a question.

Jim doesn't reply.

"What does she want with me, Jim?"

"Did you really get the police here because of those calls? Calls you never even mentioned to me?"

It's my turn to shrug. "No, they wanted to talk to me about—stuff, to do with Beatrice. Then I got a call. Perfect timing, wouldn't you say?"

"What 'stuff' about Beatrice?"

"You know what it is. I told you—the neighbor, who told the police he thought someone was there. Same story."

"What do you have to do with that?"

"Me? Nothing. They had questions about the cleaner, about George: loose ends, as they called it."

Not strictly true, but close enough.

"You haven't answered me, Jim. What does Allison want from me?"

"I didn't say it was Allison."

"But you think it is, don't you. So now what?"

"I don't know if it's Allison." He runs a hand through his hair. He looks tired, or maybe just dejected. I wonder how well the pitch is really going. I wonder what's going to happen to my money. "If it continues, we'll get the police involved," he says.

I relent. "Fine. As you wish. But I think I'll change the number. Would you mind?"

"Not at all. I agree completely. I'll do that now if you like."

"No, you go upstairs and change. I'll do it."

I study the envelope in my hand.

"What's this?" he asks.

"I don't know. Was it there when you came in?"

"I don't think so—I would have seen it."

I have a strong feeling that I should be opening this on my own, away from Jim's prying eyes, but he's curious about it. He moves to take it from me. I lift a hand to stop him.

"I think I know what this is; Frankie was going to drop it off. I wonder why he didn't come in." I say this as lightly as I can. "You go upstairs and get cleaned up."

"All right." His lips touch my forehead. "I'll clean up and get changed. We're not going anywhere today, are we?"

"No, why?"

"So I know what to wear: something casual, or something more presentable."

As if that horrible polyester tracksuit wasn't casual enough.

He puts his keys and his phone on the table, and it occurs to me again that every time I've gotten one of these weird calls, Jim has been out.

31

I dial the phone company and after the inevitable series of *press this, press that* instructions, I get to speak to a woman.

I explain my predicament. "I want an unlisted number. Can you do that?"

"Certainly. Can I start with your name and current number, and then I will ask you a couple of security questions?"

I reel off my phone number and tell her my name.

"Did you say Emma Fern?"

"That's right, F-E-R-N."

"Oh."

Silence.

"Hello? Are you there?"

"Yes, sorry. What is your occupation, Mrs. Fern?"

"I'm a writer."

"Oh. My. God," she says, in that tone young people use to show they're impressed. "You're *that* Emma Fern! The author?"

I sigh. "Which is precisely why I need my number unlisted."

"Of course, certainly, but—" She sounds flustered. "I'm sorry, Mrs. Fern. It's just that I'm such a big fan. I loved *Long Grass Running* so, so much. It's my favorite novel, like, ever!" She goes on like this for a bit, just like I did when I first met Beatrice, all those moons ago. I feel like I'm trapped in a scene from *All About Eve*.

"Thank you, um—"

"It's Nicole," she gushes, "Nicole Callaghan."

"Well, Nicole, thank you. That's kind of you."

"Oh, not at all! Really! It's such an honor to speak to you, Mrs. Fern!"

"Thank you so much, Nicole Callaghan. Now, if we could get back to the matter at hand . . ."

"Of course! Yes! I'll provide you with a new unlisted number immediately."

After it's all done, I wonder whether they'll give out my old number to someone else. Whether some poor, unsuspecting customer will be getting these crazy phone calls. I wonder if the caller, whoever she is, will even realize it's not me at the other end.

◆ ◆ ◆

"All done?" Jim looks shiny, his hair wet and brushed back, his clothes freshly ironed.

"Yes, new number, unlisted."

"Good. Is my fruit and yogurt ready?"

"Sorry, I completely forgot with all this. I'll get it for you right away."

"Don't worry about it. I need to go into the office now anyway."

"What? But it's Saturday."

"I know, sweetheart, but something came up and I need to work on our strategy for the big pitch."

"Can't you work here? In your office?"

"I'll get it done quicker at the Forum. I won't be long. Are you all right?"

I pout. "I guess so. It's just that, the phone call, the police—this morning has been a bit of a shock."

"Well, it's all over now. I'm so glad you changed the number. It was probably kids anyway, as you said, but still, better safe than sorry, huh? Will you write the number down for me? I should go. I'll see you later."

He bends down and gives me a perfunctory kiss. What is it about the top of my head?

He turns back to me at the door. "You won't forget, will you?"

"About the number? I'll give it to you now, if you like."

"No, about the bank transfer, about the money."

He looks so sweet, so happy, so loving.

So needy.

"No, I won't forget. I'll do it right now."

"Thank you, partner," he bumps my shoulder with his fist, chuckles. "I love you."

"I love you too."

I log online into my bank account and transfer all my money to the Forum's account. It makes me a little nervous. I hope this deal works out, because it's all the money I have.

Then, when I can't put it off any longer, I open the envelope that's still lying on the table in the hall.

I'm so nervous. This can't possibly be good. It has to be from whoever's been calling. I don't know what's in it, but I know it's going to be awful. I almost anticipate seeing a pig's head or something. But no, it contains only a single sheet of white paper, printed.

Don't make me tell you again. One million dollars. More soon . . .

Oh no. No no no no. Suddenly everybody wants my money. Or maybe that's not a coincidence. Maybe whoever sent this is in cahoots with Jim. But why? Jim must have known I'd say yes.

No, this isn't from Jim anyway. This is from my evil Amazon stalker, I have no doubt. What did they say? That I can make it all go away. And now they've explained to me how. I'm sure I'll log onto Amazon and find more disturbing comments. By the time they're done with me, I'll be begging for instructions to give them whatever money they want.

In a funny way, I feel relieved. This isn't someone trying to right a wrong, this is a common criminal indulging in a little blackmail.

I want to log back on and see if there's time to cancel the bank transfer, but no, I won't do it. Fuck off, whoever you are. Whatever it is you're selling, nutcase, I'm not buying. I know the rules: I give you a million dollars now and then you'll want another one. I silently repeat my mantra: *There's no proof.* Even that so-called outline of Hannah's is easily explained. And when I write that book, my memoir of Beatrice, that's going to settle everything. Beatrice used to say the hardest thing when starting a new book is to be in control of the narrative. Well, I'm about to exert total control on this one. I tear the sheet of paper in as many little pieces as I can and shove them to the bottom of the garbage can. I'm scared, but I feel very brave. I know it's the right thing.

With the trepidation I'm getting used to, I log in to my Amazon account and check the book page. I look and look and keep looking, but there's nothing from *Beatrice_777* anymore. When I go to look at the profile, the review is no longer there. I hold my breath while I check for *Beatrice_1234*, and *Beatrice_isdead*, but they're all gone, all of them. *Beatrice_whatever* no longer exists.

I let my breath out.

32

"This is ridiculous! Am I under arrest? Should I call a lawyer?"

"No one is detaining you, Mrs. Fern, and you can make any calls you want. Like I said already, we need to clear up a couple things and we really appreciate you helping us out here."

This is probably the longest sentence Detective Carr has ever said to me. We're sitting at my kitchen table, and I can't wait for them to go away. I honestly thought they'd leave me alone, after they left my place the other day. After they saw the state I was in when I got that horrible phone call. But no such luck. Two days later, they're back.

"Do we really need to do this again? I don't know what you need from me. I'm sorry I don't remember exactly where I was that terrible day—what do you want me to do?"

"Just answer the questions, Mrs. Fern. That's all we want."

I turn to Detective Massoud. "Did you find out who has been threatening me?"

"You declined to file a complaint, so no, we haven't followed that up."

"So if I get murdered, will I need to come back from the dead and file a complaint for you to look into it?"

They look at each other.

"Mrs. Fern, we believe that someone was in the apartment when your friend was killed."

Oh Lord. The emphasis on *your friend* isn't lost on me either. Passive-aggressive behavior is what I call it. You want to help *your friend*, right? You wouldn't impede the police looking into *your friend*'s death, would you?

"So you think someone killed her?"

"We're not saying that exactly. It's still possible Mrs. Johnson Greene's death was an accident, but we have reason to believe that someone else was in the apartment at the time." She looks up at me. "Was it you?"

I feel my head vibrating back and forth. I can't control it.

"Just answer the question, Mrs. Fern," Carr says.

"No, I wasn't there."

"But you can't tell us where you were?" Massoud asks.

"I did tell you!" I wail. "I went to get my hair done!"

"But before that?"

"I was shopping! I told you!"

"All right." She looks at her notes. "We would like to look at your shoes, Mrs. Fern."

"My shoes?"

"We're hoping you will cooperate. We just need to rule you out. You were a close friend of the deceased. You would have been at the house often, am I correct?"

"Yes! I was there a lot. Ask George."

"Can we look at your shoes?"

I remember now, I know exactly what's happening here. When I crouched down next to Beatrice, I stepped just on the edge of the blood that was pooling around her head. Just the tip of my shoe; it must have made a mark on the rug somehow, and the police were there, examining every fiber in the area. I'm sure that's it, the shoes issue.

"Of course you can, if you must. I have a lot of shoes. Which ones would you like, Detective Massoud? The Louboutin sandals?" I bend down to look at her feet under the table between us. "No, wait—you're more of an Oxford girl, am I right? Comfort-before-style sort of thing? Well, sorry, I don't own any of those."

"What is it, Mrs. Fern?" Carr asks.

"What's what?"

"The problem."

"You mean, being harassed by the two of you on a regular basis? Jeez, I don't know."

"Fine," Massoud says. "We can do it your way, Mrs. Fern. We'll get a warrant for the shoes. We won't ask for your cooperation any longer."

I shake my head and put my palms down on the table. "No, that's fine. You can have my shoes. Do I bring them down here?"

"No need, we just want to take a look, take photos. There may be one or two pairs we might want to take away with us."

"Is it just my shoes you're looking at? Can I ask that?"

"No, we're looking to exclude footprints from all friends and relatives."

Footprints. Exclude. They're lying to me, of course.

"It's been a tough month, Detectives. My best friend died, and now I'm being stalked by some insane person. I'm sorry if I've come across as . . . uncooperative, but as you can see, I'm having difficulty coping."

"We can get a warrant," Massoud says, "if we have to."

"It doesn't need to come to that. We just appreciate your help, Mrs. Fern," Detective Carr says. So this "good cop, bad cop" thing is real then, not just the stuff of pulp fiction.

I stand up from my chair. "Okay, fine. Let's go take photos of my shoes. This way please," I say, as if I'm hosting these two guests instead of putting myself at their mercy.

We walk through the bedroom to the small walk-in closet, which has barely enough room for Jim's and my clothes. Every time I see it, I think that either we're going to move, or I'll put all of Jim's shirts and suits in the spare bedroom. He'd hate that.

"Here." I point down toward the two dozen or so pairs neatly arranged on the floor. "There's also a couple pairs of sneakers in the front hall, and my slippers in the bedroom. Should I get those too?"

Massoud pulls a surprisingly large camera from her shoulder bag.

"We don't need the slippers," she says. I bend down to pick up a pair of Nikes that have been pushed below the bottom shelf. I want to be helpful, move things along, get them out of here.

There's a hand on my arm.

"Don't do that," Massoud says brusquely.

"I've worn them, all of those, I think, since Bea—you know."

"That's all right, please don't touch anything right now." She has gloves on, and she bends down and picks up the first pair, puts them sole-up on the shelf closest to the door. She examines them briefly and lifts the camera to her eye.

She thinks now I know they're looking for shoes that have touched a pool of blood, I might quickly interfere or something, scrape a nail against an inconvenient dark red scuff mark.

I cross my arms against my chest and watch them handling my shoes, taking photos. It's crowded in here, but I don't want to leave.

"We will need to take these," Carr says.

He's holding up a pair of low-heeled black pumps. Not a bad match, actually.

"Yes, of course. Take what you need."

He puts them into a plastic bag and jots something down on what looks like a receipt book.

"Would you mind?" Massoud is pointing at my feet. I sigh and lift a foot behind me, reach back and remove my shoe. I hand it to her. She points to the shelf, and I do as she indicates, and deposit the shoe on it.

She turns it around and photographs it, and I repeat the exercise for the other foot.

"Are you taking them?" I ask, my feet bare on the carpet.

"No, you can put them back on," Massoud says. Not a match then. They really do know what they're looking for.

I stand in the doorway while they work, and I pull my cell phone from my pocket; I can't help it. There's a new message on my dashboard from Amazon, in reply to my zillions of requests.

> Dear Mrs. Fern,
> Thank you for contacting our author relations department. We apologize for the delay, and in future please note that your publisher is responsible for advising us of any errors related to your account.
>
> We have determined that the reviews being investigated violate our terms of service, and in accordance with our policies, the users responsible have been suspended permanently.
>
> Please contact us if you have any further questions.
>
> Regards,
> Amazon Author Relations

Okay, finally. I breathe and breathe as if my body has been starved of oxygen for weeks.

Thank the Lord.

I guess even Amazon agrees that those reviews were "not helpful." I wonder if *Beatrice_pissoff* will try again. Probably. She or he just needs to create a new account every few days, and we'll restart the whole damn rigmarole. The money from the book sales is still coming in steadily, but it's going to take a long time to get a million dollars together. I'm not kidding myself. All I did just now was buy myself a little time.

When Massoud has photographed every shoe from every angle, she puts her equipment back in her shoulder bag.

"We'll let you know when we can return these." Massoud's holding up a clear plastic bag that holds two pairs of shoes. Carr hands me the receipt and asks me to sign it.

"No problem," I say, "I'm happy to help."

I literally run to the kitchen after I close the door behind them.

◆　◆　◆

I check my Amazon dashboard again, then I open my email, and my vision goes blurry. There are a dozen or so new emails in my inbox, all with the same subject line.

What have you done, Emma?

Will I never get a break? Will they never leave me the fuck alone?

My hand's shaking and it takes a few tries before I manage to open one of those emails.

Liar
noun
A person who tell lies.
Origin: Old English

I randomly open more emails; they all say the same thing, and they're all from *beatrice_wrotethebook@outlook.com*.

My heart's beating so hard I can feel it in my throat. I sit on my hands to try to steady them, but my whole body's shaking, and I can't breathe anymore.

I don't know how long I sit like this, but at some point I find myself standing at the sink, taking big gulps of water from the tap. Then I lean back and stare at the screen over on the table, like it's some kind of evil object.

I have to do something. I have to make this stop. Getting the reviews deleted isn't going to deter this nutcase. I need to make them stop. I have to find a way.

My despair slowly turns to anger. How dare they, whoever they are? How dare they invade my life? They want money? Of course they do—this is just an ordinary, pathetic little blackmail job. I don't know what they think they know, but unless they have a manuscript that bears Beatrice's signature on every page, then they have nothing, and I doubt very much they have that.

I dry my hands and return to the laptop and hit "Reply".

No, wait. Don't give them anything yet. Think, Emma, think.

I delete my new message, bring up the browser, and type *how to find out who sent an email* in the search bar.

I know that anyone can sign up for an Outlook email account, so that's probably a dead end.

The first result is promising: *How to track the original location of an email via its IP address.*

All the other results are similar, and half an hour later I start to feel a lot more hopeful. Because unless *Beatrice_dofuckoff* is some kind of IT professional, it's likely they don't know zip about email headers and IP addresses, and have sent me a lot more information than they realize. Once I've figured out how to view the email headers, I jot down the IP address for each email, and guess what, they're all the same.

I begin to understand the significance of what I'm looking at. An IP address seems to be like a unique serial number attached to a person's modem or computer, and if you know what you're doing, you can figure out the geographical location of the computer that was used to access the Internet. That's how all those kids who download music or movies illegally end up getting caught.

It seems just about possible that I will be able to figure out who *Beatrice_makesmylifehell* actually is, or at the very least, where they live.

I sure hope it's not here, in this house.

33

After I called the phone company to change my number, they emailed me a survey to fill out, something along the lines of "Nicole helped you with your inquiry today. How was your experience?"

Which is helpful because I would not have remembered the young woman's name; the young woman who was gushing about *Long Grass Running*.

"AT&T customer service. May I have your name, please?"

"Yes, hello, this is Emma Fern speaking. I wonder if I could speak to Nicole? I don't have a last name, but I think it was Callaghan. I realize it's a bit of a long shot, but she works in a similar capacity—as you, I mean."

There's a short pause.

"Can I ask what this is regarding?"

"It's just that Nicole helped me last time, and I wanted to—" I have no idea what to say. I feel stupid. I haven't thought this through at all.

"Was there a problem with the service you received?"

"No, not at all, on the contrary. I just wanted to thank her personally. She was very helpful."

"I'm sure Nicole will appreciate it, Mrs. Fern. I'd be happy to pass on the message."

"No, please, can I speak to her directly?"

"I'm sorry, Mrs. Fern. There are so many of us working here, and I don't know who Nicole is, or if she's working right now, but I'd be happy to check that information in the logs and—"

"Would you? Check the logs, I mean? You see, I'm a writer, and she knows my book." I chuckle. "She's a bit of a fan of mine, so I wanted to send her a signed copy, as a thank you."

Lame, right?

"One moment, please."

But incredibly, I may well succeed in my quest, as I'm now listening to what was once referred to as elevator music. Everyone knows what that means, right? And yet has anyone ever been in an elevator that plays music?

"Hello, Nicole Callaghan speaking."

Incredible.

"Nicole, it's Emma Fern here. How are you?"

"Mrs. Fern?"

"Yes. How are you, Nicole?"

"Oh, I'm fine, thanks. Is everything okay? With your new number, I mean? It's not listed—I made sure of that."

"Yes, thank you. It's perfect—thank you so much. You were very helpful."

"Oh, I'm glad. Was there something else then?"

"I—you were very kind when I called, and I thought you'd like a copy of my book. I wanted to sign one for you, and I can send it to your workplace."

"Oh, Mrs. Fern, that would be amazing! Just amazing! You would do that? It's my favorite book, like, ever! *Long Grass Running*—I love it sooo much! I gave it to my mom, you know, for her birthday. She loves it too!"

"That's great to hear. Thank you, Nicole. I'd like to send you a special copy, yes. I was pleased to hear how much you liked it. And your mother."

"That's so nice of you, Mrs. Fern, so nice. I didn't tell anyone you were a customer, just so you know. I wouldn't want you to think that."

"Thank you, Nicole. I appreciate that. What's your address? Give me your work address and I'll mail it there."

She reels off the address.

"I'll pop that in the mail first thing, Nicole. But listen, you've been so knowledgeable, I wonder if you could help me with something else."

"Of course, I'd be happy to try. What product is it?"

"No, nothing like that. It's for my next novel. I'm researching something called IP addresses. Do you know what they are?"

"Your next novel? Oh, Mrs. Fern, I can't wait! What's it about?"

"It involves IP addresses for a start," I laugh, "but I'm not terribly knowledgeable about those things. I thought you might be?"

"Internet protocols—yes, sure. I'd be happy to help if I can."

"Great. So from what I understand, if I were to give you all the numbers for an IP address, could you tell where the computer is? Physically, I mean?"

"Like the actual address? Like 123 Main Street, Washington, DC?"

"Exactly."

"Um, let me think. You could get the country easily from an IP address."

"But more precise than that?"

"IP addresses get assigned randomly and they change all the time, for us anyway. They get rotated." She sounds very professional now. "They get assigned to your modem by our servers, if you're our customer using the Internet. I'm pretty sure that's how it works."

I sigh. I'm barking up the wrong tree here. She's not the solution to my problem after all.

"What is it exactly you're looking for, Mrs. Fern? I mean, I'm sure you could search online and find out everything you need—not that I don't want to help or anything. I'd really love to. Can you explain a bit more what you want to know?"

Worth a try, I suppose. "I guess I'm wondering, if I were to give you an IP address, could you tell me how to find out where the person using that IP lives?"

"I'm pretty sure you need the exact time they were assigned that IP address. Like I said, they get assigned randomly and then rotated again. To get a match, you need to know what time exactly they were online from that IP address."

The time—yes, this is great, because I have all the times and dates and Lord knows what else.

"Okay, that's really useful, Nicole. Thank you for that. So if you have the IP address, and you have the time and date, what do you do next?"

"Oh, I'm not sure, Mrs. Fern. I wouldn't know what to do at that point. I'm sorry."

"That's all right, Nicole." But it's not all right; it's crushing.

"I could ask my boyfriend if you like. He knows much more than I do about this kind of thing."

"He does?"

"Yeah, he's a network engineer here. He knows everything there is to know about IP addresses, Mrs. Fern. I guarantee it," she laughs.

"Call me Emma, please."

"Really? Wow, okay then, Emma."

"You would do that for me?"

"Are you kidding? I'd love to help you, and he won't mind—he loves talking about this tech stuff."

"If I give you the IP addresses and the times, then you can ask your boyfriend? Where they came from? I've got all the details right here!"

There's a short silence at the other end, then she says, "What would be the point? It's not real, right? You don't have actual IPs and actual times? You're researching this for your novel. I don't see how Gary can—"

I don't know what to do. I'm desperate. I try to think up a reason why, yes, we're dealing with real IPs here, real people, and I need to track them down, and no, this is not a novel, ha ha, you've got me, but I just burst into tears instead.

"Help me." I'm trying to hold back the sobs and it comes out as a whisper.

"What? I didn't get that, Mrs. Fern."

"Help me, Nicole, please." I feel so stupid, crying like this to a young woman who barely knows me. She's going to hang up on me, I can feel it, she'll think I'm crazy, probably dangerous, and she needs to get off the phone pronto.

"Okay, Emma." Her voice is steady, deeper, in control. "Tell me everything."

So I do. I tell her everything, every little thing. No, I don't—not everything, obviously. But I tell her about being stalked, and scared, and that I went to the police but they won't do anything, they won't listen, and I'm desperate, Nicole, I say, I don't know what to do, I'm at the end of my rope, I'm not sleeping, I'm not writing. I tell her about the phone calls I used to get and why I had the number changed.

"This is awful, Emma. You have to be careful, you know. There really are crazies out there."

I know, I say, tell me about it, but what can I do?

"You have to go back to the police, and you have to show them the emails. That's the first thing, Emma. This is serious."

"The police say they don't have enough information, but if I can point them to an address, then they could go and talk to this person. That would make them stop, wouldn't it?" I say. "No one wants the police on their doorstep when they've been sending crazy threatening emails to famous people, do they?"

"And I bet they're doing it to other famous people," she replies.

"Yes! Exactly! We're all being scared out of our wits here, Nicole, but we haven't done anything wrong—I haven't done anything wrong— and yet no one will help me!"

"Email me the details and I'll talk to Gary. It's just too horrible, Emma. You poor thing! Don't worry about it anymore, all right? We'll find out who that crazy person is and send the police after them. They'll get their comeuppance, you'll see. Leave it with me," she says.

God bless her.

34

I feel wretched and relieved all at once after I hang up. Nicole promised she's on the case on my behalf, and she clearly has excellent customer service skills. A ringing endorsement for the company she works for. God, I'm desperate to lie down, I could curl up right here, on the kitchen tiles. My phone rings and I close my eyes in frustration. I've had enough for today. But it's Jim.

"Emma! Sweetheart! We did it!"

"You don't need to shout, Jim, I can hear just fine. What did we do?"

He takes a breath. "The Treasury," he says. He sounds almost reverential.

"The Treasury? I'm not sure—"

"The Treasury! Sweetheart, we got it—we got the contract!"

"Oh my God! Jim, that's amazing, that's wonderful! That's . . . so soon?"

"Do you know what this means? Do you have *any* idea what this means?"

"You're awfully smart?"

"You bet! Oh, Emma. You have no idea, this is my lifelong dream come true! I can't get my thoughts in order. We have an opportunity to change society like never before, Em! Make a better life for all, at the expense of none. I'm rambling now, but you know, we can put in place all these proven theories, finally. As a nation, we're going to lead the world in productivity and well-being!"

"Darling, that's amazing. I'm so happy for you. I'm so proud of you! And this was so fast! I only transferred the money, what, last Saturday wasn't it?"

There's a short silence.

"What?" he says.

"Isn't that what you needed the money for?" I ask. "To seal the big deal? This is the big deal, right?"

"Yes, yes, of course. We had to show we could follow through. It's a big investment on our part too."

"Well, you deserve it, Jim. This is really wonderful news. I'm truly happy for you."

"And it's just the beginning! Sweetheart, we're celebrating, as you can imagine, all of us, admin staff too, the whole lab, tonight. Em, I think this is the happiest day of my life! No, wait, the second-happiest—the day I married you was the happiest."

"Celebrating? Tonight?" I ask.

"Of course! What do you think! This is the biggest thing that's ever happened to me. Millennium is going to change the world. Damn right we're celebrating! Jenny booked a large table at Perry's Corner. I probably need to get a move on, but I wanted to tell you right away."

I look down at myself, my jeans and baggy T-shirt. "I'll run up and get changed then, as soon as we get off the phone. It won't take long."

"Emma, darling—"

"I can be at Perry's in forty minutes, tops."

"It's a Millennium event, sweetheart."

I wait.

"You understand, don't you?" he says.

"For a million bucks, I'd have thought I had earned at least an honorary seat at the table."

I can hear his short intake of breath. "We couldn't have done it without you, that's true. I know that."

We. I wonder who *we* is, because suddenly I'm pretty sure it doesn't include me.

"Hey, we'll have a celebratory glass of champagne together when I get home, all right? I shouldn't be late. And I do want to celebrate with my wife. Will you put a bottle in the refrigerator for us?"

You have to be kidding me. Is that all I am? An afterthought? What am I supposed to say to that? *Yippee?*

"I think it would be nice to include me, Jim. I did finance this . . . contract. Is it such a big deal if I come and join you?"

"It's just that it's only us, the lab, and—"

"The lab and the support staff, you said. What am I, a potted plant? An ATM machine?"

"Don't be difficult, Em, please. Not today. It's a great day. Let me have my moment, all right?"

I grit my teeth and bite my tongue, all at the same time. "All right." It comes out heavy, resentful. I try again. "Of course. I understand. You have fun, and we'll toast to the Treasury when you get home."

"Good. I really need to get going now. Everyone's waiting for me. I'll see you later, sweetheart, all right? I won't be late."

"I love you," I whisper, but he's gone.

I grab fistfuls of my hair and pull, letting out a kind of scream, the guttural kind, the kind you don't want anyone to hear, but that takes effort to release, and I let tears gush out of me. It takes ages for me to calm down, but eventually I manage it.

Don't be difficult, Em.

No, of course not. That would be unconscionable, not when you've had such good news. So what if I made it all possible? If I gave you *all* my money, simply because you asked?

Don't be difficult, Em.

The words go around in circles in my head, on a loop. We'll have a glass of champagne when he gets home. I should put a bottle in the fridge, but then I see there is one already. There's always champagne in my refrigerator these days.

Why doesn't he want me there? I love it when Jim comes with me to functions. He should be proud to have me by his side. That's the way it's supposed to be. I thought that was the way it was. People look up to me now—just ask Nicole. Oh, and I gave him all my money so that he could close his stupid deal.

I go upstairs and take a couple of the pills that Dr. Craven prescribed for me. Frankie will be pleased with me when I tell him that I went to see the good doctor, as instructed. And he was right, dear Frankie, I do need some help. I'm falling apart. I know that.

"Don't take too many," Dr. Craven admonished me. "They're fairly strong, but they will help you sleep. If you feel any anxiety, take one, but don't drive."

I'm not feeling any anxiety, but I as sure as hell need to calm down, and if I have nowhere to go, then I may as well sleep.

But I can't. I'm too wound up, and I don't want to take any more of those pills and pass out. I go back downstairs to the kitchen and pull the bottle of champagne from the refrigerator. It takes a bit of brute force to get it open, and some of it flows onto the floor when I finally manage it, but I don't care. I grab a glass from the shelf and fill it up.

Cheers, Em, thank you so much for being so supportive, so willing to help, so selfless. I couldn't have done it without you, sweetheart. I'm a very lucky man indeed.

Don't be difficult, Em.

I was taking summer college classes when I met Jim. I was there to study business and accounting, but I'd taken this extra class in English literature for my own enjoyment. He was still a student, but he was teaching math at the same school to make ends meet, and one day when I was rushing to get there on time, I literally ran into him, and the coffee he was carrying spilled all over my shirt. He apologized profusely, as if it were his fault, and I thought he was the most impressive man I'd ever met. He dressed well by any standard, let alone for a student—a little old-fashioned, maybe, but it gave him an aura of respectability. We saw each other in the hallway over the next few weeks, and one day he asked me out and we went to the best restaurant I'd ever set foot in. When I went to his house to meet his parents, I couldn't believe how wealthy they were. They're not really, I realize that now, they're simply middle-class, but to me, they were at the top of the food chain, and I was a bit of plankton that had drifted into Jim's wake.

I think I became obsessed with him, when I look back on it. I worked hard to improve my appearance: I dressed better, I spoke better, I educated myself so that I could contribute to conversations about politics, social issues, international affairs.

Eventually, Jim proposed, and our wedding day really was the happiest day of my life. But I still try to be that person that I think Jim wants me to be, and I still don't know who that is. No matter how many books I write, how many awards I win, how much money I give him, I'm still that awkward, self-conscious woman, inadequate in all the important ways, pretending to be a grown-up. But is that what he wants? Because I know deep down that Jim isn't at the restaurant with the Millennium team. Otherwise he would have included me. Of course he would have. I financed the whole thing, for Christ's sake. No, Jim's with that little witch Allison, who stalks him and stalks me, and won't let go until she's gotten her hooks into him, and has peeled me off him, and can have him all to herself.

I go upstairs and change into my sexy black dress. It fits me perfectly, now that I've lost that extra weight. I put on makeup, which is no easy feat when you're crying. I pin my hair up; it takes forever. I keep dropping things: hair clips, lipstick, tears. I'm glad the police were not interested in my Louboutins. I get out the door and half stumble to my car. I shouldn't be driving, but I don't care. I just want to get there as quickly as possible.

35

When I tell the waiter at Perry's Corner that I'm with the Jim Fern party, he stares at me a moment longer than he should. He recognizes me, Lord bless him. Who knew waiters were so cultured? But then again, this is one of the best restaurants in the city; maybe a mental index of who's who is a prerequisite.

"Are you all right, madam?"

"Of course, why wouldn't I be?"

"You may want to use the ladies' room, madam. It's this way." He points toward the back of the dining room and as I turn to look I catch sight of myself in the mirror by the coat check. My mascara's all over my face. It would be funny if it weren't so pathetic. I step over to the mirror to take a better look, rifle through my handbag for a Kleenex and clean it up as well as I can, reapply some lipstick.

"It's fine, really. Thank you." I've recovered quickly. I don't care what he thinks.

He nods and extends an arm, showing me the way. I crane my neck from behind him, looking for Jim and Allison in the main dining room, but I can't see them.

"This way," he says, and then I catch sight of him. He's sitting at the head of a long table. There's Carol, Terry, Jenny, and at least half a dozen other people, some of whom I vaguely recognize, some of whom

I've never seen before. They're in the middle of a toast, their glasses raised toward Jim while he's speaking, or holding court rather. It's like a tableau.

"Hello, everyone!" I say brightly. Every face turns and looks up at me in unison. I smile and nod enthusiastically at them all. "I'm not too late, I hope? Oh good, you've already ordered," I say to no one in particular in a very cheery tone, a bright smile plastered on my face. I put a hand on the back of the nearest chair to steady myself, and turn to Jim.

He doesn't say a word, just glares at me, his lips pressed together in a thin pale line. His eyes are narrowed, hard. I cringe, almost, at how furious he looks, and then feel a flush of embarrassment. I'm standing like a dork, with no idea what to do next, but Terry comes to my rescue and a waiter is quickly summoned to set up a place for me. People shuffle their chairs noisily to make room; no one has asked me where I'd like to sit but I end up near Jim, between two young women I've never met, who look vaguely put out at the disturbance I've caused.

Carol is sitting on Jim's left, and she extends a hand across the table toward me, which I grab, awkwardly.

"It's nice to see you, Emma. I'm so happy you could be here."

"Really? That's nice of you. I wish my husband would say the same."

Jim has picked up his knife and fork, and he's making a show of cutting up his asparagus. There's a vein throbbing on the side of his neck, and a crimson patch on his forehead, just between his eyes. He gets like that when he's stressed. Or angry. Or absolutely enraged.

"I interrupted you all. Sorry about that—you were having a toast, right? Let's do that!" I stand up and push back my chair, but I've misjudged the movement and it clatters backward to the floor. "Oh, leave it, leave it!" I say, waving my free hand, even though no one has made a move to pick it up. "Come on, everybody! Let's have a toast!" They're not sure what to do—they're all looking at Jim for a clue, instructions, anything.

"Sit down, Emma," he mutters.

"No! Come on! It's a celebration, right? Stand up, everyone!" I move my hand up and down, palm up, in case they don't know what "up" looks like. Terry, Lord love him, gets up from his chair, lifts his glass high. "To the Millennium, and its talented director!" Finally, hesitantly, everyone follows suit, and repeats the toast to the sound of scraping chairs.

"And may this be the first success of many! To the Treasury!" Terry adds.

"To the Treasury!" answers the chorus.

"To my million bucks that made it all possible!" I shout, raising my glass so fast half the contents spill onto the tablecloth, and I quickly drain the rest in one gesture. But this time, the chorus is silent. They're all looking at me, and then at Jim.

Jim has stood up. I can see it from the corner of my eye. He grabs me by the elbow. His whole face is a deep crimson now. I worry vaguely that he's having a heart attack as he pulls me roughly away from the table and I stumble, almost fall. My heel catches the chair leg and comes off my foot.

"Stop it—stop!" I shout, but he's walking too fast, his fingers digging into my arm, pulling me along. The restaurant staff stare as we go past, but no one tries to stop him. They're probably thinking the same thing: the sooner I'm out of there, the better for everyone.

He shoulders the glass door open and yanks my arm, grabs my shoulder with his other hand, and pushes me outside.

I've fallen on the sidewalk. "You're drunk. Go home, Emma," he says, staring at me with disgust.

I heave myself up with both hands flat on the ground and manage to sit. A waiter slips by beside Jim, his arm reaching out to me. I lift a hand to take his, grateful he's going to help me up, but no, he's holding my other shoe, which he places into my open palm.

"Can we call you a taxi, madam?" he asks.

"No," I gulp, the sobs bubbling up my throat. "I'm fine." I manage to stand up and point to the opposite side of the street, where my car is parked, very badly actually.

"You can't drive," Jim scoffs.

"What do you care? Don't tell me what to do, you—asshole!" I shout.

I stumble across the road to the car. My knee hurts from the scrape I got. I keep dropping the keys and it takes forever to open the door. I look behind me to see if he's watching, but his back is turned, he's going inside. He's waving a hand at the side of his head, as if to dismiss this annoyance that I am.

I gently lean my forehead on the steering wheel and let the humiliation wash over me. I'm crying so hard I can't breathe properly. I'm engulfed in abject misery so deep I can't imagine ever crawling out of it. I don't want to start the car, I don't want to do anything but sit here, taking great big gulps of air.

My phone rings, and I ignore it at first, because I've been thinking in this wretched moment that I have never been so lonely, and that I have no friends. Not a single friend. No one to call for help. I let it go to voice mail.

It rings again. Whoever it is, they really want to talk to me. I empty the contents of my handbag on the passenger seat and pick it up.

"Hello?" I manage to whisper.

"Emma, it's Nicole. I hope it's not too late to call."

"Nicole?"

"Nicole Callaghan—you know, from AT&T?"

"Oh, Nicole, hold on a sec, please." I put the phone down and blow my nose, wipe my face. "Okay, sorry, Nicole. Go ahead."

"I just wanted to let you know I have an address for you."

I jolt myself upright. "You have an address?"

"Yes, my boyfriend tracked down those IPs for you. I didn't want to wait. You have a pen?"

"Huh, one sec." I rifle through the objects on the seat and pick up a pen and an old receipt. "Okay, I'm here," I say. She reels off the address and I jot it down. It's not mine. I don't know why I thought it would be—I really am going crazy—but I was genuinely starting to believe that somehow, Jim was behind this.

After I hang up, I stare at the piece of paper, the address a blurry scrawl. I'm in no state to confront a blackmailer, but I have to know who's been torturing me, and put a stop to it. I grab my wallet from the passenger seat, lurch out of the car, and head for a coffee shop at the end of the block.

◆ ◆ ◆

An hour and a half later I'm parked opposite a beautifully preserved brownstone with a slate roof. I don't know who lives there—I have never been here before—but I'm about to find out who hates me so much that they have made my life hell for the past couple of weeks. God, is that all it is? It feels like a century. Well, anyway, whoever it is, it seems like they don't need my money. This isn't an apartment building, it's a single-family home. The house is dark, so they're probably asleep; it's almost midnight. I'm sipping yet another cup of hot black coffee and I'm starting to feel normal again—well, not drunk anymore, anyway. I'm ready to go and confront my nightmare. I should be frightened. After all, this is someone who knows something about me, something very secret, and I don't know the first thing about them. But I'm past being scared now. I am vibrating with anger.

I'm taking my time, studying the windows, wondering who's asleep behind the curtains upstairs. I have all the time in the world, and I wait until I'm sufficiently sobered up. A cab pulls up and stops in front of the house, and after a moment someone gets out and climbs the stairs to the front door. When the cab drives off I softly open my door and cross the street. The figure turns at the sound of my heels clicking on the pavement.

"Emma! What are you doing here?"

36

It doesn't take long for Hannah to figure out that I know. She can tell from the shock on my face that I wasn't expecting her to be there. Her face hardens, but she lets me inside.

"What do you want, Emma?"

"I think the question is, what do *you* want, Hannah?"

I follow her into the living room. She removes her coat, and drops it on the back of the couch, and I do the same. Still not looking at me, she walks over to an antique bar cabinet, and pulls out a bottle of Scotch and two glasses. She pours and hands me one. I accept it, even though I have no intention of drinking it; it's taken me almost two hours and gallons of black coffee to sober up.

"Don't you have anything better to do," I ask her, "than to stalk me? Harass me? What the hell is wrong with you?"

She laughs, not a very nice sound this time.

"Who do you think you are?" she snarls, the laughter gone. She downs the Scotch and quickly pours another one. She still has the bottle in her hand.

It's quite surreal, standing here in her living room with a drink in my hand. From the outside it looks like we're socializing. From the inside, well, that's another story.

"I've gone to the police, you know."

"I doubt that very much."

"They don't take kindly to anonymous threats, blackmail, all these lies you've been putting on my Amazon page."

"Emma, please, let's cut the crap, okay? You and I both know you didn't write a single word of that book." She puts the bottle of Scotch down after one last top-up and sits on the couch.

She's very different from the usual gentle Hannah. It's like a mask has been removed; she looks tired, hard.

I haven't really thought this far. For a moment, I contemplate throwing my glass at her and walking out, but I need to know what she knows, and especially what proof she has. If any.

"Why would you even say that?"

"Because it was my idea." She leans forward and pokes an index finger into my chest. "*My* idea, you little bitch."

I don't say anything. I can tell from her tone she's desperate to tell someone, and who better than me? I don't need to incriminate myself with questions. I put my handbag down on the bar, next to the bottle; settle myself on the armchair opposite her, make myself comfortable, and wait for the rest.

She leans back on the couch. "I told Beatrice," she says, "don't publish this under your name, they'll crucify you, the critics will. You're a woman, you're a commercial fiction writer. Test the waters first."

She takes a sip.

"She was going to do it under a pen name, but I told her, forget it—it's too hard. You can't do interviews, you can't do photo shoots. No, you need a stand-in."

A stand-in. I heard that very word from Beatrice, that fateful day.

"And then you came along. She called me. 'I found her,' she told me, 'the stand-in. She's perfect. You absolutely have to meet her, Hannah.'"

"At dinner, at her house," I say.

"And, boy, you were perfect. A puppy dog, madly in love with Beatrice. I told her, 'You couldn't have picked a better one if you'd put an ad on Craigslist.' Oh, how we laughed at you."

She looks quite deranged, a grimace on her face, her head thrown back. It occurs to me she might be more dangerous than I anticipated.

"Still laughing?" I ask her.

She snaps her head back toward me. "But you had to go and ruin everything. Frankie Badosa!" She sputters his name with contempt. "I was supposed to represent you, obviously, to sell the book to a prestige imprint."

"You're sure about that, Hannah? Because Beatrice certainly gave me the impression that you were *not* supposed to represent me."

"What do you mean?"

"She said if it was you, then people might guess she had written it. Too close to home, she said. In fact, she was very insistent that she would find someone new."

Hannah reaches behind her to grab the bottle and refills her Scotch. I know the feeling.

"Beatrice was a bitch," she says, matter-of-factly.

"Tell me about it." I didn't mean literally, but it's too late.

"I worked with that woman for twenty years. Twenty years of my life I spent massaging her ego, making her a success, taking an unknown and turning her into the bestselling female crime writer of the last decade, did you know that?"

"I'm sure you did well for yourself out of it," I say, looking around the expensively furnished room.

"But she lost it—she lost her mojo. Did you read her last two books? They were awful. She wasn't into it anymore. They didn't sell well and she blamed me." She does that finger-jabbing thing again, at her own chest this time. "Me! I made her, but even I can't turn water into wine. So she wanted to dump me, change agents. She said I'd become complacent, that I wasn't working hard enough for her anymore."

"Wow, that's harsh."

"She fired me via email, can you believe it?"

"Well, look, I'm sorry to hear all that—sounds rough, it really does—but what does it have to do with me? If she fired you, then you wouldn't have been the agent for *Long Grass Running* anyway."

"She wanted to change genres, and she didn't think I was a *good fit*." She almost spits out the last words. "Frankly, changing genres now, at this point in her failing career, wasn't a good idea. Certainly not switching to literary fiction, that's for sure. What a bitch! I can't say I was sorry when I heard she'd died. I wouldn't have wished it or anything, and the timing was off. If she could have fallen down the stairs after revealing herself as the author, well, that would have been much better."

"So if you knew about the novel, why did you call me about that old outline you'd found?"

She laughs. "There was no old outline, Emma. I was just messing with your head."

"I see. And the Amazon reviews, the phone calls; that was all to blackmail me? You want a million bucks—I get it. You people are all the same. Well, as it happens I don't have a million bucks. So you can get back in line."

"A million bucks? You must be joking. I want to be your agent, and I want back pay—you bet I do."

"But the note—" I don't finish the sentence. Instead I mentally facepalm. What are the odds that Jim would ask me for a million dollars, and the next day there'd be a note asking for the same amount on my doorstep? Was that even intended for me?

I wave the thought away. I can't make any sense of it yet.

"Okay, so here we are"—I look again around the room admiringly—"having a drink together, which is nice. We've been trying to catch up for ages. Anyway, I'm glad we've finally managed it, but again it begs the question: What is it you want, Hannah?"

"Are you deaf or something? I just told you. I'm your agent now. You and I will sign a contract right here, and you will reimburse me all the commission I should have been earning. And more—we'll call it interest on past due amounts."

"I see." I'm not exactly sure how she thinks she's going to make me, but no doubt I'll find out.

I lower my hand beside the armchair without changing my gaze, and gently pour the Scotch onto the carpet, very slowly, so it doesn't make any noise, still looking at her. Then I stand up and go to the counter where the bottle is.

I reach out my hand toward her constantly empty tumbler—that woman can drink me under the table—and she hands me her glass without looking.

"Do you have any ice?" I ask. She turns her head to me, about to tell me to fuck off or something, but then goes out of the room, presumably to the kitchen.

I rifle through my bag and pull out the bottle of pills Dr. Craven prescribed. I'm in awe of my own steady hands. I didn't know I had it in me. I grab a cocktail muddler from Hannah's impressively complete set of barware and crush at least half a dozen pills into the bottom of her glass, getting them down to a fine powder by the time I hear her start to walk back from the kitchen. Just as Hannah comes back with a small bucket of ice—the vintage type, with silver mesh on the outside, very pretty—I pour two fingers of Scotch into her glass, then mine. I grab the tongs and drop a couple of cubes into my Scotch.

I turn to her, holding up the tongs. "You?"

She shrugs. *Good*, I think, *it'll be easier to mix and mask.*

I hand her glass back to her and go back to my very comfortable armchair.

"You need to start on that memoir, if you haven't already. I can sell that," she says, as if it's all been settled, then downs half her drink in one gulp.

"I'm still gathering my thoughts."

"Well, don't gather too long. I'm going to type up that contract." She walks toward the door with her Scotch, taking sips as she goes, and I assume she's going to a study of some sort somewhere else in the house, but no, she pulls out a portable desk from a little nook I hadn't noticed. There's a small laptop and a printer. She pulls up a chair, sits down, opens the laptop, and starts typing. The woman is efficient, I'll give her that.

I have no idea how many pills it'll take to put her to sleep, let alone what I should do when she is. I'm making a show of scanning the bookshelves opposite, when suddenly there's a loud thump, and I turn and have my answer: Hannah has fallen off the chair and is sprawled on the carpet.

I crouch next to her and shake her. "Hannah, wake up. Are you okay?"

She opens her eyes slowly, mumbles something I don't understand.

"It's okay. Here, let me help you up." I reach under her arms and try to lift her, but she's too heavy. "Hannah, come on—wake up!" I slap her, like I've seen in the movies. It feels fantastic.

She mumbles again and dribbles a little but manages to move her arms, and after an eternity I maneuver her upright and drag her back over to the couch.

I'm panting with exhaustion. I tell her I'll go find help and look around the living room until I spot a scarf hanging off the back of a chair.

I wrap the scarf around my hand and run out of the room, looking for her bathroom. I find it and rummage through the vanity drawers until I see what I'm looking for—a bottle of sleeping pills, almost full—and I give a mental prayer of thanks to the pharmaceutical industry of this country, which has made sure every household is well stocked with barbiturates. I snatch a bottle of Asendin while I'm there—better safe than sorry—and I also grab a lipstick from the top of the vanity.

Back downstairs, Hannah's still moaning and drooling on the couch. With my hand wrapped in the scarf, I open the mail application on her laptop and search for *Beatrice Johnson Greene*. An email thread titled "the puppy" draws my attention, and I read it. It makes my stomach churn.

The puppy refuses to be trained, it starts. Beatrice is complaining bitterly that I'm not following her orders and lists many "mistakes" I apparently have been making. My name's never mentioned, nor is the title of the book. She closes with: *That's it, I'm pulling the leash.*

But it's the latest email thread I'm interested in. The one dated two days before Beatrice died.

> Re: Sales Report
> Hannah, thank you for forwarding the monthly sales report. I note your comment that it's not our best. I'd like to correct you there: it's not *your* best. It reiterates what I have been discussing with you over the last few months. I am appalled at your attitude and lack of professionalism. I have been in discussions with Evans & Marks and have decided to retain their services as of today. Therefore, please consider this email notice of the termination of our contract, effective immediately.
>
> Regards,
> Beatrice Johnson Greene

I press "Print" and gingerly lift the page from the printer, making sure not to make contact between my skin and the keyboard or the paper.

Then I fill up Hannah's glass with the rest of the Scotch and swirl it around.

"Here," I tell the whimpering, dribbling Hannah, "it will make you feel better."

I take her right hand in my wrapped one and make her hold the lipstick. "Let me help," I tell her. I hold the printed email against my knee, propping it up so that she can reach it.

You're a fucking bitch, is what we manage to write with the lipstick across the page—and it's no easy feat, let me tell you. It's sort of legible, enough anyway. I drop the page on the floor, let the damaged lipstick fall onto Hannah's chest.

I pop as many pills as I can into her drink, using the muddler to crush them as much possible. Then I lift her head and pour the contents between her lips.

"Come on, there you go, gulp gulp gulp—that's it, good girl. Here, this will help you." I pour some more Scotch into her mouth, but she coughs and half of it trickles onto her chin.

Stupid woman. Her head's wobbling on top of my hand, like one of those weird toys people used to put on their dashboards, those dogs with the head bobbing up and down and sideways. It's also surprisingly heavy.

"Make an effort, Hannah. You're not a child, for Christ's sake—hurry up!" I give her more Scotch, and now she's swallowing: great.

I keep feeding her pills, and when I've made sure she's ingested them all and the rest of the Scotch, I gently rest her back on the couch and watch her for a moment. Her eyes are open. I don't know if that's a good sign, and when I say "a good sign," I mean a sign that she's about to check out. I can barely see her pupils, they're so far up her eyelids.

If this doesn't work, I have a whole lot more of my own pills, but I really hope I won't need to use them. I leave her there, softly open the front door, and check outside. It's very quiet at this time of night. I make sure the front door is going to stay ajar, then crouch down, quickly cross the road to my car, and quietly open the trunk. From beneath the spare wheel, I pull out the plastic bag that holds the shoes I was wearing when I killed Beatrice. Did those detectives really think I would put them back in my closet? Seriously, with police work like that, no wonder this country's going to the dogs.

Softly, softly, I close the trunk and crouch down again, listening. Still deadly quiet. I sprint back across the road and through the door, which I close gently behind me, and run up the stairs to shove the bag into her closet, right at the back, after I wipe off the bag and the shoes to get rid of my fingerprints. I am leaving nothing to chance. I thank my lucky stars that we're the same shoe size, which I know because she tried my shoe on that day, the day I first met her.

Back downstairs, I stand in the doorway and look at her poor sad body on the couch. Considering the massive cocktail I've just administered, I don't need to take her pulse to know it's over, but I do anyway. Measure twice, cut once, right?

I make sure to wipe anything I touched earlier, like the tongs from the ice bucket, and clean any traces of the crushed pills off the muddler. Then I take the glass I drank from and shove it into my bag. This time, when I walk out the door, I make sure it's securely shut behind me.

There's no sign of life in this quiet, expensive neighborhood. I turn the key one notch in the ignition, without starting the engine; shift into neutral; release the handbrake; and gently, slowly, let the car roll down the hill.

37

All I want to do is go to bed, by the time I get home. I am more exhausted than I can say, but also extremely satisfied after a job well done.

"Where have you been?"

I turn on the light in the living room. "Christ, you scared me, Jim. Why are you sitting here in the dark?"

"You should have been home hours ago. Where were you?"

"Oh, you know, here and there, busy busy busy. Had fun at your dinner? Nice people, I thought."

And then I see it—the large suitcase on the floor by his feet.

"Oh, sorry, darling, you're going somewhere. You probably told me, but I completely forgot! Honestly, my brain these days!" I remove my own coat and fold it over the back of the nearest chair. "Although in my defense, I've had a lot on my plate," I add.

"I'm leaving, Em." He stands up and buttons his coat. I've never seen this coat before. It's some kind of raincoat, nicely cut, expensive.

"I can see that, Jim, and I'm glad I caught you. Where are you going again?"

"I'm leaving you." He bends down and picks up his suitcase. "This can't be a surprise."

"I don't understand what you're saying."

"I'll get my things picked up later in the week."

"You're leaving me?"

"Come on, Em. This must be what you want. It's not like we've been close. You're too busy with your publicity tours, your book signings, your career," he snarls. "Anyway, it doesn't matter. There's someone else in my life now. There has been for a while and I'm going to be with her. She understands my needs."

"Someone else?" I'm struggling to make sense of the words. He ignores me. "What do you mean? Who is it, Jim? Allison?"

"Don't go into hysterics, please."

"Is it because of the dinner?" He's standing in front of me. I'm blocking the way to the front door.

"Can I get past, please?"

I'm rooted to the spot, completely paralyzed. He pushes me aside, walks past me. I'm grasping at straws.

"You can't leave! Jim, please! Let's talk about this!" My voice has gone up an octave.

"Don't be difficult, Em, not this time."

"Difficult? Jim, Christ, I've had a really, really hard day here, sit down and talk to me, explain to me what's going on here. Are you going to be with her? With Allison?"

He shakes his head at me, just like at dinner, a look of disgust on his face. "You need to be an adult about this."

"What about the money?" I ask.

"You'll get it back—I told you. Don't make this about money, Em, all right? When you've calmed down, call me at work and we can make a time to discuss the details of our separation. You have a lawyer, right?"

"A lawyer?"

"For the divorce. I'll have mine get in touch and you can discuss it with him."

He opens the front door. Nothing he's saying or doing makes any sense, but my heart is breaking nonetheless.

"Goodbye, Emma," he mutters, before closing it behind him. And that's when I faint.

◆ ◆ ◆

I don't know how long I've been out like this, on the hard, wooden floor in my hallway, but the sun is up when I come to. I lift myself on my hands and knees and hold on to the corner of the hall table to help myself up. I feel bruised and broken as I move slowly to the kitchen. I sit at the table, bury my face in my arms, and I cry like I've never cried before, not even when my mother died.

I don't understand what's happening, after everything I've just gone through. I was so close to being free—free to be happy with my life, free to really be the better me—and for what?

I remember the pills in my handbag. That's what I'll do. And I'll leave a note and make sure that Jim knows I'm dying for him, the bastard. See what the papers make of that! I'm already composing the suicide note in my head.

> My darling,
> I can no longer bear your cruelty. My life has become unbearable. I have tried everything to make you happy. I have given you all I have: my love, my tenderness, my support, and of course, all of my money, just as you asked, every cent I earned from the novel I wrote—the one I dedicated to you, remember? But none of that matters. Those sacrifices I have made gladly.

It cheers me up no end to fantasize about what the papers will print, because of course I will find a way for them to get hold of it. Maybe I'll email them a copy. Would that be weird? Maybe I should text Frankie to come and get me—*I've taken the whole bottle*, I'll tell him. He'll come right away, he'll save me, he'll find the note . . .

No. I can't let this happen. I have done so much for this man, and how's that for a cliché? I really did give him all my money, my hard-earned money, because no one can say they worked harder than I have to be where I am.

I need to pull myself together. I go upstairs to shower and change. I go through the motions without thinking about the last few hours, what I've just done. I only think of the present. Of all people, I cannot let Allison beat me, not after everything I've gone through.

Poor Allison. She doesn't know me at all. She has no idea who I am, what I am, what I am capable of.

I chuckle to myself at the thought that I even contemplated letting Jim leave me, as if I didn't have a choice in the matter. Surely murder is a lot like having children, or getting a pet: it's the first one that changes your life. After that, well, it's just incremental. Not such a big deal any-more. I've killed two people, for Christ's sake, and frankly, I'm getting rather good at it, even if I do say so myself.

Allison Vickars.

I'm almost vibrating with excitement when I get into a cab, armed with her address. I don't know what I'm going to do yet, but let's be honest, I'm really very good at improvising.

Just as I get out of the taxi I catch sight of her, outside her building, unlocking her bicycle. There's a rush of anger through me that makes me grit my teeth so hard I wonder if they'll break. Look at her, little perky Allison, with her little leather jacket and her cute haircut. It baffles me what Jim sees in her, honestly. She looks like a . . . student. The kind who struggles with student loans, the kind who works at the grocery store checkout on Sundays to make ends meet. I can't see her on Jim's arm myself, but maybe now that he's scored all my hard-won cash he'll spend some of it on her. She could really use it. I had no idea Jim had such bad taste. What on earth do they talk about? *America's Got Talent*?

"Hey, Allison!"

She turns around.

"Well, well, Emma Fern. That's interesting. What are you doing here?"

"Well, you know, I was in the neighborhood and I thought I'd pop in and smash your face."

"Ha! Nice one!" She doesn't look remotely guilty or even nervous. "I must say, I'm surprised to see you here. I didn't think Jim had the guts."

"You're going to leave him alone, Allison, and I say this politely because that's the kind of person I am, but I need us to be very clear about this. You will have nothing to do with my husband ever again."

"Oh, don't worry, Emma—can I call you Emma? I got what I wanted. I'm not going to milk this anymore. That was the deal, like I said. The originals are all here." She pats the large bag hanging off her shoulder. "He sent you to pick it up, huh? I was on my way to meet him. I guess he didn't trust me!"

I have no idea what's going on, but it sounds interesting. I can smell it. So I'm just going to play along.

She opens the bag and pulls out a couple of large, bulky beige envelopes.

I hold out my hand.

"All yours, Emma. Like I said, these are the originals; there are no copies. I'm not stupid. I know if I try to wrangle more money out of him, it won't end up nice for me. Like I said, I got what I wanted."

I take the bulky envelopes from her.

She cocks her head. "Tell me something, I'm just curious. Does he really think he can fix the problem between now and then?" She chuckles. "Tell him from me, good luck with that. Like I said, no skin off my nose. You people do what you want: I got my million bucks."

She grabs hold of her bicycle, which was leaning against the wall, and rests one foot on the pedal.

"Thanks for saving me the trip, Emma, but don't come here again, okay?"

I turn around and walk down the block.

She's pedaled away by the time I've turned the corner. I walk a couple more blocks until I come across a small park. I go in and sit on a bench. A million bucks. He gave her my money, the swindling fucking bastard. What kind of creep did I marry?

I take the first envelope, tear it open, and pull out the thick stack of papers. At a glance, the top page is dense with text and charts and tables. Something jiggles at the bottom of the package. There are CDs in there, and a couple of flash drives. I pull out one CD; it's marked "Data dump 1" in thick black marker.

I look at the papers more closely, then flick through them quickly. It looks brain-numbingly technical—stacks of spreadsheets filled with numbers, more graphs, and pie charts. Then I find the summary section.

> The application of the forecasting model as described has yielded inconclusive results in all data subsets [1971–1980], [1981–1990], [1991–2000], [2001–2010], [2011–2015].

It goes on like this, and it's complete gibberish to me, but I take my time. There has to be something in there if Jim paid all that money for it—all my money for it—so I keep reading:

> As a result of the empirical analysis of the data for seven OECD countries involving the variables detailed in Appendix H, the economic model as described does not yield sufficiently conclusive results to be considered viable.

I read that part back again, from the top, twice, three times. Then I reread it again, just to be sure. I flip through the pages, scan certain sections that make a little more sense to me; I go back to the summary and concentrate on each word; I study the spreadsheets and graphs, actual results against the predicted results of Jim's economic model that's going to Change The World As We Know It.

I get it, I'm sure. I know what's going on here. I'm smiling. Then I'm grinning.

And then I laugh, a big belly laugh, the tears streaming down my face, and finally, this time, not from grief.

38

Obviously Jim hasn't made a big announcement about us because when I get to the lobby of the Millennium Forum, Jenny greets me with a smile and a "How are you, Mrs. Fern? It's nice to see you again." I can't tell if she's being sarcastic or just very polite, but I am in such a great mood that I don't care. I take the time to have a little chat about this, that, and the other. Eventually I climb up the stairs to Jim's office with a fat envelope in my hand and a spring in my step.

"What are you doing here?" he barks. He's standing by his desk, his coat on, with the air of someone who has just walked in and isn't happy about something. His hand is on the phone on the desk.

"Calling Allison? Don't bother. Think of me as your personal messenger service." I drop myself heavily in the chair opposite. "I am beat! What a day! And it's still only morning, can you believe it?"

He's not angry. I can see it in his eyes. He's confused, but with just the tiniest little sliver of fear poking through.

"Emma, you can't be here, I'm busy. If you want to talk about anything, make an appointment, all right? Better still, call my lawyer."

I smile at him benevolently. "Of course, darling, I understand, but this won't take long."

"What do you want?"

"Missing anything?" I slap the envelope onto the desk.

He picks it up. "What's this?"

"And here I was, thinking you were the smartest man I'd ever met. Lord, when I think about it I want to laugh!" Which I do. Heartily.

He flips through the pages. "Where did you get this?"

"There you were, acting so superior all the time, prancing around like you were some kind of genius, and making me feel like I was cramping your style, because what am I—a shopkeeper, you said once. But no, wait, a Poulton Prize nominee, bestselling author, on the *New York Times* bestseller list, and still I'm not good enough for you. Little old me, I couldn't hold a candle to you, my genius of a husband!"

I shake my head, laughing. I'm having so much fun, but I don't think Jim is, because he has turned very pale.

"And all this time, you were just a common little con man. Out for a buck, just like the rest of us." I lean forward, rest my arms on his desk. "What will they think now, Jim? Your donors, your clients? When they hear that all the research is fake? That they've been conned? That your ooh-la-la PhD research that has made you famous, has given you all this"—I look around the room as I say this—"is fake? That what you were trying to do was never going to happen? It was impossible, wasn't it, analyzing the past and coming up with a magic formula for the future, so we could all be comfortable, employed, own property, have healthcare, la-di-da, except, oops, it doesn't work."

"You don't know what you're talking about."

"Oh, I think I do. It's all in here." I pat the envelope on the desk. "No, wait, actually it's not all in here. That's only a little bit. I kept the rest. I didn't think you needed to see it anyway—I mean, it's your research, right? You know it by heart. You know how bad the numbers are, how fake the data is."

"Where did you get this, Emma?"

"You know very well where I got this. Oh, don't look at me like that. I was just trying to be helpful, save you the trip. Allison was grateful. Anyway, she said to tell you not to worry because she won't take it any further. She will honor the deal, and between you and me, Jim, I think she realizes she doesn't have a choice. So don't worry about it. If she ever rears her pretty little head, I can take care of it. I seem to have developed quite a knack for taking care of people."

He doesn't seem relieved by that.

"She also said to tell you—now, how did she put it? Ah yes, 'good luck with that.' I'm not exactly sure what she meant, but if I were to take a wild guess, I'd say she meant: *Good luck applying that model or whatever you call it, and getting the kind of results you've been trumpeting about.* Which I think is a little harsh myself. I'm sure you're close, aren't you? Well, I hope you are, otherwise you're one hell of a fraud, my love. But you get an A for audacity."

"You don't know what you're talking about. These numbers"—he slaps the sheets of paper fanned out on the desk—"they're old. I've refined it since then, I've cracked it. This means nothing."

"I see. So that million dollars you gave her was for . . . ? No, don't tell me, let me guess. Furthering her education? Because I'm with you: I think she needs it. No? Okay, don't tell me, don't tell me, you gave her a million dollars because . . . hmm, what could it be? She was your student, she was assisting you in your research, right? It says so in here." I point to the papers. "She knows as well as you do that your research is bogus. She never wanted a job, did she? She was blackmailing you, because you have no model, or whatever you call your magic formula—magic mushroom is more like it! You're just winging it! Or should I say lying?"

"Shut up, Emma! You're shouting!"

"Am I? Sorry about that, just the excitement of it all, and I've not slept for two days, can you believe it? Well, I did have a little nap on the floor of the hallway after you left but I don't think that counts. So my senses are a bit, you know, off-kilter. Anyway, where were we?"

"What are you going to do?"

"Nothing, Jim."

"I don't believe that."

"Come on, what kind of wife would I be to turn on my husband like that? Do you really think I'd do that to you—humiliate you? Publicly? Ruin you? You'd never work again in your life, Jim. You would be a shell of a man, the remnants of great promise, begging on the streets for small change. No, of course not. I love you, you know that. It will be our little secret. But I think you should come home now, don't you?"

"You bitch!" He hits the desk loudly with the palm of his hand. "You can't do this! What do you want? Your money back? I'll get you your money back!"

"Who's being loud now, Jim?" And just as I say this, the door opens and Carol walks in, all wide-eyed.

"What's going on?"

"Hey, Carol, how are you? Nice to see you."

She walks over to Jim and puts a hand on his shoulder. She looks into his face. "We can hear you all the way down the hall!" Then she gives me a hard stare: the protective type.

Huh. Carol?

"I think you should leave now, Emma."

"Wow, okay, I did not see that coming. Carol, congratulations. I really thought you were a lovely person. I had no idea you were scuttling behind my back and fucking my husband."

"It's not like that, and I'm sorry if you're hurt. It just happened between us. We didn't want it to happen, but it did."

"Huh, original. Oh well, never mind, not to worry, Carol. I'm sure Jim will give you an appropriate reference." I stand up. "Coming, darling?"

"He said you would be difficult," Carol says with narrowed eyes.

"He said that? Jim, you really need to get some new material. Anyway, who cares, he's changed his mind about that. Haven't you, sweetheart?"

Jim's rooted to the spot. He's red in the face, staring at me. We're both looking at him, Carol and I—she with confusion, me with a benevolent smile—but we both know that because he hasn't said anything yet, the die isn't cast. The corners of her mouth droop and tremble. She's genuinely surprised that he hasn't contradicted me. I feel very sorry for her. No, I don't.

He turns to her and gently removes her hand from his shoulder. "I'm sorry."

"Jim, it's all right. We discussed this," she says this in a tone more appropriate to the nursing staff at the local hospital.

"No, Carol, I'm really sorry. I made a mistake. I'm going home with Emma. I'm really sorry."

She looks crestfallen but already a shadow of acceptance has appeared on her face. Not a fighter then.

I get up and point at the desk.

"Don't forget your papers, darling. You'll want to take these home with you."

39

The New York Times

Poulton Prize Winner Emma Fern and the Mentor Who Inspired Her

By Pushpa Sharma

When this year's Poulton winner Emma Fern was asked where she got her inspiration from, she replied, "In a dream, it all came to me in a dream." Emma Fern's win was a surprise—she's only the second first-time novelist to win the coveted prize—and she knows it. "I never thought I would win, not in a million years. I am very humbled and thrilled that my little novel has pleased so many readers around the world." *Long Grass Running* has sold over two million copies and been translated into seven languages.

So, what's next for this talented young writer? "My husband's taking me away on vacation. We both had a big year and we're looking forward to some time together." They certainly have had a big year. Emma Fern's husband is the eminent economist Jim Fern, the man who made economics sexy and whose groundbreaking work was recently adopted by the Department of the Treasury. "But I am working on a memoir, of my very dear friend and mentor Beatrice Johnson Greene." Mrs. Johnson Greene, a bestselling crime novelist, was murdered by her literary agent, Hannah Beal. Ms. Beal committed suicide two months ago.

Will there be any mention of this tragedy in Mrs. Fern's memoir? "Well, yes, I believe I must. I will be writing about the truth here, so I have to include these tragic events, as sad as that is for me."

So will we have to wait a little longer for her next work of fiction? "Not too long, I hope! Of course, this memoir is one hundred percent non-fiction, definitely," Mrs. Fern says, "but after that I will be dedicating myself to my next novel. My fans demand it, and so does my heart."

We simply can't wait.

ACKNOWLEDGMENTS

Until I Met Her has been through quite a journey now, and this new edition comes with my heartfelt thanks to the wonderful Jane Snelgrove and the lovely team at Thomas & Mercer for all their work in making it happen.

Thank you, dear EB, for reading the first draft and helping shape the writing. You're a wonderful friend.

To Katrina Diaz and Aja Pollock for their brilliant editing work on the original edition.

A huge thank you to my friends and family, whose affection and enthusiasm mean the world to me, and especially to my husband, my love, who makes everything possible.

ABOUT THE AUTHOR

Natalie Barelli can usually be found reading a book, and that book will more likely than not be a psychological thriller. Writing a novel was always on her bucket list, and eventually, with *Until I Met Her,* it became a reality. She hasn't stopped writing since.

When not absorbed in the latest gripping page-turner, Natalie loves cooking, knits very badly, enjoys riding her Vespa around town, and otherwise spends far too much time at the computer. She lives in Australia, with her husband and extended family.

Printed in Great Britain
by Amazon

63910004R00170